JUMPING TO CONCLUSIONS

JUMPING TO CONCLUSIONS

A FANTA DELANEY MYSTERY

A.V. HOWLAND

Author Photo Credit: Haley Desilets

First edition

ISBN: 979-8-89820-015-2

Cover art by Level Best Designs

This book was professionally typeset on Reedsy.
Find out more at reedsy.com

Mom and Dad

Praise for Jumping to Conclusions

"A captivating blend of horses, secrets, and suspense—*Jumping to Conclusions* is a must-read for fans of cozy mysteries with a rural twist. Set in the competitive world of equestrian sports, this whodunit cleverly weaves together buried secrets, hidden motives, and unexpected turns. With richly drawn characters and a determined heroine who's not afraid to dig for the truth, this debut novel proves the author knows the horse world—and the cracks that lie just beneath its polished surface."—Desmond P. Ryan, author of *A Pint Of Trouble* series

"Horse girls and mystery lovers take note! A.V. Howland's sparkling debut mystery, *Jumping to Conclusions*, is for you. The plot is fast-paced, the characters are relatable, and the horse show details are spot-on. Ride along with Fanta Delaney and her horse Des as they compete for ribbons while chasing down a killer."—Laurien Berenson, author of the *Melanie Travis* and *Senior Sleuth* mystery series

"I galloped through this exciting novel. Readers will love how A.V. Howland takes them behind the scenes of competitive show jumping to craft a murder mystery that will keep them guessing right to the end."—Don Macdonald, author of the *Michael Shelter* mysteries

Prologue

Fanta landed face-first in the straw with a jarring thud. She gasped, twisted around, and looked up in fright. The angry stallion towered above her on his hind legs, shaking his thick neck and pawing the air with his hooves, razor-sharp metal horseshoes glinting in the harsh light from the stable aisle. Fanta cowered, hot tears on her cheeks. The stallion squealed, the sound more terrifying than any battle cry. His nostrils showed crimson, his ears were flat to his head, and his eyes were black and furious. Fanta scrabbled at the straw, hands slipping, feet sliding. She had to move, or she would be trampled beneath his hooves. There had already been one dead body in this whole mess. She was about to be next.

Chapter One

"Okay, so we've got the shooting in the west end, the transit issue at city council, and layoffs at that manufacturing plant east of here. Let's get the opinion piece on the mayor's development plans written today."

It was another morning meeting. Fanta Delaney wished she could be anywhere else, but it was all part of life at the North City Newser, where she'd been hired only a few months before as a features writer. She looked around the group of hard-nosed editors and reporters. She'd never thought a newsroom could be so cut-throat. Now, here she was, in the middle of it all. Her idealistic days at university seemed like a dream, or maybe a joke.

She shifted uneasily on the hard plastic chair with the metal legs that wobbled whenever she moved. Everyone always left it for her to sit in. She looked at her notes, at her feet, at her knees poking out of her plain brown skirt. If she could just give her update, she could melt away into the background and out of imminent danger.

"What's happening with features?" Abby Neville, the Newser's managing editor, perched on the edge of a metal desk in the newsroom. Her red blazer with its glossy oversized buttons was paired with a slim black skirt and sky-high patent stilettos. "How's that birdwatching piece coming along?"

"Yes, hi , everybody." Fanta looked down at her notebook like she didn't know exactly what was written there. She tucked a strand of reddish-brown hair behind one ear with a shaky hand. Her freckled cheeks flushed.

"Why are we writing this stuff?" the business editor cut in. His eyes bulged unnaturally from their sockets and his lips were thick and fleshy. "We should be tackling substantive pieces related to the issues of the day. Birdwatching," the man spat, "we don't have resources for fluff stories like that." He threw a challenging stare at his colleagues.

Abby regarded him dispassionately. "I'm glad you've shared your opinion, I just don't agree with you." She cocked her head. "I think Fanta's piece relates perfectly to our coverage of environmental and greenspace issues. Issues we know our readers care about."

The business editor pursed his lips and shoved a hand through his greasy comb-over. People moved restlessly in their seats.

"Fanta?" Abby prompted.

"Thanks, yes, so, the birds are doing really well." Fanta plucked at a loose button on her blouse and tugged at the frayed hem of her skirt. She hated when everyone was watching her. "I've interviewed several birdwatchers in the community—birders, that's what they call themselves—and they've shared stories about how they, well, watch birds."

A reporter sitting nearby snickered. Fanta glanced her way. Like she was working on the next Watergate. More likely, she was writing about the sewer line being constructed in the newest subdivision or the zoning changes being considered by council. At least birds had some life and color to them.

"It's great to have these personal anecdotes from readers," Abby commented.

"Right?" Fanta threw a grateful look at her boss. "So I'm going to center my story around those. It should be a nice feature for the weekend." She tried a confident smile that wavered only a bit at the edges. The group seemed ready to move on.

"What's next?" The business editor couldn't contain himself. "An exposé on crocheting?" His flabby lips parted in glee.

Fanta's stomach dropped. All eyes swiveled back to her.

"Well, I'm planning a piece on ballroom dancing," she stuttered. "The tango, waltz, stuff like that. You know. Cha cha cha!" She shimmied in her seat, causing the wobbly chair to squeak dangerously. Her semi-confident smile collapsed. Ballroom dancing had seemed like a fun concept; flirty but not dirty, traditional but not old school. Maybe she wouldn't know a good story if it dropped from the sky and plonked onto her desk with a big red label: AWESOME FEATURES IDEA—WRITE THIS ONE.

The business editor opened his mouth as if to chomp into something juicy, wonky teeth protruding in at least five different directions.

"I'll look forward to that," Abby interjected smoothly. "My husband and I love to go dancing. It's a great way to practise collaboration and self-control." She twirled the exquisite gold Patek watch on her wrist and gazed around the group. People exchanged wary glances.

Fanta took a deep breath. "Totally. So I'm going to visit a few dance studios in the area and pick up more of those personal anecdotes." There had to be points for pleasing the boss. She wanted nothing more than to scurry back to her desk before someone else took a bite.

"Perfect, thanks, Fanta," Abby said, turning away.

"Oh, sorry, and before I forget," Fanta jumped back in, waving a hand like a kid in the schoolroom, "I'm going to be at the horse show this afternoon, you know, competing." She lifted her chin proudly. Her colleagues might not be impressed with her work, but surely they'd be dazzled by the exciting world of equestrian sports.

The business editor turned to the tousle-haired man beside him. "That's what we're missing in the sports section," he guffawed, spittle flying. "Are you gonna send a writer to the horsey show? Maybe we could put it up front with the hockey championships. All those riders walking around in tight pants might make for some good pictures."

Fanta scowled. Did the guy not realize he was the only one laughing? His retirement day could not come soon enough.

Abby glanced his way. "Perhaps you can come and see me after the meeting. I'd like to chat."

Fanta barely suppressed an eye-roll. It was like high school all over again. When she had started at the Newser, she had thought it would be about doing the work, surrounded by like-minded professionals, pulling toward a common goal. Instead, she had to deal with this motley collection of personalities who wouldn't pull toward a common goal even if it shimmered before them like an oasis in the desert.

Abby looked back at Fanta. "Thanks again and best of luck at the horse show." Then she turned smoothly to the sports editor. "How is the section shaping up? I've heard there are some interesting races in the league competitions."

Fanta hustled to her desk, irritation trailing after her. She may as well have announced that she was going to spend the afternoon throwing horseshoes at a garden party with a bunch of geezers. The fact that she was going to be rubbing shoulders with some of show jumping's elite meant nothing to these people.

She plunked herself in her office chair, which had obviously made the rounds of the newsroom for some years. The seat was crusty and stained, and there were random hairs that Fanta didn't recognize as her own stuck on the headrest. At least she'd finally managed to wrangle the thing into some sort of ergonomic comfort. She poked the space bar on the keyboard and rested her chin in her hand. She would fiddle with the birdwatching piece before heading to the horse show. She really wanted it to shine; maybe it would even go viral! She was sure the Newser's readers would be enthralled. In the background, she heard the morning meeting breaking up. Next thing she knew, Abby was standing next to her.

Fanta looked up in surprise. How did Abby get her thick chestnut hair to look so perfect? Fanta could barely afford a basic trim every six months, much less a blowout every day.

"Listen, Fanta, I wanted to talk to you before you go," Abby said in her silken tone.

Fanta's stomach churned. Of course, her work was foolish. She didn't have what it took to be a journalist. Abby had just been sparing her feelings in front of the group.

"Okay," she managed in a small voice, bracing herself on the armrests.

"It's something all reporters have to learn," Abby started, "so don't feel I'm singling you out. But your work is good, and it's important to the Newser. Don't let anyone discourage you. You've got to stand your ground. Give us a good pitch! Then everyone will see what you have to offer." Abby smiled down at her kindly.

Fanta tried to keep her lip from trembling. Abby was the best. "Okay, thanks. I understand. I can try that." She nodded with more confidence than she felt. "I'll do it next time."

"Great." Abby stepped away. "I'm sure you will." She strolled away toward her office, zig-zagging through the desks in the busy newsroom, stopping to chat and answer questions. Fanta tried and failed to picture Abby's sublime stilettos on her own feet.

She glanced at the clock. She had to get going. She grabbed her purse from the bottom desk drawer and turned off her computer. With the morning meeting behind her, she was anxious to get to the showgrounds. The pristine riding clothes she wore at the horse shows were nestled in a garment bag and stowed in the trunk of her car alongside her polished leather boots. Her coach had trailered the horses from Bay Ridge Farms to the show that morning. Fanta looked forward to seeing her horse, Des. He was her best friend.

She took a last look at her desktop, making sure she hadn't forgotten anything. Her eyes landed on the horse calendar she had pinned to her cubicle wall. A chubby white pony galloped across a flowery field. June. She puffed out an uneasy breath. This would be the first show of the summer season. It had been a long winter practising her riding in the indoor arena at Bay Ridge. Thank goodness Des had lots of experience in the show ring. Her own skills would be rusty, if not completely disintegrated.

She looped the strap of her purse around her shoulder and stood up from her workstation. She had been thrilled to start at the Newser, her first real job after university. The trade-off was she couldn't spend as much time riding. As a teenager, she'd hung out at the barn, taking lessons, doing chores, and just enjoying the horses. Riding had been the highlight of her life. Of course, her parents had paid all the bills.

Now she had to pay her own way, and, while she longed to be a journalist, it sure wasn't going to make her a millionaire. At twenty-five, with her pitiful salary, she struggled to cover Des's upkeep at Bay Ridge. Going to the horse shows stretched her budget to the max. She pushed the manky office chair under her desk, the little wheels squeaking in protest. Still, she was proud to have purchased a horse of her own, with only a little help from her parents, and to do the sport she loved.

She skirted the newsroom and walked out into the parking lot. The sun threw a painful glare in her eyes. Slipping on her shades, she spotted her Honda in a far corner. A mini heatwave billowed out as she opened the door. The black upholstery was like a lit stovetop. She turned the engine and cranked the AC. It would be great to get out into the countryside.

She exited the lot and slipped into the flow of cars. Someone honked at the intrusion. Fanta shook her head. Whatever. She lived and worked north of Toronto, but the big city never seemed very far away, especially on a workday. Traffic was crazy, and people were always in a hurry, going to work, to school, to the mall. She hit a red light and glanced around at the other drivers. A young woman swiped mascara on maxed-out lashes, eyes stretched wide. A middle-aged couple with an empty baby seat in the back were having a heated argument. An older man belted out a tune in the privacy of his car. A slick young professional, earbuds jammed in his head, was shouting into space, face apoplectic.

The usual. Fanta flipped on the radio. The noon news was on.

"In the headlines today, the mayor has given the go-ahead for a major extension of the transit system, despite taxpayers' objections. Police are looking for the public's help in identifying a suspect wanted in connection with a shooting in the west end. And we take a look at how layoffs at the Toptile manufacturing plant will affect local residents. Now to our top story..."

Fanta clicked it off. It was depressing for so many reasons. The light flipped to green and she pressed on the gas, willing the car in front of her to move faster, riding its bumper. Despite Abby's reassurances, the comments from the morning meeting echoed in her head. Maybe there was truth to them. It was fun writing features, but there were so many important stories to be told—ones that could really help people and make a difference in the world. Not birdwatching or ballroom dancing. Maybe her work was a joke.

Fanta frowned as she crawled along in the heavy traffic. Surely some people enjoyed her writing. Her parents, for example. They were always encouraging—mostly. A recent conversation with her mother slipped through her mind.

"You're such a talent, honey. I think they could use someone like you at City Hall or on the business beat. Don't you think? You could really keep people on their toes. Tell it like it is."

Fanta's frown deepened. What did her mom know? She had never started out on the bottom rung of the newsroom. Fanta accelerated as the traffic cleared. Her career was going just fine, thank you very much. Right now, she just needed to get to the horse show.

Chapter Two

Fanta bumped the Honda carefully over the rutted terrain, looking for a spot in the vast field that served as a parking lot at the horse show. Vehicles were jammed in higgledy-piggledy; BMWs next to rusty pickups, giant SUVs crowding out compact cars. Finally, she squeezed into a precarious spot near a drainage ditch, hopped out, and popped the trunk so she could collect her riding gear. Her nerves fizzed. She had to find the Bay Ridge stalls, get Des ready, and head to the warm-up area in time for her class.

She trotted over the sunbaked ground, toting her gear. Up ahead were a dozen or more big white tents that served as temporary stables for the hundreds of horses that came from miles around to compete at the show. Fanta looped from one tent to the other, her stomach churning. What if she couldn't find Des? Just as a wave of panic was cresting, she spotted the big burgundy banner: Bay Ridge Farms. With a sigh of relief, she hurried over.

She peeked into the tack room and then down the aisle. No one was around. Her coach, Penny Wilson, who owned Bay Ridge along with her husband, was likely up at the show ring. Fanta spotted Des's familiar face, watching her from his stall. He nickered as she approached.

"Dessie!" Fanta poked a carrot through the bars of the stall. Des grabbed it with his lips and pulled it into his mouth, crunching happily. His mane was already braided, and he was picture-perfect for the show ring. "You stay here. I'm going to get changed."

Fanta hurried to the tack room, glancing about as she went. Except for the horses, there was no one to be seen. She dipped into the tack room and tucked herself into a dark corner, where she stepped out of her work skirt and pulled on her tan riding breeches. They were skintight. She struggled with the clasps. Had she gained weight since the last show season? Fanta sucked in a breath, and the zipper lurched to the top. Great, one more thing to worry about. She peeled off her white blouse and exchanged it for her long-sleeved riding shirt. Then she stepped carefully into her tall leather boots and zipped them up the back.

Finally, with Des wearing his saddle and bridle and her in full horse show regalia, she started toward the show ring, goose-stepping in her stiff boots. The quiet of the stable gradually gave way to a busy scene filled with horses, riders, trainers, grooms, and spectators. Golf carts zipped about, ferrying people and equipment from one place to another. The air was charged with energy. She passed by a canteen, a food tent, and vendors selling horse-related wares. She tried not to stare at the big-name riders going by.

Just ahead, Penny waved from the middle of one of the warm-up rings. A tall woman with a loud voice, Penny was hard to miss, even in the busy warm-up area. She wore her usual baggy high-waisted jeans and floppy t-shirt, a baseball cap pulled low over her eyes.

"Great timing! Hop up, get Des moving, and we'll try a few practice jumps. He doesn't need much more than that."

Fanta's stomach flip-flopped. Des might not need more than that, but she probably did.

"I'll help!" Bonnie Stephens, one of the Bay Ridge grooms, hurried over, a bucket of brushes and gear in one hand and a big smile on her face. Bonnie was always positive and cheerful. Fanta didn't know what she'd do without her.

Once in the saddle, Fanta asked Des to walk, trot, and canter. They hopped over a couple of practice fences, weaving through the other riders, Penny calling out instructions. Then, all too soon, she and Des were at the in-gate, next to compete. The summer sun shimmered over the show ring. Fanta's stomach felt like the heat waves rippling over the sand. Sweat trickled into the snug waistband of her breeches. She prayed she wouldn't puke.

"You guys will be just fine." Bonnie patted Des and glanced up at Fanta with an encouraging smile.

"Thanks." Fanta tried for a confident grin that was probably more of a sickly grimace. Fortunately, Des didn't seem to be picking up on her nerves. He stood calmly, his ears pricked forward, watching the goings-on in the ring with his big, dark eyes.

Fanta shifted in the saddle. Was it even sane, the whole horse show thing? Here she was under the blazing summer sun in her long-sleeved shirt and black tailored jacket, tight breeches, riding helmet, and boots. It just wasn't normal.

"Hey there, Fanta, are you with me? I said you'll have to be careful with that first fence." Penny peered up at her, her broad face chapped and sunburnt. "I can see you're feeling a bit queasy. Try to relax. It's the first show of the season. Des will take care of you. Just remember to keep your pace."

Fanta watched the competitor in the ring finish the course and slow her horse to a trot, receiving a smattering of applause.

"Have fun," Penny instructed, giving Des a pat on the rump.

Fanta clenched her jaw. That was just what she'd do. She gathered her reins and urged Des forward. Show time!

Entering the ring, she asked Des to pick up his canter, taking the time to establish a steady pace. The noise of the showgrounds faded and the wind rushed in her ears. It was just her and Des. She placed her eyes on the first obstacle, a brown brush box. What had Penny said about it? She couldn't remember. She saw a perfect take-off spot and they jumped over easily.

Riding deep into the corner, Fanta pinned her gaze on the next two jumps positioned along the side of the ring. She knew there were five strides between them. Keeping her rhythmic pace, she got to the first fence perfectly and kept Des moving smoothly to the second, completing the five strides flawlessly. Fanta's tension uncoiled. Maybe she hadn't completely forgotten how to do things.

She rode Des through the next corner and aimed him squarely at the jump in the middle of the ring. She sat up in the saddle, beginning to enjoy the moment. Things were going better than expected. Maybe she would even win a ribbon. Des cantered down and jumped the single obstacle in textbook fashion.

Swinging into the next corner, Des swished his tail and did a frisky hop. Fanta smiled. He was enjoying the jumping. She steadied him for the next two fences, which were separated by four long strides. At her command, Des slowed his pace. But then…uh oh. Des jumped the first obstacle from too far away. Fanta felt a burble of panic. She needed to move forward to make the four strides and clear the second fence. She urged Des on and he rushed ahead, making a mighty leap over the second obstacle.

Fanta was almost unseated. She struggled to right herself, puffing for air. Sweat dripped from under her helmet. She gripped the reins with her leather gloves, attempting to steer Des through the last corner and toward the final two fences.

Before she could fully regroup, the next jump was upon them. Des leaped awkwardly, barely clearing the obstacle and landing at a standstill on the other side. Fanta cursed. She had to get moving. Penny's voice was in her head: heels down, sit straight, shoulders back, look up. She pushed Des forward and clung on as he rocketed over the last fence.

She slowed to a trot, patted Des, and walked out of the ring on a loose rein. Penny was waiting for her, head cocked to one side. Fanta knew exactly what she would say.

"You lost your pace." Penny gave Des a pat. "We'll try again tomorrow."

Fanta nodded. Breathe in through the nose, out through the mouth. Or was that the other way around? She really was out of shape. Penny marched away, calling out to another Bay Ridge rider who was getting ready to compete.

Fanta steered Des to a quiet corner. She wanted nothing more than to go back to the stables and shed her riding gear. Her shirt was stuck to her body like a second skin. Her hair under her helmet felt plastered to her head. She wiped the sweat out of her eyes. The show continued over the weekend and she would go back in the ring a few more times. Now, she was done for the day.

She dismounted and patted Des, who rubbed his great head against her, leaving a trail of white hairs on the sleeve of her black riding jacket. Fanta pushed him away gently and gathered her reins, preparing to lead him back to the stables. "Sorry, Dessie, I'll do better tomorrow," she muttered.

Turning, she spotted a horse being prepped for the ring by a young groom with wispy blonde hair that was fast escaping a skinny ponytail. A poised, perfectly attired rider sat in the saddle.

"This course shouldn't be a problem for you…nothing you haven't seen before." Someone stepped out from behind the horse and rider.

Fanta gasped. Greg Grenier! She stared dreamily. Greg was the professional rider and coach at Two Gates Stables, not far from Bay Ridge. He stood with his hands on his hips, looking up at the rider. His flaxen hair gleamed in the sunlight, his white breeches fit him impeccably, and his boyish face was lean and tanned. Fanta swooned. Then a thought hit her. What if Greg had witnessed her pathetic attempt at the course? A hot flush spread across her cheeks. Of all people. He was probably thanking his lucky stars that she wasn't one of his pupils.

"Absolutely, thanks, Greg." With a cue to the horse, the rider started toward the ring.

"Go see what's keeping my next horse, will you?" Greg shouted over his shoulder.

The young blonde groom stuck a filthy towel in her back pocket, grabbed her gear, and scurried away toward the stables like a frightened mouse.

Fanta stared at Greg. He had the command of a captain, the grace of a dancer. Her mind slipped back to her life as a young pony clubber. She had avidly followed Greg's riding career from afar, reading every article, staring at glossy photos, obsessing over his social media. It had been a bit pathetic, she had to admit. She had never actually met Greg, but it felt like she had from all the times she'd seen him at horse shows. Of course, she'd invented every possible sort of encounter, all of which had ended with her and Greg riding off together into the sunset. Her favorite was the one on the beach, with him shirtless, riding a prancing steed bareback through the surf, her perched in front of him in a frothy white gown, his tanned hands resting in her lap, holding the simple rope reins. It was ridiculous for so many reasons, but still…

Fanta froze. Greg was coming her way, strolling along, his eyes on the ring where his student was competing. He was so close! Maybe he would bump into her, offer a smile. Or she could reach out, introduce herself. Greg walked by, his attention never leaving the ring.

Fanta pooched out a long breath. She turned back to Des, giving him a scratch between the ears.

"It's time to get cleaned up, Dessie." He nibbled at her sleeve with his velvety lips. "Let's find Bonnie. She'll get us sorted out."

Chapter Three

Fanta headed back to the stables, Des in tow. The noon sun beat down, the high, wispy clouds doing little to lessen its heat. Farm fields and tall trees pushed up against the edges of the sprawling showgrounds. The hum of a nearby six-lane highway floated on the breeze. A jumbo plane lumbered through the sky on its way to the big international airport.

Back at the white tents, people were busy bathing horses, filling water buckets, and toting hay and shavings to the stalls. Fanta headed toward the Bay Ridge set-up.

"How did it go?" Bonnie reached out to take Des's reins.

"Des did well." Fanta grinned sheepishly. "I'm a work in progress." Penny had always taught her: a good horsewoman never blamed her horse. She had given Des the wrong commands; he had only done what she'd asked of him.

Bonnie laughed. "Aren't we all!" She gave Fanta's shoulder a squeeze. "It's only the first show. You guys are just getting warmed up. It will go even better tomorrow, you'll see."

"Thanks, you're the best, did I mention that?" Fanta started to pull her riding gloves off, one finger at a time. "I saw Greg Grenier up at the ring," she said, waggling her eyebrows. She could tell Bonnie anything, no judgment. "He's so hot," she added wistfully.

"Right? Who doesn't love Greg." Bonnie gave a cheeky grin and a wink before heading toward a grooming stall, Des following happily.

Fanta trudged into the tack room. She'd survived her first class, but that was about it. She peeled off her jacket and removed her helmet. Talk about hat head. She fussed uselessly with her chin-length hair. Burrowing in her tack trunk, she came up with an old sun visor and slipped it on.

"I'm going to grab something to eat," she called, shoving her debit card in her pocket. "You want anything?"

Bonnie waved. "I'm good, you go. Des and I are just fine."

Fanta retraced her steps toward the show ring. Her stomach grumbled. She hadn't had anything since breakfast. Even then, she hadn't wanted much. Horse-show nerves kept her from eating. Plus, the horsey set was notoriously thin and beautiful. Fanta watched as a beachy blonde with a dynamite smile strolled past, flawless in white breeches, chatting on her phone. In the warm-up ring, a lithe man swung himself into the saddle atop a massive show jumper.

Fanta tugged at the pinchy waistband of her breeches. She'd barely been able to slip her phone into the front pocket. She shook her head, the visor slipping down over her eyes. How many times had someone called her a "big girl" when she was young? It was some useless euphemism for fat. No wonder she was scarred for life. She still hated eating in front of other people, even though she'd lost the extra weight—the "baby fat." Plus, she knew full well that she needed her energy for riding. It was stupid, but she often ate popsicles at the horse shows. They had zero nutritional value, and she was pretty sure she looked like an idiot eating them.

Fanta walked up to the canteen. This time would be different.

"What can I get you?" the pleasant-looking man called out.

"I'll have a—" Hot dog? Hamburger? Salad? Grilled cheese? "Orange popsicle, please."

Fanta pulled some napkins from the dispenser, took the popsicle, and waved her debit card at the machine. She wandered over to the big show jumping ring, where there was always a buzz in the air. Sucking the popsicle—maybe licking would be better?—she gazed at the tall metal bleachers and swanky VIP seating area. Flags waved atop tall poles, bold advertising banners were slung along the fence lines, and stunning luxury cars were parked this way and that around the ring. Fanta took it all in. It was completely different from where she and Des competed, in a smaller ring in the show hunters. There, horses and riders were judged on how well they navigated a simple course of natural-looking fences like gates and hedges. Show jumping was a whole other ball game, with huge, colorful jumps and twisty courses. The key was not to knock any rails down and go as quickly as possible, especially in a jump-off against the clock.

Fanta watched the horse and rider in the ring leap over the last big jump and surge through the timers. What a rush! So different from the calm pace of the hunter ring. She hoped to try show jumping one day, but she had to prove herself in the hunter ring first.

"Hi there," said a voice at her side. Startled, Fanta glanced over. It was Terry Miller, one of Greg Grenier's students at Two Gates. Terry also rode in the adult hunter division, which was filled with entrants like Fanta who rode for pleasure, although some took it more seriously than others. Terry and his dapple gray mare Pearl were pretty much unbeatable.

"Hey, Terry, how's it going?" She was surprised Terry had stopped to speak with her. She was not high on most people's networking lists. She looked more closely at him. His curly hair was flat and his beefy face flushed. "How did you do in the class?" she asked.

"Pearl was on form today, we won," Terry replied glumly.

Fanta blinked. She would have been happy just to do well, much less win the class. She hoped Terry hadn't seen her make a fool of herself.

"I guess you and Des had a miss there," Terry observed.

Fanta groaned silently. She would improve, she vowed. Terry had more money and more experience than she did, it was easier for him to do well.

They lapsed into silence. Fanta focused on finishing her popsicle before a giant orange splotch landed on her white riding shirt. Beside her, Terry fidgeted, standing on tiptoe, eyes roving the crowds. Fanta leaned away. It was irritating. She swallowed the last bite of popsicle and wrapped the wooden stick in a napkin. Time to head back and see Des at the stables.

"Oh, there he is, the boy wonder," Terry breathed sarcastically, his eyes riveted on something in the distance.

Fanta wiped her tacky hands with the napkin, white bits sticking to her fingers. What was Terry talking about? Then she saw Greg at the in-gate, next to go aboard his horse Dash.

"Oh, there's Greg. This should be good, right? Dash is awesome," Fanta said, uncertain. Had Terry been talking about Greg? Surely not. Everyone knew Greg was a demi-god.

She gazed at Greg, sitting confidently astride Dash. He was so attractive, and he just had that thing—that way of making everyone stop and stare. Fanta sighed. At one point, she'd considered boarding Des at Two Gates, mostly because Greg was there. Fanta cringed at the memory. She hadn't been able to afford the expensive barn. Just as well. What would she have done, follow Greg around like a lovesick puppy? She would probably have been too dorky to even speak to him. No, she was happy at Bay Ridge.

She sighed again. She hadn't been surprised to hear that Greg was dating an American show jumping rider with a pile of money to go along with her string of top horses. The two of them were the horsey version of Ken and Barbie.

She turned to Terry. He was still staring, bushy eyebrows drawn together in a fierce frown.

"If Greg goes clear and gets into the jump-off, the other riders better boogie," Fanta tried. Dash was not a big horse, but he was a speedy and careful jumper.

Terry sneered, "Oh yeah, Greg's the best, alright. Just don't try to actually talk with him. I'm one of his top clients, but do you think I can get a minute of his time?" Terry's shoulders slumped and his unruly curls flopped into his eyes. "Sorry. I'm just dealing with a lot right now."

Fanta glanced back at Greg, puzzled. Terry was way off-base. Who could possibly be angry with Greg, show jumping's lustrous ambassador to the world? Then her breath caught in her throat and her heart seized. A tall brunette was giving Greg's leather riding boots a last-minute polish as he sat on his horse. She had stupidly long legs showcased in skinny jeans, a butt that was rounded just so, and a taut crease in the bust line of her tight t-shirt. It was easy to see the hint of some really sexy underwear.

After one last caress of Greg's calf encased in the leather boot, the brunette checked the girth to ensure it was snug and wiped the foam from Dash's mouth. Then she stepped back as Greg urged Dash forward into the ring at a rapid-fire trot, quickly picking up a fast canter.

Deirdre Lalonde. Fanta knew her all too well. She and Deirdre had been pony clubbers together. Fanta had been chubby and freckled. Deirdre had been olive-skinned and curvy. When Deirdre saw that Fanta was crushing on Greg, she had made it her mission to tease and torment her. The situation had become unbearable.

Fanta shuddered. One time, Deirdre had painstakingly cut out a bunch of glamorous photos of Greg from the horsey magazines and glued them all over Fanta's locker at the stable. Then she had affixed a particularly unflattering picture of Fanta in the middle of the whole thing, creating some sort of monstrous collage. The other pony clubbers had been beside themselves, tittering and whispering behind their hands as Fanta walked innocently into the barn. Seeing her, Deirdre had started miming an exhausted dog, tongue lolling and eyes bugging. "There's Panta Fanta," she'd jeered, sending the pony clubbers into new fits of laughter. "When you gonna hook up with Greg?"

Fanta shook her head, trying to clear the memory. She would never erase it completely. Fortunately, Deirdre had moved away not long after that. Now, here she was, a groom at Two Gates, working with Greg every day. Fanta felt all the old jealousies and insecurities roil in her gut.

A roar went up from the crowd. Fanta blinked as Greg and Dash surged through the timers with a burst of speed and a clear round. Greg fist-pumped. Dash snorted and shook his head.

"That's super, he'll be in the jump-off," Fanta exclaimed. She watched Greg as he dismounted and gave Dash a nice pat. The heinous Deirdre reached for the reins. Then…no! Greg swept Deirdre into a hug and pressed her body tightly against his, gazing down at her intensely. Deirdre—no surprise— returned the embrace wholeheartedly, rubbing herself against him like a hungry cat. Fanta could only watch in dismay as Greg stroked Deirdre's cheek and pushed a strand of silky brown hair off her face.

"Oh, that's just great, that's just what we need," Terry groused. "The guy's a liability wherever he goes. Can't he keep his hands to himself?"

What? Terry needed to get his facts right. Obviously, Greg was blameless. Deirdre was the pitiless troublemaker. Fanta turned to Terry, ready to set things straight, just in time to see his face open in suspense. "Here comes trouble," he whispered.

Fanta swiveled back to the in-gate. Greg's girlfriend was approaching from the other side of the warm-up ring. Lana Taylor was a petite blonde who looked cute and perky but was not known for being kind or forgiving. Fanta held her breath. It was like watching a car crash in slo-mo. Greg and Deirdre stepped away from each other as if hit by an electric current. Lana walked around Dash and greeted Greg with a smile and a peck on the cheek. Fanta exhaled. Apparently, Lana had missed the moment of passion between Greg and Deirdre. Greg smiled, said something in Lana's ear, and turned her deftly in the opposite direction, walking off, hand in hand.

"Gotta go now," Terry called, chugging away in Greg's wake.

Deirdre was left holding Dash. Fanta was thrilled to see that she looked completely deflated. Dash would need to be kept ringside so that Greg could ride him in the jump-off, which was coming up soon. Deirdre would have a nice stretch of time to think about Greg with his super-hot, super-rich, super-talented girlfriend Lana, fooling around in some hidden corner of the showgrounds. Fanta regarded Deirdre through slitted eyes. Surely she didn't think she could tempt Greg with her lacy bra and superior grooming skills. Good luck with that.

Fanta crumpled the popsicle stick and napkin in her fist and pitched them in the first trash can she saw. There was some weird stuff playing out at Two Gates. None of it was her problem.

Back at the Bay Ridge stalls, she found Des tucked up for the night with a full hay net. She went to her tack trunk and pulled out some carrots. Des's ears pricked as she opened his stall door.

"Here you go," she whispered, offering him a carrot and giving his forehead a kiss. "Sorry I let you down today. Things will go better tomorrow, Dessie. I'll get it right, don't you worry." Des munched happily, eyes half-closed.

In the tack room, Fanta cleaned her saddle and bridle and made sure everything was ready for the next day. Then, tired and sweaty, she went to find her car in the parking area. In the distance, she saw Greg riding triumphantly back to the stables with a first-place ribbon pinned on Dash's bridle. Lana walked alongside the horse, looking up at Greg and talking with him. Deirdre followed quietly, a bucket of grooming gear in one hand and Greg's riding jacket slung over her arm. Fanta smiled. Perfect.

Chapter Four

Fanta's apartment was located near the offices of the Newser. The top-floor unit in the low-rise building had a small bedroom and a den that led out to a pleasant deck where Fanta enjoyed sitting, almost as if she were in the treetops. She lived alone and had decorated her space to her own taste. She had tried for comfortable and stylish, although, as much as she loved all the latest home fashions, she couldn't afford most of them. Still, she always had fun trolling the clearance racks at the nearby big-box stores.

After a long, hot shower, she heated a frozen pizza and guzzled down several glasses of water. She totally needed to hydrate, or her skin would start wrinkling before she could say SPF. She flipped on the TV but couldn't find anything in the zillion or so shows listed. She felt restless. Maybe it was time to let loose. Penny wouldn't mind. And she would still get plenty of sleep and be ready to ride Des properly the next morning.

After some debate, she selected a pair of artfully ripped jeans and a summer top with a retro vibe. She restored her hair to its slick bob and dusted sparkly powder over her cheeks. She stared at her reflection in the bathroom mirror. She looked boring. Grabbing her cosmetics bag, she slicked on a coat of blackest-black mascara, a hint of beguiling eyeshadow, and a swish of juicy red lip gloss. She pouted at her reflection. Better. She might not stand a chance with Greg, but maybe someone interesting was out there.

Firing up the Honda, she headed toward the Carleton Hotel. It was a rundown but handy place near the showgrounds. Lots of horse people stayed there during the shows. One of its main attractions was a nice little dance bar. Fanta smiled as she pulled into the packed lot. As expected, the place was hopping. Horsey people liked a good party almost as much as riding and competing.

Fanta stepped into the bar, trying to look cool and independent. The place was festooned with twinkling lights. Tables and chairs were tucked away in intimate corners. The music pumped, the lights strobed, and a disco ball spun from the ceiling. The dance floor was packed with partiers and the bartender was doing a brisk trade.

Fanta perched on a stool at the bar and ordered a beer. She checked herself in the dusky mirrors. Beer in hand, she practised looking aloof yet approachable, self-assured yet friendly.

Sara Robinson hitched herself up onto the seat next to her. She plonked a glass on the bar, empty save for a battered paper umbrella and a limp chunk of fruit. She wriggled on the small round stool, trying to get a purchase. Her neon blue miniskirt crawled dangerously up her thighs, while her spangly top slipped down precariously. Sara didn't seem to notice. Fanta gave her the side-eye. By all appearances, Sara had been at the party for a while.

"Hey, how did it go today?" Fanta tried an easy opener. She wasn't sure what to make of Sara, who also rode at Bay Ridge. The rumor was that Sara's parents had bought her a horse, hoping it would distract her from partying. Fanta seriously doubted the strategy was working. She glanced again at Sara. She had an attractive face with strong features (not well-served by a heavy-handed makeup job—was blue eyeshadow a thing again?) and full lips (currently dripping in a blood-red gloss that would not have been out of place in a vampire movie). Her hair looked like it had been chopped off with dull scissors in a dark bathroom.

"Thanks," Sara said groggily to the bartender, who handed her a fresh drink before offering a knowing look to no one in particular. Sara spun slowly around on the stool, drink in hand, and surveyed the room.

"Oh, hi, Fanta," she drawled. Her tongue, which featured a little silver stud, played with the swizzle stick in her drink. Some poor guy passing by sped up noticeably as Sara threw him a lascivious wink. "Everything was *suuuper* today, couldn't have gone better."

Fanta doubted that was true. Sara usually struggled with her young horse, Rose, who needed a rider with a steady hand and a calm demeanor. Sara didn't fit the bill on either count. Fanta wasn't sure what to say. Fortunately, Sara wasn't interested in her opinion. Instead, her blue-crested eyes widened and she waggled her extravagant eyebrows like conjoined caterpillars. She pointed with the swizzle. "What's going on there?"

Fanta followed Sara's stare to a dark corner of the bar. What? She drew in a sharp breath. "Is that Chessy with Greg Grenier?" Fanta hissed. "They know each other?" Life was utterly unfair.

Chessy MacKay was another of the riders at Bay Ridge. She had sleek blonde hair, a heart-shaped face, dewy skin, and green eyes. Then there was her classic rider's physique—long legs and arms and a lean torso. Perhaps worst of all, she was an awesome horsewoman, with seemingly boundless natural talent. Fanta wanted to like Chessy, she seemed nice enough, but her drive to become a top equestrian was hard to take. Everyone knew she was Penny's favorite. The whole scenario made Fanta green with jealousy. Now, here was Chessy, chatting up Greg Grenier. Fanta felt her evening buckle and collapse like a sand sculpture at high tide.

Sara tittered, her head bobbing side-to-side on her skinny neck. "Looks like Little Miss Equestrian has figured out there's more to life than saddles and stirrups."

Fanta tried not to stare. Chessy and Greg sat with their heads bent together in what looked like an intense conversation. They made a nice-looking couple, she had to admit. The music was loud, but Greg seemed to be sitting closer to Chessy than was necessary.

"Penny wouldn't like Chessy cozying up to Greg like that," she heard herself whisper in a snarky way.

"Oh, why not?" Sara jabbed at the cherry in her drink and popped it into her mouth. "Penny would never find fault with Bay Ridge's own super trouper." She rolled her eyes, the sky-blue eyeshadow having a creepy effect, like an evil clown in a horror movie.

Fanta lifted her beer to her lips and discovered it was gone. She could ill afford another. "That's true," she grumped, "as if the rest of us aren't valuable paying clients."

She hated the words as soon as they left her mouth. It wasn't hard to see that Chessy benefited from a number of freebies at Bay Ridge. Fanta tried to clamber onto the high road. That was because Chessy worked hard with the horses and was always there to support Penny. Although, maybe someday she'd have to pay her own way like everyone else. Fanta fell back onto the low road with a bump.

Sara was droning on. "*Sooo* right. I mean, we're all equally talented. I could ride any horse just as well as Chessy. I'm sure you could, too, Fanta." Sara's tone suggested more than a hint of doubt.

A mild disgust crept into the pit of Fanta's stomach. She was a far better rider than Sara would ever be. She might not be in Chessy's league, but still. Sara was on glue. There was no way she was going to be lumped into some category with her.

"*Oooh*, don't look now." Sara placed her empty glass on the bar behind her and stared as if watching the dying moments of a big-screen thriller.

Fanta followed her gaze. "There's Lana," Fanta breathed, "she must be looking for Greg. This can't be good."

Lana stood at the entrance to the bar in a shimmery emerald-green dress and spiky heels. Her curly hair was carefully styled and her striking makeup featured a vivid red lip. She looked brightly around the crowded room.

"Wow, she's gone all out," Sara giggled. "She might be in for a disappointment," she sing-songed gleefully.

"Maybe she won't see them?" Fanta couldn't tear her gaze from the unfolding drama.

Lana's eyes seemed to dilate as she zeroed in on Greg and Chessy, chatting away at their corner table. Lana glowered, drew herself up like a small but mighty dictator, and executed a quick about-face. Her dainty heels tip-tapped off into the lobby like tiny gunshots.

"Whoa, Chessy better watch her step. I wouldn't want to be in Lana's bad books." Sara slid off the stool and planted her feet on the floor with only a slight wobble. "See you later, Fanta, don't stay out too late." She offered an ingratiating smile and gave a royal wave before weaving through the crowd.

If only Sara followed her own advice. Fanta was glad to see her go.

She turned back to the dizzying tableau of Chessy and Greg. Surely they weren't on a date. If they were, it didn't seem promising. Chessy was wearing a polo shirt and dirty jeans. Greg was outfitted in something similar, if a bit cleaner. As the conversation progressed, Chessy looked increasingly uncomfortable. Greg looked irritated. Then, Chessy rose from her seat. A tense exchange seemed to follow, with Chessy standing, arms akimbo, and Greg sitting, shrugging his shoulders. Fanta could practically see the thought bubble over his head: *What's up with this chick?* It wasn't a nice thing to think. But who would deny Greg whatever he might want? Finally, Chessy walked out of the bar. Greg sat for a while, a cross look on his face, before also getting up and starting for the door.

Fanta placed her empty beer bottle on the bar. What in the world was happening at Two Gates? Whatever it was, did it involve Chessy? Or even Bay Ridge? Suddenly, the effects of the long, hot day and the one beer washed over her. It seemed like months ago she'd been toughing it out at the morning meeting at the Newser. She would steer clear of whatever was going on with Greg. Still, she felt badly for him. Shouldn't someone offer comfort, a shoulder to cry on, a safe place to vent? It didn't seem as if Lana would be playing that role any time soon.

She imagined herself pulling Greg into a soothing embrace, lifting her trusting eyes to his, his cupid lips reaching down for her mouth. Whoa! Like that was ever going to happen.

She paid her tab, slid off the stool, and wound her way out to the lobby. She glanced around in distaste. It really was shabby. The fake leather furniture was worn and patched. The linoleum floor had seen more than its share of foot traffic. Not to mention the display case of desserts, probably meant to look sugary and enticing, but under the fluorescent lighting appearing oily and possibly even moldy.

"I understand your concerns. I wouldn't do anything without telling you. I think you're jumping to a worst-case scenario. I'm sure it will all work out for the both of us."

Fanta rounded a corner and walked smack-dab into Greg's backside. He bumped forward, issued a curt goodbye into his phone, spun around, and looked directly at her.

All the air whooshed out of her body. She goggled at him. Her jaw flapped up and down. She had to say something.

"Oh, hi, Greg, you don't know me, I'm Fanta, Fanta Delaney, but I wanted to say what a great ride you had this afternoon." After all these years! Here he was in his faded jeans and white polo, standing before her. He smelled so nice. It was everything she'd ever dreamed of.

"Thanks, Dash is super." Greg paused, uncertain. "I guess you're a horse show person. I don't suppose you've seen Lana?" His voice was tinged with anxiety.

"I spotted her in the bar earlier. She may have been looking for you, actually. Maybe she headed out? These long days are a killer. I don't know how you pro riders do it," Fanta babbled. She just needed to shut up.

"Dammit." Greg's beautiful face creased in irritation, his thoughts obviously zig-zagging around in his head. Then he remembered Fanta. "Right, sorry. I better go find her. Have a great horse show." He turned on his heel and headed for the elevators.

Fanta arrived back on Earth from another lovely, lovely planet. She had actually spoken to Greg! Was that good? No. The conversation replayed in her mind. The whole thing was beyond cringeworthy. She glanced around the lobby, praying fervently: *Please, let no one have witnessed the encounter.* Her eyes landed on Deirdre, standing near the front desk. Disaster! But Deirdre wasn't looking at her. Instead, she was staring after Greg with a cunning gleam in her eye, undoubtedly plotting the next flagrant step in her seduction scheme.

Fanta hastened to the exit. She did not want to interact with Deirdre. Not in any way, shape, or form. Both of them were older now, but Fanta had no doubt that they were doomed to play out their childhood roles for eternity. She scuttled through the revolving doors, hoping they didn't hurl her back into the lobby. Poor Greg! His girlfriend was mad and MIA, Chessy had rebuffed whatever advances he may have made, and he was becoming entangled with the sorceress that was Deirdre. Not to mention whatever hissy fit Terry seemed to be having. She hurried to her car. Of course, Greg didn't seem to be making things easy for himself. But he better be careful. Because while she seriously doubted that Chessy was interested in him in any romantic way, she could easily imagine Deirdre pulling out all the stops to blow his relationship with Lana to bits.

Chapter Five

Saturday dawned rainy and cool. Fanta rose early and drove to the showgrounds. The wide streets were virtually empty and the jewel tones of the traffic lights glowed on the wet pavement under the overcast skies. She pulled at the waistband of her breeches. It was still too tight. She'd never admit it under threat of death or even being locked in a closed room with Deirdre, but she'd cut a little gap—okay, maybe two—in the elastic waistband with some cheap nail scissors. Her belly had plumped out in relief. No one would ever know, unless somehow she ended up at the local emergency room. Even then.

She fidgeted in the driver's seat. The morning would feature the adult hunter division's under-saddle or flat class, where horses were judged on their walk, trot, and canter and not required to jump. Fanta felt good about it. Des usually did well. Her fellow competitors could be merciless, though, jostling each other, cutting off other horses, pushing poor lost souls out to the edge of the ring where the judges would never see them. Fanta would be on her guard. Des didn't usually let any of the shenanigans disturb him.

The second class over fences was in the afternoon. Fanta's gut constricted. She wasn't so sure about that. Would she be able to up her game from the day before? The pressure was on to put in a good showing.

Driving by the Carleton, Fanta's thoughts turned to Greg. Somewhere, in one of the hotel's ticky-tacky rooms, beautiful Greg lay outstretched on a bed, tanned skin and flaxen hair against tousled white sheets, sleeping soundly. Fanta blissed out at the thought of it. Or, maybe Greg was not alone. Perhaps Lana was curled beside him, petite and lovely. Or Deirdre hovered over him, ready for a morning wake-up call. Fanta's brow furrowed. On the upside, now that she'd spoken to Greg, albeit briefly (perhaps foolishly), maybe next time he passed by, she could give a small nod, even exchange a greeting. The possibilities were endless.

Fanta turned onto the road that led to the showgrounds. Who was she kidding? Greg was totally into Lana. And why not? Lana had everything going for her. It was a smart move on Greg's part to hook up with her. So why the feverish scene with Deirdre? And the confab with Chessy? Fanta slumped in her seat. She was older now; she could see things for what they really were. Maybe Greg's laurel crown was a little skewed, his golden luster a bit tarnished.

But no. Fanta turned on the clicker and headed into the showgrounds. It was all Deirdre's fault. She was the temptress, the siren. It was totally down to her that Greg was distracted and not treating his girlfriend and maybe his clients as he should. Deirdre was a wrecking ball in anyone's life.

Fanta slid the Honda to a stop in the rain-soaked field, grabbed a few items from the trunk, and headed toward the Bay Ridge stalls. The stables were in full swing, despite the early hour. Des had eaten his oats and was standing in the grooming stall with Bonnie, who was brushing his gray coat and cleaning out his hooves. Fanta could tell that Des was happy with the attention, his eyes half-closed and lower lip drooping. There was a tight row of small braids along the ridge of his neck and one in his forelock. Show hunters were required to be immaculately turned out for competition and Des was rocking it.

Bonnie played with the strands of Des's long tail. "Hey, Fanta. What do you think? It's going to be a messy one today." With some braiding, Des's grayish-white tail could be kept out of what was sure to be sloppy, dirty footing.

"Yeah, if we can do a mud tail or something, it would look good," Fanta replied. Bonnie was a wizard with such things. Fanta headed to the tack room. She already had her breeches, riding shirt, and tall boots on. She just had to add her tailored riding jacket and helmet. With the weather, at least she wouldn't be so hot and sweaty in the whole outfit.

Carrying Des's saddle and bridle and trying not to get dirty, she returned to where Bonnie was working in the grooming stall. Fanta smiled fondly. Des stood patiently, beautifully groomed and dolled up for the show ring. Then her smile faltered. Once out of the stables, it would take no time at all for his legs and belly to be spattered with mud. It was going to be a fun day cleaning equipment and hosing off horses. Not to mention potentially riding in a driving downpour. Fanta sighed. The show always went on.

"Cheer up, Fanta." Lyle Sampford strolled up beside her, a garment bag slung over his shoulder. His wiry hair was carefully brushed and he had taken time with the sparse hairs on his chin that might possibly have required shaving. His woodsy cologne with floral undertones was overpowering and reminiscent of the fly spray they used on the horses. He wore faded jeans, a white shirt, and pointy cowboy boots. "It'll be like a do-over for you and Des this afternoon. You can't mess it up a second time."

Fanta threw an exasperated look at Lyle. He was a fixture at Bay Ridge, having ridden there since he was a child. He was a good rider and he obviously loved the horses, including his own little bay Trifle. Fanta pursed her lips. Lyle loved the horses, but she knew for a fact he was also pretty happy to scope out the many cute, athletic girls who competed in the sport.

Sara hurried up the aisle. She looked as if she'd just stepped out of a hurricane. Fanta was sure she could see smudgy traces of the heavy makeup from the evening before on Sara's face. Gross. Where exactly had Sara spent the night? It didn't bear thinking about.

Sara shooed Lyle out of the way, whipped open one of the large Bay Ridge tack boxes, and began rummaging through it with a frantic energy. "Pay no attention to him, Fanta. He has no clue what he's talking about, as usual," she said, her head disappearing into the trunk.

Fanta stepped away as Sara and Lyle started their usual dickering. It was incredible how Sara's moods could swing from one extreme to another. Fanta didn't know what to make of it. Her own mood stayed pretty much the same from day to day. Should she change it up? Something to consider. She would welcome more happy positivity and less endless worrying.

"Here's your boy." Bonnie was leading Des toward her.

"He looks amazing, thanks! Did I mention you're the best?"

Fanta grinned at Bonnie, who helped her hop up onto Des's back. She started toward the warm-up ring. Des walked along happily, despite the raindrops spattering his coat. Fanta could see her dark riding jacket beginning to get damp. There was nothing to be done about it.

Reaching the warm-up, she took in the swirl of other horses and riders prepping for the flat class. In show hunters, it was ideal to have a horse with a long, low stride that covered the ground and was comfortable for the rider to sit. From her pony club days, Fanta knew that show hunters had their origins in the traditional fox hunt, where riders spent a long day in the saddle, riding cross-country. Comfort was paramount.

Terry trotted by on the gorgeous Pearl. There was the class winner, Fanta thought, not without a hint of jealousy. Pearl was a classic. Des was not in her league, but he usually won a ribbon in the flat class. Fanta started to put him through his paces in the warm-up.

Soon, the competitors were called into the show ring. The class started with everyone at a walk, spread out around the large ring. Already, Fanta sensed some of the riders vying for the best position from which to catch the judge's eye. She concentrated on keeping Des's stride long and loose. He seemed happy to oblige.

"Trot, please!" commanded the ring steward.

Fanta asked Des to pick up his pace. Fortunately, the sand ring was not too wet. Still, many of the horses fussed, not keen on the rain and puddles. Others pinned their ears and swished their tails, not liking so many horses moving beside them. Des swung along easily. Across the ring, directly in the judge's line of sight, Pearl floated over the ground, calm and graceful.

Then came the command for the canter. Fanta tensed, ever so slightly. Things might get interesting. The faster pace was exciting for the horses. On the outskirts of the group, she saw a rangy chestnut explode with a huge buck, his back hooves kicking gaily into the air, his rider holding on for dear life. A dark bay nearby pulled hard at the reins, obviously wanting to gallop off willy-nilly across the ring. The rider pulled back with all her might, face grim.

"Thank you, reverse please!" came the command.

Obediently, the group returned to a walk and changed direction. Horses needed to be balanced on both sides. Like humans, they tended to be stronger one way than the other. Fanta knew Des preferred going around the ring to the left.

Once again, they went through their walk, trot, and canter. Des was the perfect gentleman, even as a snippy chestnut mare bared her teeth at him and a gray horse shaped like a dump truck rumbled right under his nose. Fanta was just as happy when they were all asked to line up down the middle of the ring.

The announcer wasted no time. "In first place, we have String of Pearls, owned and ridden by Terry Miller." The result was no surprise.

Terry pulled out from the line, looking tired but pleased. Fanta kept her ears cocked as the announcer continued. Then, "In fourth place, we have Desmos, owned and ridden by Fanta Delaney."

Fanta urged Des forward, a smile on her face. The judges and stewards congratulated her and pinned a fluttery ribbon on Des's bridle. They walked from the ring, Des with his head held high, Fanta grinning. She was dying to get back to the stables and see Bonnie, who would fuss over them like a mother hen.

Sure enough, when she arrived, Bonnie was ready to help.

"Look at you guys! Congrats, Fanta, way to go. Good boy, Dessie." Bonnie took the reins from Fanta and patted Des, even giving him a smooch on the nose. Des played it up like a ham.

"I'm afraid we got a little dirty." Fanta eyeballed Des's lower legs, which were covered in sand and grit. "Sorry about that."

"Oh, don't worry. Nothing a little warm water can't fix." Bonnie led Des into the grooming stall. He would have some time to rest and hang out with his hay net before the next class over fences.

Fanta pulled the leather gloves from her hands and plucked her raincoat from the peg where she'd left it.

"I'm going to grab a coffee. Can I get you anything?"

"A hot chocolate would be great, thanks," Bonnie replied, slipping off Des's saddle.

"I'd love a tea, if you don't mind." Sara appeared out of the aisle. "But it has to be organic. And not too hot. And if they have cardboard cups, not Styrofoam, that would be great."

"Coffee for me, black," called Lyle from the tack room.

Fanta rolled her eyes. Lengthy beverage order in hand, she put on her raincoat and headed to the canteen. She patted her pockets to make sure she had her phone and wallet. She surreptitiously slipped a finger under the waistband of her breeches. Better. She would purchase a healthy, protein-packed breakfast item. At least a banana. Not one of those delicious-looking muffins. Everyone knew those were basically just big pieces of cake.

She hopped through the puddles, trying to keep her leather riding boots dry. Over the usual horse show hubbub, she heard raised voices. She glanced around. Terry was standing beside one of the rings, arguing with another man. Looking more closely, Fanta recognized Dave LeDans, Greg's business partner at Two Gates. Dave's pot belly strained against a stained polo shirt and his thick black hair was greasy and uncombed. He and Terry stood close together, gesticulating, their faces red and flustered. It looked unpleasant. Fanta wanted to scoot by as quickly as possible.

"I have no idea where the guy is, Terry. He's probably trying to avoid you. Can't you give him a break about your invoices? Don't you trust us to get things right?" Dave shouted.

"I have every right to inquire about the billing, Dave," Terry replied frostily. "And it's more likely that Greg is trying to avoid you, since you're always hassling him about his plans. No wonder he wants to be done with you."

"What? I don't think that's true. How could you say such a thing?" Dave reared back. "In any case, we need to find him, and fast. He's got horses to ride today, and I don't want to let these clients down."

Dave jerked his chin toward the warm-up area, where Deirdre was leading one of Greg's horses around in a circle. Her eyes were puffy, her skin was sallow, and she walked with an air of dejection. Fanta chuckled. Perhaps Greg had given Deirdre the brush-off, even in the face of her frilly underwear and wanton behavior. Or, if Lana ever found out that Deirdre was trying to hook her claws into Greg, who knew what fury might be unleashed.

Fanta picked up her pace toward the canteen. She didn't want to be in earshot of much more. She had no idea what it was about, but it sounded bad. In her haste, she almost missed another commotion going on near the entrance to the main jumper ring.

"Greg Grenier, please make your way to ring one, you're wanted in the ring. Greg Grenier, ring one," crackled the PA announcer.

The ring stewards craned their necks while riders circled on their mounts, waiting to see what the holdup was. That was odd. Fanta paused. Horse shows usually ran efficiently, with riders going in the ring at appointed times and classes running to schedule. This was especially true in the main jumper ring, which hosted big-money classes that were often televised.

Everyone's head swooped around as Greg's young blonde groom came running toward the in-gate from the stables. Her cheeks were patchy red, her breath came in panicky gusts, and her skinny arms windmilled as she ran, trying not to trip on the uneven ground. She looked like someone fleeing a house fire.

"He can't come, he can't come!" she cried, dropping her hands to her knees and heaving in great gouts of air. "He's...he's dead!"

Everyone stopped. Then, just as suddenly, a frenzy ensued. Everyone started talking. A swarm of people formed at the in-gate while others ran off to spread the shocking news about Greg.

Fanta halted in her tracks. She couldn't take it in. She had just spoken to Greg the night before. She had mooned over him for years. How could he be gone? She had the sensation of being on a rapidly sinking ship in the middle of stormy seas.

Dave and Terry steamed off toward the stables with the young groom scurrying in their wake. Deirdre followed more slowly with Greg's horse. Fanta resumed her walk to the canteen in a daze. Her brain was like a computer on the fritz. She managed to rhyme off the Bay Ridge drinks order and then stood in the throng of people waiting for their food near the silver truck.

"Can you believe it?" one misty-eyed lady breathed at her companion.

"What a thing to happen. Greg was so lovely."

"Lovely? That's not what I heard," came the reply. "I don't think there's a woman on these showgrounds who hasn't had something to do with Greg Grenier. And not always in a good way, let me tell you."

"What? Now that's not nice," chimed in another voice. "Just because you weren't on the receiving end of his attentions."

"Ha! You listen to me, missy—"

"Maybe it was a heart attack. From all his exertions."

"Or someone killed him!"

"I bet you it was that groom of his, you know, the snarky one."

"Or that little mousy one. It's the quiet ones that will surprise you."

"I saw Terry yesterday and he looked fit to be tied."

"Poor Dave. Can you imagine living in Greg's shadow? I bet he didn't see much action."

"What about Lana? She's a great rider, but I can tell you she's one uppity minx."

Fanta grabbed her beverages and pushed her way out of the maelstrom. She hurried back to the stables, agitated and unhappy. All around her, she could see the news about Greg hopping from one person to the next, spreading like wildfire.

"What's wrong?" Bonnie called, looking up in concern.

"You won't believe it," Fanta said, skidding to a stop. She bobbled the tray with the hot drinks. Carefully, she held it out in front of her. She'd completely forgotten to get anything for herself.

"Try us, Fanta. We're not as easily shocked as you are," said Lyle, reaching in to take his coffee. Sara plucked out her cup of tea, muttering a crotchety, "This is Styrofoam, but I'm dying for some antioxidants."

Bonnie looked at Fanta with trepidation, slowly taking her hot chocolate from the holder.

"It's Greg Grenier." Fanta paused, her eyes swiveling around the group. "He's dead."

"*Whaaat?*" squawked Sara, burning her lip on the hot tea.

"Oh no! That's so sad," Bonnie cried. "He was so young. And so, you know, pretty."

"Whoa, maybe he was whacked," said Lyle. "It could have been any one of a dozen jealous girlfriends." His tone was more than a bit envious. He cracked the lid on his coffee and took a slurp.

Bonnie frowned at Lyle before turning back to Fanta. "Does anyone know what happened?"

Fanta shrugged helplessly. She was like some useless messenger with only half the message. She sorely needed some deets. But who knew what had happened?

"Did I hear you say that Greg Grenier was…was dead?"

Chessy appeared out of the tack room. Her usually glowing face was white and wan, her confident voice hesitant. Dressed in boots, breeches, and a riding shirt, she twirled her baseball cap uncertainly in her hands.

Fanta nodded mutely. She had no words of comfort, much less explanation.

Chessy blinked, sniffed, and hurried away down the aisle, eyes downcast.

Bonnie and Fanta exchanged a wary look. Everything had just gone sideways. The horse world had lost its wayward adonis, and so young, too. The show would undoubtedly go on, but the shock of it all would be hard to absorb.

Chapter Six

Fanta slumped in an old lawn chair that she had dragged up beside the hunter ring. Her second class over fences was a few hours away, and already she was nervous. Busy pro riders probably didn't have time for nerves. Busy pro riders just like…Greg. Fanta's chin fell to her chest. His death felt like a personal loss. A young life cut short! She started to question all the things that were happening in her own world. She was overcome by a sudden urgency to accomplish stuff. She needed to work harder on her riding. She had to do better at the Newser. She had to make more money, meet a great guy, start a family, buy a big house, plan for retirement. She couldn't keep up with it all. She barely knew where to start.

Someone flopped on the wet grass beside her. Fanta glanced over, startled. It was Greg's young groom, the one with the wispy blonde hair. Her face was tear-streaked and dried snot made nasty slug trails out of her nose and onto her upper lip. Fanta did a double-take. Of all people, it was Romy Mitchell.

"Hi, Fanta," Romy sniffled, staring unseeingly at the hunter ring, where a rider was taking a chestnut horse around the course. The rain had stopped, but a fine mist lingered. Spectators were few and far between. There was a definite pall in the air.

"Romy, wow, I haven't seen you in a while." Fanta tried to think of a way to navigate what was sure to be an awkward conversation. "So, I guess you work…for Greg?" Worked? She was already off on the wrong foot.

Romy shared a withering look. "That's right, I did. He's dead now," she said flatly. For shock value? Sympathy-seeking? Because she was drained of all possible emotion?

"Yes, yes, I'd heard." Fanta nodded thoughtfully. "I'm so sorry for your loss." That seemed like a safe rejoinder.

Fanta's eyes trailed over Romy's ill-fitting, unstylish jeans and her little girl's t-shirt with some sort of rainbow/cloud motif or maybe a fluffy bunny on the front. Was she still wearing a training bra? Yet again, Fanta was transported back to pony club days. Golden summer afternoons of sheer torment. She and Romy had been the awkward girls, the outcasts, always on the fringes, always looking for allies. Where Fanta had been chubby and shy, Romy had been stick-thin and oddly belligerent. They had drawn together in misery, constantly fending off the likes of Deirdre. Still, Romy was a few years younger than Fanta and they had not become close friends. Over the years, Fanta had sometimes seen Romy at the horse shows. Every time, it had been a reminder of all her childhood struggles. She had avoided Romy, she was ashamed to admit, like a bad smell.

"How are you doing?" Fanta asked gently. She was surprised that poor Romy wasn't...what? Packing up Greg's gear and heading home to Two Gates? It all seemed incredibly sad.

"I had to take a break." Romy's voice cracked. She glanced at Fanta, obviously needing someone to talk to. "It's a complete disaster at Two Gates. Dave is dealing with the police, Terry is trying to take charge of the horses, and Lana has just...disappeared. No one can find her. Deirdre and I are caught in the middle of it all."

Fanta tsk-tsked. Poor Lana, she must be heartbroken. As for Deirdre, well, she couldn't work up too much sympathy there. Maybe the stress she'd put on Greg with her over-the-top romantic advances had caused him to have some sort of breakdown—a heart attack even. It would be good for her to put in some real elbow grease for once, think of others before herself. Fanta looked more carefully at Romy, who had always put Greg on a pretty big pedestal.

"I heard that they're going to have a moment of silence for Greg tomorrow, before the big jumper class," Fanta offered. At least it was something.

Romy nodded. She had a faraway look. Fanta thought back to how Romy had run to the in-gate with the news of Greg's death. Usually, Romy went unnoticed by people. She reminded Fanta of a Venus flytrap, strange but innocent in appearance, until someone unwittingly wandered by, close to her feisty temper. It seemed bizarre that Romy had played a major role in the day's drama.

"So, you must have been one of the first to hear about Greg's death," Fanta commented delicately. Romy didn't seem poised to snap her spiny jaws. Fanta continued, "That must have been tough. Does anyone know what happened?"

Romy's face undulated like a swimmer about to breach the surface of the water. She struggled for words.

"I was there, Fanta, it was me," Romy blurted, sobs wracking her thin body as she ferreted out some well-used tissues from her jeans pocket.

Fanta looked at her, confused. Surely Romy wasn't admitting to some sort of crime.

"I found him, dead, in his hotel room," Romy moaned. Her face crumpled and she dropped her head between her knees.

Fanta was appalled. "Oh no, I'm so sorry. I had no idea. I hope...I hope he...went quietly." She was completely out of her depth.

Romy raised an anguished face. "No, he didn't," she wailed. "I saw...I heard the police say...he was killed!"

"Good heavens," Fanta breathed. She sounded just like her mother. But breaking out with a juicy cuss word didn't seem quite appropriate. "So...what now?"

"I don't know, Fanta!" Romy keened. Then she dashed her hands across her face. "I gotta go now. They'll be looking for me. Thanks for listening."

Romy jumped to her feet and scampered away over the grassy hill toward the stables, leaving a trail of icky tissues in her wake.

Fanta stared after Romy. It was impossible. She could barely comprehend that Greg was dead, and now Romy was saying that someone had killed him? Fanta was offended. Greg was so perfect, so handsome. He was a great rider and a good coach. He had everything going for him. How could anyone want to...but maybe...Fanta thought back on the past few days. Terry had obviously been angry with Greg for some reason. Fanta liked Terry, but he could be demanding and difficult. He earned a lot of money in the city as a fancy-pants banker and he probably never let Greg forget it.

Fanta was distracted from her deliberations as Sara entered the ring on Rose, a lovely dark bay mare with a showy way of moving. Problem was, Rose was green and inexperienced and possibly not the best choice for a young rider like Sara. Fanta shook her head. The parents had likely been dazzled by the pretty horse, without a thought as to whether it suited the abilities of their daughter. Fanta was happy with Des. He might be a little older and not as fetching, but he was the perfect partner for her.

Sara circled carefully and started the course. Things looked promising. Rose cantered happily toward the first fence on her long, elastic legs and then slammed on the brakes right in front of it. Sara flew forward like a slingshot, almost going off over Rose's head. Righting herself, she circled and tried again with the same result. Even from outside the ring, Fanta could feel Sara's frustration mounting like a tsunami. The steward whistled her out after three tries. Sara walked Rose from the ring, obviously in a sulk. Penny met her at the in-gate, put a hand on Rose's reins, and started in on what looked like a stern lecture. Sara appeared chastened. Rose seemed pleased, probably thinking ahead to a fresh hay net and a nice grooming from Bonnie.

Fanta's mind wandered back to Greg's death. Of course, there was Lana. She had to be gutted. But…she had not been happy to see Greg with Chessy at the bar, blonde heads bent together in a cozy tryst. Maybe Lana had also sensed something going on between Greg and Deirdre. It was not hard to spot that Deirdre was on the warpath, with barely-there lingerie and puppy-dog eyes in her quiver of arrows. And, of course, there were all the usual rumors about Greg's various flings and flirtations. Fanta harrumphed. Greg had only had eyes for Lana…at least, if he'd been smart.

Fanta watched as Chessy rode into the ring on Kash. She and Penny had bought the stunning young horse together, with the plan to train him and sell him to another rider who would take him to the next step in his career. It was supposed to be some sort of investment scheme. Fanta thought it was all highly unlikely. She couldn't believe how quickly the costs of owning a horse added up. Like there would be any profit left over.

In her inimitable fashion, Chessy navigated the course smoothly. Kash was a superstar, performing well beyond his years, his fiery bay coat gleaming under the leaden skies. Penny beamed at the in-gate. Fanta grunted.

Back to the previous night. Chessy had been in the bar with Greg. Whatever they had been discussing had seemed uncomfortable for both of them. Did Chessy have a motive, enough to kill Greg? Fanta's mind boggled at the thought of a murderer doing the daily round at Bay Ridge. And then there was Dave, Greg's business partner. He had been fighting with Terry. It had sounded like Greg was a bone of contention between them. Was Two Gates in financial trouble?

Fanta attempted to reconcile the whole mish-mash of grievances, rejections, battered hearts, and foiled ambitions with her vision of Greg, golden boy. It just didn't add up.

A glance at her watch told her she better get ready for her class. She pulled herself out of the saggy lawn chair and stood, trying to orient herself in this new world of Greg being dead—maybe even murdered. Nothing about it felt good.

* * *

"Move that horse up off your leg, look up, look up!" Penny's voice thundered over the warm-up ring.

Fanta struggled to ride Des in the sudden downpour. The heavens had opened, just as she and Des had arrived in the warm-up, perky and prepped for success. Now, raindrops slapped her face and the reins slipped through her fingers. The saddle felt like wet cardboard under her seat bones. All she could think about was Greg lying dead in his hotel room. Glassy eyes, pooling blood, limbs spread in some macabre fashion, tongue lolling from his mouth. Enough!

"Stop fussing with Des, you need to keep your pace," Penny hollered, shielding her face from the driving rain.

Fanta jumped the practice fence again and again. She could tell even Des's patience was wearing thin. She just had to put everything aside and ride her horse. She imagined flipping a switch on her churning emotions, snuffing them out.

"Fanta Delaney, to the ring please!" the steward warbled through the maelstrom. Encased in a giant plastic poncho, he sounded like he'd far rather be relaxing at home, snug and dry. Wouldn't they all? But it was time to go to work. Fanta trotted Des into the show ring and immediately picked up the canter.

She pointed Des squarely at the first fence, flowed smoothly toward it, and hopped over. Perfect. She looked toward the next two jumps, her eyes never wavering. Her face was so wet it actually felt like she was crying. Suck it up. Without hesitation, she and Des flew over the pair of obstacles. She headed smoothly into a corner and came powering out, gliding over the jumps set diagonally across the ring. Fantastic! Her brain, scrubbed of emotion, was operating on a purely tactical level. Now, she needed to maintain her pace past the in-gate and up the next line of fences. Fanta forced herself not to blink, even as a particularly fat raindrop landed right in her eye. Des didn't miss a beat, and they jumped each obstacle like clockwork. Only one fence to go. Fanta concentrated on riding deep into the corner, eyes pasted on the last jump. The perfect take-off spot was right in front of her, yes, there it was. Des sailed over, landed in a smooth and balanced canter, and broke into a relaxed trot for the finishing circle.

She'd nailed it! Fanta almost fist-pumped. It was acceptable in the show jumpers, but probably a shocking breach of decorum in the hunters. She left the ring, patting Des like he had just won the Kentucky Derby.

"That was it, Fanta, you got it!" Penny smiled proudly, even as the rain coursed down her not-so-waterproof coat and her shoes squelched in the swampy footing. "You get that horse back to the barn for a good rubdown. He deserves it. And give yourself a treat, too, while you're at it. I have to go see Lyle, but you and Des stick around for the call." Penny winked and hurried off through the weather, which was subsiding into a steady drizzle.

Fanta waited anxiously ringside, holding Des's reins. A couple more competitors tackled the course, not doing nearly as well as she had. Her hopes rose, floating and fizzing like delicate bubbles. Of course, she hadn't seen Terry and Pearl go. They'd probably crushed it.

With a fumble of the microphone, the announcer started in. "In first place, we have String of Pearls, owned and ridden by Terry Miller. Let's have a nice round of applause for our class winner." There was a polite sprinkling of hand-clapping.

Okay, okay, that was not surprising. Fanta felt her head might explode. Who was next? She held her breath.

"In second place, we have Desmos, owned and ridden by Fanta Delaney."

Fanta tried not to whoop, holler, or bounce up and down. With a kiss for Des, she led him into the ring behind Pearl. Des strutted along, enjoying the attention and Fanta's buoyant mood. He held his head up nobly as the ribbon was affixed to his bridle. Fanta practically giggled at the officials. A second and a fourth! Only one more class to go. Maybe she and Des would be reserve champions of the division behind Pearl and Terry, who had already clinched the championship.

Bonnie came jogging up just as Fanta and Des walked into the warm-up area. "I'm just getting back from the other ring," Bonnie puffed, stopping to catch her breath. A grooming bucket dangled from her fingers. She looked like a drowned rat. "But how awesome! You guys are superstars," Bonnie gushed. Together, they started to lead Des back to the stables.

"Thanks, Bonnie, and for all your help, too," Fanta gibbered, feeling as if she were walking on air, even as her leather boots squished in the mud. "I can't believe it went so well. Des is such a good boy." She gave him yet another pat.

They approached the Bay Ridge stalls, with Fanta detailing every aspect of her and Des's performance. Suddenly, Bonnie's head popped up.

"Did you see that?" she said, looking concerned. "I just saw someone coming out of our tack room."

Fanta was enveloped in a cloud of euphoria. "Sorry? I'm sure it's just one of the Bay Ridge gang." She grinned at Bonnie. Her energy was boundless. "Let's give Des a special rubdown. And, oh, I think I have some of his favorite treats in my tack box."

Bonnie frowned. "Yeah, you may be right. It just…didn't look like anyone from our barn." She shook her head, glossy curls bouncing under her soaked baseball cap. The smile came back to her face. "Yes, let's get this boy all cleaned up. Nothing but the best for our Dessie."

Bonnie maneuvered Des into the grooming stall, patting and fussing over him. Fanta snagged the little foot ladder they lugged around with them to the shows. Proudly, she pinned her second-place ribbon alongside her fourth on the big Bay Ridge Farms banner. Stepping down, she gazed up in awe.

There was only one more class to go before the show was over for her and Des. She thought of Greg, who would never ride into a ring, hear the roar of the crowd, or experience the sheer joy of riding again. Fanta made a promise. She would put all her worries aside and perform to the absolute best of her abilities, even if it were the only tiny thing she could do in honor of her fallen hero.

Chapter Seven

Fanta sat in the tall metal bleachers surrounding the main jumper ring. The sun had unexpectedly come out and was warm on her back. Still, the air was like a sauna and big dark clouds threatened. But Fanta barely noticed. She was basking in the glow of her fabulous ride on Des. She'd left him primped and preened, munching happily on hay in his stall. Des was the best.

Fanta gazed at the maze of colorful fences in the ring. They made her teeth clench, they looked so intimidating. Still, with her newfound confidence and maybe a bit of talent, Fanta could picture herself riding into the jumper ring, piloting some awesome horse over jumps taller than she was, finishing through the timers with a flourish and a mighty fist pump. She took a big chomp of her grape popsicle.

"Mind if I join you?" Sara plunked herself on the bleacher next to Fanta. A jolt went through the thin metal. Fanta bounced and almost dropped her popsicle. She glanced over in irritation. Sara's thick hair was even more of a tangled mess and her riding clothes were wrinkled and stained. Fanta scrunched her nose. Thank goodness they were outdoors. She sighed. It would have been nice to have a few more moments to herself. Who knew what tortured round-robin of gripes and barbs might follow.

Sara settled giant movie-star sunglasses on her nose, just so. She clicked her tongue stud against her teeth. She pulled a nail file from the back pocket of her breeches and started poking and rasping. Sara was obviously in blasé mode. Fanta was no longer shocked by any of it.

Sara jutted her chin at the ring. "I think Chessy's going to be coming in soon," she said, uber-casual, "she's got Ollie in the junior jumpers."

Fanta felt her buoyant mood deflate. Okay, Chessy was a good rider, but surely Penny could see that she, Fanta, amateur equestrian extraordinaire, was ready to tackle the bigger courses in the jumper ring, twisting and turning and racing against the clock. But no, it was always Chessy, Chessy, Chessy. Fanta frowned behind her cheap plastic shades. A large purple drip fell from the tip of her popsicle, precariously close to the cuff of her white riding shirt.

"How did it go with Rose today?" Fanta smiled a mean smile. As if she hadn't seen Sara implode in the ring earlier. She felt like some hideous big-game hunter, waiting for a hapless animal to fall into the hidden trap, relishing the anticipation.

Sara issued an exaggerated groan. "Oh, well, Rose tried really hard, but I was just so tired. I have so many responsibilities these days." She rolled her neck in a circle. Nasty pops and crinkles sounded. "Rose isn't like Des. You always have to be on your game with her. She's a difficult ride, not point-and-jump." Sara started filing one of her nails to a vicious spike.

Fanta began to hyperventilate. She wanted nothing more than to shove Sara and her stupid nail file off the bench and watch them ping pong away through the metal spindles of the bleachers to the ground below. They could lie there with the rest of the trash. With any luck, the file would pierce Sara's shriveled heart, or her tiny brain. Fanta choked back her anger and indignation. Sara had no clue about how to ride a difficult horse. She and Rose had not even made it over the first fence! And, *hell-ooo*, Des was not point-and-jump.

Fanta tried to focus on the ring, where the first competitor had started the course. The horse was a fabulous jumper but had a short stride, which could make it tricky to navigate from one jump to the next. With steely determination, the rider headed toward three consecutive fences with only two or three strides in between. There was no room for error. The horse jumped through valiantly, leaving all the rails up. What a cutie! Fanta felt her mood lighten a shade. She totally needed to dial it back.

"Oh, that was nice, thought she might get in trouble there," Sara said mildly, gazing around the bleachers. Scritch, scritch, scritch went the nail file, drifts of nasty white stuff settling onto the leg of Sara's smirched breeches. Fanta sent invisible waves pulsing outward, willing Sara to move elsewhere. Alone, she might actually enjoy watching the class. Penny was always telling her how important it was to watch and learn.

In the ring, a rail tumbled down with a clunk. The rider had misjudged the take-off spot to one of the fences. She wouldn't move on to the jump-off. Too bad. Fanta shook her head. Still, the rider and horse had done a nice job, especially for the first competitor in the class.

"I would have ridden that differently," said Sara, all judgey and la-di-da. "She just didn't bring the horse to the jump properly." She looked at her nails with their chipped purple polish, her upper lip curled derisively.

Fanta felt her eyes bug and her ears throb. A red mist descended.

"Here's Chessy and Ollie." Sara pointed the nail file at the in-gate. Then she turned to Fanta and spoke confidentially, a superior imparting inside information to an underling. "You know, Penny and I have talked about me taking Ollie into the jumpers next year. Chessy will move on to something else, and there's no one at Bay Ridge who could step up. It will be great to advance my riding career. Isn't it exciting?"

"You've got to be—" Fanta clamped her mouth shut. The red mist was like a splash pad on steroids. She would take the high road, if only she could find it. She sucked in a massive breath—in through the mouth, out through the nose. Whatever! Everyone knew Sara lived in la-la land. Fanta just had to be the better person.

"That's quite something," she gritted out. Ollie was Bay Ridge's most experienced show jumper. There was no way that Penny would allow Sara to take Ollie in the jumper ring. It was ludicrous. The party girl could barely get her horse over a picket gate, much less manage a jumper course. Fanta snapped the wooden popsicle stick in two and dropped it through the bleachers, watching it helicopter to the ground. She felt a frisson of satisfaction.

She looked up in time to see Chessy canter briskly into the ring on Ollie. After taking a few moments to review the course in her mind, Chessy established Ollie's canter and turned toward the first fence. Up and over with surgical precision and on to the next two jumps with either five long strides or six short strides in between. Chessy galloped Ollie down the line in five bold strides and prepared to go deep into the corner to get the best approach to the next fence, a solid red wall that many horses found intimidating.

"She rode that well," Sara said grudgingly, blowing on her nails. Then she perked up. "Oh, what's wrong?"

Chessy rode smoothly out of the corner, Ollie in perfect control. Then, for no apparent reason, she dipped frighteningly to one side, almost dropping her reins, one hand grabbing at Ollie's thick neck. Ollie faltered and broke to a trot, unsure what to do next. Chessy struggled to right herself in the saddle. Her foot had dropped out of her stirrup and the leather strap dangled dangerously. It would not be good if Chessy tipped off underneath Ollie's big hooves. The crowd held its breath. Fanta realized she had her hands to her mouth.

After a few tense moments that seemed like an eternity, Chessy pulled herself back into the saddle, brought Ollie to a walk, and waved to the ring stewards that she would not continue the course. Looking shaken, she left the ring, holding the leather stirrup strap in one hand. Penny rushed to meet her.

"Oh, that's too bad," said Sara, looking anything but upset. "Anyway, I see some of my friends over there, I'll catch you later." She scampered over to a group of young riders from another barn, probably eager to discuss Chessy's mishap in the ring or whatever other witchcraft she had in mind.

Fanta breathed a sigh of relief. Chessy seemed to be okay, and Sara had finally gone. Things were looking up. She watched a few more riders compete, but her heart was no longer in it. The red mist had subsided, but so had her celebratory mood. Gray clouds once again blocked the sun and Fanta felt clammy and chilled. Greg's death crept back into her mind; it was really starting to sink in. And now, what had happened to Chessy? She got up from the bleachers and made her way back to the Bay Ridge stalls, where she found Bonnie cleaning saddles and bridles. There appeared to be no one else around.

"Hey, Bonnie. Did you hear about Chessy? She almost had a fall in the ring just now." Fanta jerked her thumb back the way she had come.

Bonnie regarded her silently, seeming to contemplate. Then, she beckoned Fanta to follow her into the tack room and over to the saddle rack. Chessy's saddle was identified by a small brass nameplate. Without a word, Bonnie lifted the flap that covered the top of the stirrup strap and kept the buckle from chafing the rider's leg.

Fanta and Bonnie eyed each other. It was easy to see that the stitching on the strap had come loose, allowing the stirrup to give way under the rider's weight. If that had happened just as Chessy was jumping a big fence, the consequences could have been disastrous. It had been bad enough as it was. Fanta peered at the frayed stitching. Maybe it was just her imagination, but it looked like it had not only come loose, but been purposely ripped.

* * *

Glad to be home, Fanta sat in her favorite recliner, cradling a cup of hot tea in her hands. It was Saturday night, prime party time, but she doubted anyone from the horse world would be whooping it up at the Carleton. How many people knew that Greg was not only dead, but possibly murdered? She wished she herself didn't know. She couldn't get her head around it. It seemed otherworldly.

Bored, she picked up her phone and scrolled through her social media feed. She had lost touch with most of her friends from university. She flipped through their photos and posts. They seemed like strangers now. She should post a picture of herself and Des and their two ribbons. She would grin like a fool and Des would be his awesome, lovable self. She laid the phone down on the small side table. She had never been good at self-promotion. And she looked fat in most photos.

She glanced around her small space. It always made her happy. She liked to think she had an eye for interior design. She had inherited a lot of familiar pieces from her parents' house when they had downsized and moved to

Florida a few years ago. Of course, she loved the sale racks at the home fashion stores, and she was not above picking up odds and ends she spotted around the neighborhood on trash day. She was often surprised at what she stumbled on. She pictured the amazing gilt-edged mirror that hung above the dresser in her bedroom. Some crazy neighbor had thought it was no good anymore.

She put the tea mug down beside her phone and drew a plush blanket around herself. It was a warm summer evening. The gray clouds were making way for shafts of evening sunlight. Raindrops sparkled on the leaves that hung just outside her front window. Still, she felt a chill. Her perfect, gorgeous Greg was dead. Chessy had almost had a bad fall. With the exception of her own amazing ride that afternoon on Des, it was not turning out to be a great horse show. She would compete in her class the next day and return to the office on Monday.

She wondered idly if anyone at work was up to speed on the goings-on at the horse show. The Newser no longer had the resources to staff the newsroom on the weekend. Come Monday, a mysterious death at one of the local hotels might catch some editor's eye. Fanta snorted. Even though it was related to the superfluous sport of show jumping.

A muted buzzing started up. What was that? Fanta cast her eyes about. The phone she'd been provided by the Newser was ringing from the depths of her purse, which was on the floor at her feet. She reached down, straining to grasp it. Finally, she snagged one of the handles, pulled it onto her lap, and reached in.

"Hello?" Oops. It could be an important work call. "Uh, Fanta Delaney here."

"Fanta, is that you?" a soft voice said. "It's Romy. Romy Mitchell."

Before Fanta could respond, Romy rushed on. "I hope it's okay that I've called you on a weekend and everything. I mean, I know you're not at work. I saw your phone number in the Newser, and I thought I would give it a try. But if you're busy, you know, that's okay, too."

"Oh, hi, Romy, sure. How are you?" Fanta stammered. She flashed on Romy in her fluffy bunny t-shirt, crying her heart out, having no one to confide in. The poor girl. "What can I do for you?"

"Well, I think you might be able to help me, to help us," Romy started cautiously. "I thought, you know, you're a reporter and everything. That must mean you're good at finding things out. Asking questions, that sort of stuff."

Fanta suppressed a snort of laughter. Her most recent questions had been about the best binoculars for birdwatching and what local dance studios taught the tango. Not terribly discerning. Then she reconsidered. It was nice that someone thought of her as a real journalist. Even if it was only Romy.

"Well, that's true, I am a reporter," Fanta said. She sounded like a pompous jerk. "But, I'm not sure what you're getting at. Are you interested in finding a job in the media?" Like she could do anything. She had only just started herself.

"No, no, that's not it at all. It's Greg, I was hoping you could ask about Greg," Romy said, exasperated.

Say what? Fanta struggled to get a grip on the conversation. Did Romy want to be asked questions about Greg? Like some sort of healing exercise? It reminded her of a mental health feature she had considered writing for the Newser.

"I'm sorry, I don't understand. You'll have to be more specific. Then I can figure out how to assist you." Now she sounded like one of those dreaded call center people, the ones she always landed on after pressing a zillion buttons and yelling nonsense into the phone.

Romy made a soft growling noise and launched in. "The police are investigating Greg's death. You know, I told you that they think he was killed." Romy paused. Fanta made an affirmative sort of sound. Romy continued, "Okay. But I'm not sure they know much about the horse world. I mean, horse people can be pretty weird. These investigators have no clue."

Fanta thought that police officials likely had their fill of weird. She was still having trouble understanding whatever it was Romy had in mind.

"Well, it's true that I'm a reporter, but I'm not on the crime beat," she managed, thinking as quickly as she could. "The Newser's police reporter may do a piece on Greg, especially if it's a homicide, but I don't know what she's got." Fanta had no idea if she had anything, or if it was even on her radar. "Did you want me to ask her?"

At least the police reporter was one of the more approachable people in the newsroom. It mightn't be a bad idea to reach out. Fanta was warming to the plan. It could raise her profile at the Newser. Abby would be impressed.

"No, not really, Fanta. And there's no if. Greg was murdered!" Romy's temper was taking flight. "Here's what I'm saying. I thought you might ask around, talk to some horse show people. You know what they're like, who they are. You speak their language. Then, if you found out anything, you could tell the police. It would be, like, helpful to them. To have context. To see how everything fits together. Don't you think?"

Fanta doubted it. Why would the police want some wannabe sleuth wandering around, mucking everything up? And as for horse show people… well, good luck to anyone who wanted to figure them out. "I don't know, Romy. I'm not sure it's a good idea. It's going to be an official police investigation. I'd just be in the way. I appreciate your confidence, but I don't really know anything about solving crimes."

Fanta stumbled to a stop, unsure how to proceed. The whole request was unnerving. Before she could utter another syllable, Romy gave an exaggerated sigh and the line went dead.

Fanta pulled the phone away from her ear and looked at it, as if an explanation might be written on the dark screen. With nothing forthcoming, she shoved the device back in her purse. She uncurled herself from the armchair. It was time for bed if she wanted to be rested for the next day. What was Romy thinking? Fanta had never been one for putting herself out there, straying outside her comfort zone. Romy should know that better than anyone.

She rinsed her mug and placed it in the strainer. She went through her mental checklist to ensure everything in the kitchen was ready for the morning. All good. She trailed toward her bedroom. Her alarm was set for the right time. She headed to the bathroom, her thoughts traveling with her. There was no doubt her response to Romy had been the right one. She certainly couldn't help with any police inquiry. The mere suggestion was preposterous.

She looked at herself in the mirror, brushing her teeth, counting the strokes. She tried to picture another Fanta, zipping about the horse world, asking probing questions, notebook aloft, blazing a path to justice. It was plain silly. Finally, she crawled into her neat and comfy bed. She didn't have the skills to do something like that. She closed her eyes. Did she?

Chapter Eight

Fanta left for the showgrounds early Sunday. She drove steadily along the deserted highways. The morning was bright and sunny and her eyes ached behind her sunglasses. Even her hot, strong coffee was having a limited effect. At least her riding shirt was clean and her breeches were a titch more comfortable.

She had slept poorly, her brain turning over and over like an unfortunate animal on a spit. She had not been able to stop thinking about her conversation with Romy. On the one hand, the whole idea of looking into Greg's death was overwhelming, even scary. On the other, she couldn't escape the feeling that not doing anything would be a lost opportunity. After all, it wouldn't be too hard to ask a few questions, talk to a few people, just like Romy said. Surely she could manage it. Unless she was a total wuss.

She bumped the Honda into the jam-packed parking area. After an endless loop-de-loop, she found a spot miles away from the tented stables. She trudged along, carrying her gear. She needed to think about riding Des. Not all this stuff with Greg. Her priorities were completely out of whack. Not to mention, she'd promised Abby that she would do better at work. She totally had to pick it up.

Bleary-eyed, she rounded a corner, stumbled on a grassy tussock, and came face to face with Deirdre.

"Oh, hi." Fanta was disoriented. She glanced up at the dark blue banner at the top of the stalls. Lana Taylor Stables. She looked back at Deirdre, who was calmly cleaning a bridle hanging from a hook. Her skinny jeans seemed a little less skinny, and her revealing t-shirt had been replaced with a staid polo.

"You're working for Lana now?" Fanta blurted. Leave it to Deirdre to abandon Two Gates at its time of need. The fickle witch.

"Yes, Panta Fanta, try to keep up."

Deirdre's expression was masked by sunglasses and a ball cap, but Fanta could plainly see and hear the sneer. It occurred to Fanta that, even though she and Deirdre hadn't spoken in years, here they were, facing off just like in pony club days. There would be no, "Hey, how ya doin'? Great to see you." That was not going to happen. Ever.

Deirdre was continuing, "If you must know, I left to get away from *you*, and took a job in Vermont with Lana. She was looking for someone with experience at her level. Then, for reasons you wouldn't understand, I came back to work for Greg. Let's just say, he was in need of my…skills."

Fanta gagged. She could only imagine. "Well, it may surprise you to learn, Dee-Dee, that I haven't been following your…I'm not sure of the word…career? I've been going to university and getting, you know, a *real* job."

Fanta sent a silent apology to Bonnie and nice grooms everywhere. She would be lost without them.

Deirdre offered a look of disdain, her gaze flicking up and down Fanta's body. "Whatever you say. It must be a desk job, from the looks of it."

Fanta seethed. A hideous memory flooded into her brain. Her mom had bought her a ski jacket to wear at the barn. It had seemed sporty at the time. Fanta had loved the electric blue and eye-searing yellow stripes. But it had been completely out of place at the conservative horse stables and been perfect fodder for Deirdre. One time, Fanta had left the jacket hanging in the tack room. She'd come back, put it on, tucked her hands in the pockets, and found them full of fresh manure.

Fanta blinked painfully. Her eyes snagged on one of Greg's horses being loaded onto a trailer for the trip back to Two Gates. Before she could think about it, she said, "How sad. It's such terrible news about Greg."

Deirdre smirked. "Oh, I'm sure you're broken-hearted." The tone was harsh and mocking. "Did you ever actually speak to the guy? Or did you just keep his picture under your pillow at night? As I recall, you had quite a few pictures of Greg." Deirdre cackled.

Fanta's face flamed. "I did talk with Greg," she replied indignantly. "Just the other night, I…we…had a nice chat." Had Deirdre seen that interaction? No, no, no. Fanta gave herself a mental shake. She would not give Deirdre the upper hand, not again.

She continued primly, "Anyway, Dee-Dee, I'm glad to see you haven't taken everything lying down. I'm sure Lana will teach you a whole new set of skills, ones related to horses and horsemanship. That should help get you back on your feet."

Her hatred for Deirdre ground in her gut like a blunt-toothed saw.

Deirdre snatched the bridle from its hook. "You'd best be on your way to that little backwoods barn where you ride," she hissed. "I have to get ready for the big jumper class this afternoon."

Fanta was caught off-guard. "Lana is riding today? I thought she might take some time off."

"Not all of us are as pathetic as you are," Deirdre jeered. "Lana is a professional rider, an adult. She doesn't let emotions get in the way of doing her job."

Deirdre turned and disappeared into Lana's tack room. Fanta did a full-body shake, trying to rid herself of the toxic energy. Then she continued on her way to the Bay Ridge stalls. It was all too much. First Romy, now Deirdre. Was she doomed to constantly relive her childhood?

* * *

This was it. The last class of the division. The reserve championship was on the line. It was her time to shine.

Fanta had found the same cool confidence as the day before, and Des was responding like a champ. The course was riding beautifully. She cantered deep into the corner of the show ring and turned Des squarely toward the last line of two fences. The sun threw a nasty glare in her eyes, but she could see the perfect take-off spot. If she could just nab the last two jumps, she would be sure to win another ribbon, maybe the reserve championship. She was living the dream!

Des arced beautifully over the first fence. Fanta sat tall in the saddle, ready to put the finishing touches on another flawless ride. With her eyes fixed firmly on the last obstacle, she didn't see the spectator in the bleachers take out a big pink parasol and snap it open with a flourish. Poor Des lurched to the left, startled. Fanta lurched to the right. She struggled to regain her balance as Des soldiered on down the line. They were at the final fence. Des leaped with all his might. Fanta clung on like a limpet.

She slowed to a trot and made her way to the out-gate. "I love this sport, I love this sport," she muttered under her breath. She patted Des. He had reacted as any horse would have. She gave his neck an extra rub. It was what she loved most about riding: partnering with another living creature. From across the warm-up ring, Penny gave her a big thumbs-up and a smile.

Fanta dismounted, loosened the girth, and secured her stirrups on the saddle. There would be no ribbon for her performance, and the reserve championship was likely out of reach. She meandered back to the white tents, Des following. Still, she'd done well for the first show of the season. There was nothing to be ashamed of.

Back at the stalls, Bonnie was ready to help. "I can take Des." She scanned Fanta's face. "You okay?"

"Thanks. Yeah, for sure, I'm okay." Fanta shrugged. Everything had been right there in front of her, shiny and golden. Now it was gone.

Bonnie buzzed around Des, taking off the saddle, setting in with the brushes. All the tiny braids would need to come out of his mane. Fanta knew it was a lot of work.

"I'm going to help. Let me go take off my jacket and stuff." She just had to get on with it. Bonnie wasn't paid to be some sort of therapist.

In the tack room, Fanta peeled off her show jacket. It needed to go to the dry cleaners, pronto. She pulled off her tall leather boots and exchanged them for her runners. She lifted her helmet off her head and shoved the sun visor on as quickly as possible. That felt better. Her mood was improving. She grabbed two chilled bottles of water from the Bay Ridge cooler and strolled back out to the grooming stall.

"Hey Bonnie, I got you a—"

Her words were cut short by a voice coming over the PA system.

"This week, we were all saddened to learn of the death of Mr. Greg Grenier, one of our sport's greatest young talents," the announcer intoned. Fanta looked around. Everyone in the barn area had stopped what they were doing, listening. "I don't think there's any among us who would doubt Greg's passion for the horses, his talent as a rider, and his commitment to the sport." Fanta heard a few sniffles, but otherwise an eerie quiet. "And so on behalf of the equestrian community and this show's organizing committee, I'd ask you to take a moment to reflect on Greg's career and his contributions. Thank you."

Fanta sat heavily on one of the Bay Ridge tack trunks. Her heart ached, and for someone she'd never even known. What would the show world be without Greg? She saw tears coursing down Bonnie's cheeks.

Gradually, activity began to pick up again. Together, Fanta and Bonnie got Des cleaned up and back in his stall. All the horses and equipment would trailer back to Bay Ridge that afternoon. But first, there was the big grand prix show jumping class, featuring top riders from Canada and the U.S. With a wave and a thank you for Bonnie, Fanta headed toward the main jumper ring.

By the time she found a seat in the packed bleachers, a few riders had already tackled the course, but no one had managed a clear round. As Fanta got settled, she could see that the biggest challenge was a wide water jump followed by four short strides to a tall, shaky-looking fence. Riders had to gallop to clear the water, then quickly shorten the horse's stride to jump the tall fence carefully.

Fanta was focused on the ring when a voice spoke beside her. "Is it okay if I join you?"

Fanta looked up. It was Chessy. "Sure!" Fanta scooted over to make room. She felt awkward, happy, and nervous. One of the cool kids was actually going to sit beside her.

Chessy folded her long legs into the spot. "This should be a good class.

I walked the course earlier, and it's full of tricky spots." Jumper riders examined the course on foot so they could formulate a strategy for how they would ride it.

"That's cool." Fanta performed a mental kick. Was that the best she could do? The whole situation was overwhelming. Feeling Chessy's presence beside her like an aura, she gazed with envy at the top riders competing in their white breeches and red jackets. What was it like to ride on a national team? She could barely imagine the exhilaration and terror that she would feel.

Chessy examined each rider's every move. "That was nice, but I would have asked that horse to do eight strides instead of nine," she commented, as one of the younger riders in the class finished the course with four faults.

Fanta glanced sideways at Chessy. Did she ever think about anything other than riding? She realized she knew very little about her. Of course, she was gorgeous and talented. But beyond that…Then Fanta remembered the stirrup strap and the stitching. Surely Chessy had seen it herself.

"I'm glad you weren't hurt with Ollie yesterday, that looked scary," Fanta ventured. "What happened?"

Chessy shrugged. "I have no idea. The stitching gave out. Penny was pretty upset about it." Her eyes didn't leave the ring. "Not much I can do, I guess."

Fanta decided to leave her suspicions unspoken. They were silly. Chessy would only see her as some conspiracy nut. She remembered that Chessy attended the local college. That seemed like a safer topic. "How's school going?"

"Just a few classes to finish, then I'll be able to graduate." Chessy glanced at Fanta and then back at the ring, where another rider was charging around the course.

"And then what?" Fanta asked. This was possibly the longest conversation she'd ever had with Chessy, who was turning out to be a perfectly normal person.

"Then I'll be a qualified vet tech. I hope to find a job around here so I can stay in the area." Chessy's eyes trailed the horse and rider in the ring, riding the course along with them.

"That's fantastic, what a great career choice." Fanta had never thought of Chessy outside the bounds of riding and horses.

Chessy nodded and smiled. "Yeah, thanks."

Fanta had the sense of standing at the top of a great precipice. She stepped off. "I happened to see you talking with Greg Friday night at the Carleton. It looked pretty intense. I guess you guys knew each other."

Chessy turned and gave Fanta a hard look.

"I mean, you seemed upset when you heard about his death," Fanta stammered, tumbling through a freefall. "I guess I wondered if there was something going on. You know, between you and Greg," she squeaked. What was she thinking? Everything had been going so well. "I mean, who would blame you? He was totally hot." No! Had she just said that?

Chessy stood abruptly. "I better make sure the horses are ready to trailer home." She made her way out of the bleachers without a backward glance.

Fanta's cheeks felt like a barbecue on fire. She dropped her head in her hands. "Way to go, Sherlock." She was dreaming in technicolor if she thought she had any of the skills needed to investigate Greg's death.

The announcer boomed, "I know you'll join me in giving a special round of applause for our next competitor, Lana Taylor on Palmetto."

Lana galloped into the ring on the powerful stallion. She seemed to have Palmetto well under control. The crowd roared and then tuned in to watch her every move. Surely Greg was not far from her mind.

Silence reigned as Lana and Palmetto ticked around the course. They stretched over the wide water jump and flew over the tall, shaky-looking fence. Would they go clear? That would be amazing. Then, everything fell apart. Palmetto approached the corner nearest the in-gate and began prancing sideways. Lana pulled on her left rein and encouraged him forward. Palmetto resumed his canter, headed toward the next fence, and stopped hard in front of it. Lana cartwheeled over his head and landed heavily on the sand. A gasp went up from the crowd. Fanta craned her neck. Lana was sprawled on the ground but was still holding Palmetto's reins. She sprang to her feet, dusted herself off, and waved away any offer of help. The spectators relaxed. Falls happened. Still, it would have been too much if Lana had been injured.

Fanta sat back. Poor Lana. Greg's death had taken its toll. She watched as Lana stalked from the ring, leading Palmetto, and roughly pushed aside Deirdre, who was waiting anxiously at the out-gate with her grooming gear. Fanta smiled mirthlessly. That was worth seeing. She tried to stretch her legs in the cramped bleachers. At the very least, it was nice to know that even top riders had their moments in the ring.

She watched a few more competitors go. There were a handful of clear rounds, so there would be a jump-off. The crowd was happy and buoyant. But Fanta was tired. It was time to call it a day.

She inched her way out of the bleachers and headed toward the crowded parking area. She had been woozy that morning. Where had she left the car? Her head swiveled like a periscope. Over there? She changed direction and walked alongside the tented stables. People were packing up and getting ready to trailer home. She thought of Des, happy to be back in his familiar stall at Bay Ridge. She would let him rest and go see him later in the week.

She stopped to get her bearings. She suddenly felt anxious to get away from the barn area. She would crumple up and die if she bumped into Deirdre again. A woman's voice floated out from the tent next to her.

"I can't believe this is my life right now," the voice hissed. "What a fiasco in the ring. I thought Palmetto had gotten past behaviors like that." There was a sound like a foot stomping. "And I wish everyone would stop being so nice to me. It's not helping. No one can understand what I had with Greg."

Fanta froze. It had to be Lana. Who was she talking to?

"You're just lucky I've taken you back, Deirdre," Lana continued her harangue. "I saw you flirting with Greg. Did you seriously think he would have dumped me for you?" There was a dismissive laugh. "Then there's that girl Chessy. I don't know why Greg gave her the time of day. What did she expect to happen? She needed to back off."

Fanta held her breath. Lana was in full flow. "All you young girls. There's just no respect. You think you can have whatever you want. Just send some guy a pic of your—" Lana heaved a mighty sigh. "So listen, Deirdre. You'd best behave yourself, if you know what's good for you. With your reputation, not many barns would take you. Think about that."

Footsteps faded away inside the tent. Wow! Fanta started to exhale. Lana was a force to be reckoned with, and Deirdre had gotten the smackdown she so richly deserved. Amazing! But wait. Fanta stepped back. Someone was coming her way, and fast. Fanta plastered herself against the tent as Deirdre, face stormy and eyes downcast, flew by and disappeared around the corner.

Fanta strolled into the car park, whistling a tune, twirling her keys. She found the Honda, unlocked the door, and flopped happily into the seat. Forget the panties and push-up bras, Deirdre better break out her steel-toed boots. By the sounds of it, Lana was going to give her the ride of her life. Fanta chuckled. The Honda wallowed over the uneven ground. She slipped on her shades and gazed at the setting sun. There really was a god.

* * *

Fanta relaxed on her small deck with a steaming cup of chamomile tea, enjoying the evening. The birds were flying home, the breeze dying to a whisper, and the darkness creeping across the sky. She totally needed to unwind before starting another work week. The morning meeting was only—she checked her watch—twelve hours away. Someday, she vowed, she would have real news to share with the group. Maybe even tomorrow. Did she have any information to relate about Greg's death? Fanta wasn't sure.

From the apartment below, she heard a screen door being pushed back, followed by snuffling and snorting. Fanta peered through the railing and saw Lottie, her downstairs neighbor's small white dog, checking out the evening air, her nose pushed against the spindles.

"That you up there, Fanta?" Mrs. Hooper's wizened face looked up at her. She wore a well-worn flowery housedress covered by one of her many vintage aprons. She held a thin tea towel in her veiny hands.

"Hi, Mrs. Hooper, yes, it's me." Fanta spoke loudly enough so the elderly woman could hear, but not so loud as to disturb her neighbors. Many of them were irritated by Mrs. Hooper, who struggled to pick up after Lottie in the scruffy yard near the parking area. Someone had even come up with the phrase, "Use the pooper scooper, Mrs. Hooper."

Lottie growled. Fanta assumed the fierce little dog was a wonderful companion to Mrs. Hooper, who lived alone in her apartment.

"Are you and Lottie enjoying the evening?" she called.

"Yes, oh yes," came the shaky reply. Mrs. Hooper paused, wringing the towel. "I'm going to visit my daughter next month, out west. I was wondering, Fanta dear, would you mind keeping an eye on our Lottie?"

Fanta regarded Lottie dubiously. "I think I could do that, Mrs. Hooper. We'll have a great time together, won't we, Lottie?" The little dog bared its teeth.

"Oh, that's good to hear, takes a load off my mind." Mrs. Hooper squinted up at Fanta in the gathering dusk. "You got yourself a boyfriend yet, young lady? Nice girl like you should have a man around."

This was a consistent theme. Fanta had gotten adept at dodging it. "Oh, Mrs. Hooper, I have to fight them off with a stick."

Mrs. Hooper giggled. "Such a card you are, dear." Fanta heard shuffling steps. Mrs. Hooper disappeared from view. "Goodnight! Come on, Lottie, before you catch your death out here."

Fanta waved, even though Mrs. Hooper couldn't see her anymore. She wondered what sort of life Mrs. Hooper had led, what her family was like. She wondered about her own old age. Would she be happy and healthy? It all seemed impossibly far away. At least she wasn't afraid of being on her own. It would be nice to meet someone, but it wasn't at the top of her priority list.

No, what she wanted to do was take charge of her life, of her future. If she asked a few questions, proved herself useful in investigating Greg's death, maybe everyone at work would take her more seriously. She would get bigger and better assignments. She would be on her way.

Fanta settled into her comfortable deck chair as the trills of birdsong made way for the steady chirp of the crickets. Something wasn't right at Two Gates, and maybe she was the person to find out what it was.

Chapter Nine

The newsroom was humming. Fanta was at her desk, finessing her birdwatching piece before turning to ballroom dancing. She would win a provincial award for feature writing. She would solve the mystery of Greg's death. She would rise to the tip-top of the Newser.

She read the birdwatching story one more time. She had been interested to learn that recordings of birdsongs could help a birder identify the species. There were also different types of feeders that attracted certain types of birds. Maybe she could adapt one for her deck.

She re-read her opening line: *"When Mabel Dougherty saw the glaucous-winged gull, she ticked one more entry off her birdie bucket list."*

Her work phone buzzed on her desk. Fanta reached for it.

"Fanta Delaney here," she said in her most pleasing, professional manner. She crossed her fingers that it wasn't one of the dance studios phoning to cancel an interview.

"Fanta? It's me, Romy. Romy Mitchell. Can't you see on the screen that it's me calling? It should show my name, you know, my ID."

"Yes, of course, Romy." Fanta actually hadn't noticed. "But that's part of my job as a journalist. Never take anything for granted. Always check your facts." She threw a glance around the newsroom. The morning meeting would start soon.

"Huh, okay."

Fanta could practically hear Romy shrug on the other end of the line.

Romy went on, "I wanted to check in with you on this Greg thing. You know, like I asked you about. Maybe you've given it more thought. Changed your mind. Because, you know, it's important." Romy sounded prepared to fight her corner.

Fanta wasn't about to be pushed about. She was no one's patsy. "Certainly, I've given it due consideration, and I will continue to do so. But there are many factors to be weighed. It's not the sort of thing I would do lightly." She wasn't about to tell Romy that she'd more or less decided to give it a shot. What if it all came to nothing?

"Oh, for—" Romy groused. "Okay, well, make it snappy. Things are moving quickly here at Two Gates. You need to get in the game." There was a pause. "What's happening there, at the Newser? Is someone on it? You know, covering the story? Whatever?"

Fanta tried not to grind her teeth. She wasn't about to let Romy know just how far out of the loop she was. "I'm about to discern that, Romy. We have our morning meeting shortly, where I will confer with my colleagues. I'll share with them what I know. I'm sure it will be helpful to them. Without my guidance, they may not recognize the importance of the story." That was great! Where did she come up with this stuff? Fanta smiled demurely.

"You're kidding, right? A guy's been killed, Fanta! Murdered in cold blood! How can that not be news?" Romy cried. "I get it that you're only a junior reporter. Maybe there's someone else I should talk to?" Romy sounded hopeful.

"No, Romy, no, there's no one else," Fanta sputtered. "Listen, I'll let you know how things go. But rest assured, I have things handled on this end."

"Let's go, everybody!" Abby came striding through the newsroom.

"I've got to go now, Romy. That's my boss. We'll talk later." Fanta stabbed the little red button and slapped the phone on her desk. Romy needed to back off. How could she be effective with someone breathing down her neck?

Fanta hit the save button on the birdwatching piece and scurried over to where everyone was gathering for the morning meeting. Somehow, she would figure out how to bring up the issue of Greg's death and convince the group that it deserved coverage. She knew well enough their views on the silly world of show jumping. She sat down as hastily as she dared in the wobbly chair.

"So some guy from the horse show was killed over at the Carleton on the weekend." Sue Goodwin, the Newser's police reporter, jumped right in.

All eyes swiveled to Fanta.

"Did you know the man, Fanta?" Abby inquired.

"Oh sure, I mean, everyone knew Greg. I didn't know him, like, personally, but for sure, you know, I knew him." Fanta's chair dipped to one side and she grabbed the seat. How had she not foreseen this?

Douglas Bell, the business editor who delighted in giving her a hard time, chuckled humorlessly, his Adam's apple bobbing in his turkey-like neck.

Sue took back the floor. "The police aren't releasing the guy's name pending the notification of next of kin, but I understand that it was—" she referred to a crumpled notebook in her hand—"Greg Grenier." She cocked an eyebrow at Fanta, who nodded mutely.

Sue shrugged, tucking her pen behind her ear. "Well, it seems like a homicide from what I'm hearing." She looked again at her notes. "Apparently, the guy was hit from behind with a blunt object sometime Friday night, probably before midnight. The investigators don't have much to go on and are asking for witnesses." Sue's brow furrowed. "A young girl found him, but I hear she's a tiny thing. I doubt the police see her bludgeoning a big guy with a heavy object."

"Do you have any insight into this, Fanta?" Abby asked.

"Oh well, nothing substantive," Fanta blustered. Her eyes skittered over the group. She held tight to her chair. Douglas had an amused look on his face. Fanta plucked up her courage. "I mean, I know some things. Terry— one of Greg's clients—was really upset with him, he told me so. And Greg's girlfriend, she thought he was cheating on her. And his business partner was angry about something. So, you know, there could be lots of suspects."

"This is a crime, not the plot of some tacky soap opera," Douglas blared.

"Anyway," Sue jumped back in, "the police say they're pursuing a line of inquiry, which may mean they have a suspect. There was also a big drug bust on the weekend, so I'm guessing resources are stretched pretty thin." She ran a hand through her short, sandy-blonde hair.

"Okay, thanks, Sue, let's keep on top of it. Fanta, let us know if you hear anything more." Abby was all business.

After the meeting, Fanta stalked back to her desk. She might have been unprepared, but Douglas's comment was plain wrong. Everyone knew that crimes were committed out of passion. And there seemed to be a lot of that at Two Gates.

She had an interview that morning for her feature on ballroom dancing. Maybe after that she would pop in at Two Gates and see if Dave LeDans was there. It would be interesting to find out what had been going on between him and Greg. It seemed like a good place to start.

She powered down her computer and took her purse from the desk drawer. At the very least, it was a pleasant day and the drive would be nice.

Ignoring a chorus of indignant honks, she swung out of the Newser's parking lot and onto the wide highway that was flanked by big-box retail. After a few minutes, she turned into a quaint neighborhood featuring small businesses and old-world charm. Her interview was at Belle of the Ball Dance Studios. She had mixed feelings about it. She didn't know much about dance, it looked dainty. She usually thumped around in leather riding boots and a clunky helmet. She couldn't imagine donning ballet slippers or tap shoes, much less a tutu. But it was always fun to meet people and learn new things.

She squeezed her car into a parking spot, jogged across the leafy street, and pulled open a glass door. She walked directly into the studio, which had mirrored walls and shiny hardwood floors. She was scheduled to meet with the instructor, Larry Kempworth, who owned the studio with his wife.

Fanta presumed the lean middle-aged man in the center of the dance floor was Larry. A young couple was attempting to move around the floor in a tight embrace.

"For heaven's sake, man, you're not handling dumbbells. That's your wife in your hands! Dip her, dip!" Larry chided.

The woman twisted awkwardly and almost lost her balance. Her husband grasped at her desperately. Then the couple laughed and prepared to try it again.

Larry glimpsed Fanta in the mirror. "Ah, you must be from the Newser," he said, gliding toward her and offering his hand. "I'm Larry, such a pleasure to have you here." He gestured to the young couple. "There's hope for them yet. You know what they say, a couple that can dance together, stays together."

"Oh, that's good." Fanta scrambled to find her mini recorder or at least a pen and paper.

"I mean, look at Fred and Viola," Larry continued, pointing to an older couple moving about the floor in a stately way, having an animated conversation as they stared into each other's eyes. "If you can dance and talk at the same time, you're halfway there," said Larry, gazing fondly at the pair.

"This is great stuff, Larry, and thanks for your time today. I can see it's busy," said Fanta, finally getting organized. She flipped to an empty page in her notebook. "Can you tell me about your studio? How did it all start?"

"Well, maybe it's easier just to show you." He indicated a woman coming toward him, floating over the shiny floor. "Please meet my wife, Babette," he said with a flourish.

Babette was the type of woman Fanta envied. Light, athletic, graceful, petite. Fanta felt like a total klutz just standing beside her.

Without a word, the pair joined hands and took to the floor. The other couples moved aside. Fanta didn't need to hear any music to recognize the dramatic opening steps of the tango. Larry and Babette began in slow motion, pulling toward and away from each other in a teasing manner. Then Larry grasped his wife by the waist, drawing her to him with controlled power, and the two began a series of rapid, intricate steps, flowing across the floor in incredibly close contact. As Babette curled her leg around her husband, Fanta could feel the sexual tension searing off the couple. With a final dizzying twirl, Babette fell backward in Larry's arm, her head almost touching the floor.

Everyone applauded. "That's pretty much how it started," said Larry, beaming at Fanta. "Babette always makes me look good."

"I let him think he's in charge," added Babette with a wink.

After gathering more details, interviewing some of the students, and attempting a few dance steps herself, Fanta said her goodbyes. She was stoked. Hopping into her car, she squeaked out of the parking spot and turned in the direction of Two Gates Stables.

Chapter Ten

Two Gates was named for its forked entrance that merged into a long, straight laneway up to the stables. Driving up the lane, Fanta saw a large indoor arena, several outdoor riding rings, a stable, and a scattering of outbuildings. She'd visited Two Gates before and knew that the grooms lived in a small motorhome near the stable. Dave lived in a gray brick bungalow set apart from the other buildings. She'd heard that Greg had kept an apartment nearby. The place seemed bland and impersonal. Fanta preferred Bay Ridge, with its older buildings and welcoming atmosphere.

She parked her car in the lot and stepped into the shade of the stable. The long cement aisle was swept and the stalls were freshly mucked. A ginger barn cat lay sprawled on the cool floor, licking its paws.

Fanta ventured in farther. A beautiful horse stood in each box stall, a blanket and halter hung neatly on the door. Fanta paused to admire Terry's horse, Pearl. The mare stood calmly, one hind leg cocked, looking at Fanta through dark, half-closed eyes. Peeking into a tack room, she saw rows of saddle racks, lockers for equipment, and bridles hanging on hooks.

Fanta approached the stable office and spotted Dave at his desk. He looked up from his paperwork and smiled.

"Hello, there," he called. He regarded her thoughtfully. "We've met before, right?" He tapped his forehead. "It's coming back to me. You were interested in boarding. Decided to move that horse of yours here after all? We've got just the spot for him." Dave looked pleased. Then his brow creased. "Sorry, I've forgotten your name."

"Fanta, the name's Fanta." She stood in the doorway.

"What type of name is that? Does your mom drink a lot of soda pop?" Dave forced a loud laugh. His face was flushed, his clothing needed a good wash and dry, and his hair was tousled. He drew a deep breath and wiped a hand across his forehead. "Sorry, that was stupid. Forgive me."

"Actually, it's short for Fantasia. My mom likes Disney movies."

Dave looked nonplussed. "Oh. What can I do for you?"

Fanta hesitated. She hadn't thought about how to conduct the discussion. Great reporter coming to the interview with no plan.

"Well, it's this business with Greg," she started. "I work at the Newser, and I thought maybe a feature on Greg would be a good idea. Something about his riding career and accomplishments, with some quotes from people who knew him best."

"Well, that sounds nice." Dave paused. "I wish I could say I knew him best, but it turned out maybe I didn't know him at all," he added ruefully, a twist to his mouth.

Fanta pulled her notebook and pen out of her purse.

"You know, we were best buddies in college." Dave leaned back in his chair, arms behind his head, a smile playing on his lips. "Studied together, partied together, the whole nine yards. Of course, we both liked horses. I was thrilled when Greg agreed to become my partner here."

His smile faded. "If I'm honest, though, I was worried. He'd been serious about someone when he was young, but in college, the guy was a real Lothario. Always lots of girls hanging around. I don't know, I guess women found him attractive." Dave shrugged, baffled.

Fanta wondered what it had been like to be Greg's less attractive friend, to stand alone as girls swarmed like flies over the campus hottie.

Dave's face grew serious. "We needed to keep things professional here. There was no room for fooling around. I just hoped that Greg's...tendencies wouldn't be a problem, you know, with the clients, even the grooms."

Fanta waited, pen poised. "And were they?"

Dave snorted. "Not as much as I'd feared, so that was a relief. Then Greg met Lana and they started to become serious. He seemed more... focused. I'm just not sure Lana knew what she was getting into. I don't know whether Greg was capable of changing his ways." Dave raised his eyebrows suggestively.

"Listen," he continued, holding up his hands in a placating gesture. "Greg sure was a great rider and a decent guy, and he didn't deserve to die the way he did. I guess no one does."

Fanta lifted her pen from the paper. "So, the two of you got along okay?"

Dave paused, assessing Fanta. "Well, in the past few weeks, he wasn't in my good books, I can tell you."

Fanta waited. Dave cocked his head.

"You may have heard that he was planning to move to another barn. In fact, he'd been talking to some of my best clients, behind my back. I spoke with Greg several times, trying to reason with him, but no luck."

"I had no idea," Fanta broke in. "Was he going to move to Lana's barn in Vermont?"

Dave gave a wry smile. "Maybe he had plans with Lana, I don't know. I think he really wanted to strike out on his own, even if it meant leaving me and Two Gates behind." He looked wistfully at the paperwork scattered across the desk. "He didn't seem to care that it would be tough for me to keep the business going here, trying to find a new pro rider and another partner and everything."

"What will you do now?"

"I'm not sure, to be honest. But for now, all of the clients are staying, which gives me time to regroup and find another pro." Dave rubbed his calloused palms together. "The real death blow would have been if Greg had left and taken those clients with him."

He stopped abruptly. "For the business, I mean. Of course, I would never hurt the guy, like I said, he was my best friend since college."

Dave started shuffling papers into piles. "Listen to me babbling away. I better get back to work. Bills to pay! Good luck with your article. I don't mean to sound negative about Greg, just business issues, you understand."

"I understand. I hope everything works out for you, Dave. Thanks for your time." Fanta turned and made her way back down the stable aisle.

Bingo! She hadn't known that Greg was planning to leave Two Gates with a bunch of valuable clients. No wonder Dave had been angry. Where did Terry and Lana fit in? Just as she had that thought, Fanta saw Lana's stallion Palmetto in one of the box stalls. She supposed it didn't make sense for Lana to take her horses back and forth to Vermont if she could keep them at Two Gates for the show season. There were obviously advantages to being Greg's girlfriend.

Fanta approached Palmetto's stall. The horse pinned his ears back, shook his head, and bared his teeth. Thank goodness she didn't have to muck out his stall. She had heard about horses that were territorial. It did not surprise her that the temperamental stallion was one of them.

Fanta headed out into the sunshine, happy to leave the subdued atmosphere of the stable behind. It was odd that there were so few people around. Although, it was midday and the horses were likely being rested after the show. As she leaned down to open the car door, she spotted activity near one of the large sheds. Deirdre and Romy were standing on a big wooden wagon, throwing hay bales into the loft. Fanta felt uncomfortable just watching. Haying was everyone's least favorite task.

She lowered herself into the car and started slowly down the long lane. She wasn't sure what to make of her interview with Dave. Obviously, things between him and Greg had been tense. Maybe it would be a good idea to check back in with Romy. She had a front row seat to everything that happened at Two Gates.

* * *

"The regional police homicide unit is investigating after a body was found in a room at the Carleton Hotel in the north end early Saturday morning. Officers discovered the man's body in the hotel on Route 5 near Highway 11 shortly after 8 a.m. Saturday, after receiving a call from the public. The police later announced that the death is considered a homicide. Police sources have told the North City Newser that the man was participating in the nearby equestrian competition, which was

occurring over the weekend. No arrest has been announced. Police are continuing with their inquiries and said Monday they're still in the process of notifying next of kin."

Fanta read and re-read the little blurb from Sue Goodwin on the Newser's website. It was pretty bare bones. Did Sue not have more info? Fanta craned her neck, looking in every nook and cranny of the newsroom. Sue's cubicle remained stubbornly empty; chair tucked in neatly, computer screen black. Dammit.

Fanta returned to her own work. She'd spent the afternoon transcribing her notes from the interviews at the Belle of the Ball Dance Studios. There were some awesome quotes. She was looking forward to writing the piece. It could be a lot of fun. Plus, she'd snapped some cool pics with her phone.

"Hey there, Fanta, do you have a moment? I don't mean to disturb." Abby's silken tones sounded in her ear.

"Oh, hi, Abby." Fanta looked up, startled. "For sure, no problem. How are you?"

Abby smiled. "I'm just fine, thanks." She hesitated, perhaps choosing her words. "I was interested this morning to hear what you had to say about this man who's been killed. It sounds like you have some great insights."

Fanta smiled back uncertainly. That was nice of Abby. She was pretty sure there was a "but" coming.

"But it would have been even better if you could have alerted the newsroom over the weekend." Abby held up a hand as Fanta tried to jump in. "I understand that we don't really have any weekend staff anymore, but you can always reach out to me. I hope you know that."

Fanta scrambled to get ahead of the conversation. "Oh, for sure, Abby. That was stupid of me. I guess I was so concentrated on my riding. And the whole thing with Greg…well, it just seemed so impossible." She wasn't going to tell her boss that she hadn't even been sure it was a news story. Talk about a career-stopper.

"Of course," Abby said smoothly. Her lipstick was some striking yet subtle shade that Fanta coveted. Not to mention the stunning pantsuit with the cream silk blouse. Abby continued, "These days, with resources so thin, we're relying on smart employees like you to be our eyes and ears in the community. That's how we find out about all the great stories there are to tell. Not that a homicide is a 'great' story." Abby chuckled softly, making delicate little air quotes. "But seriously, in this situation in particular, Fanta, you will be an amazing asset to Sue and the news team."

Fanta blinked. Wasn't she part of the news team? She wasn't sure she liked where the discussion was going.

Abby started to turn away and then paused, holding up a manicured finger. "You know, I realize we haven't always shown much interest in equestrian sports, and I'm sorry for that. It's a big part of life here in the region. But sometimes a news story is first and foremost a news story, regardless of the context. After all, we're here to inform the public, especially when it comes to crime and safety." Abby smiled once more. "Have a great afternoon, Fanta, and keep up the good work."

Fanta sat stunned at her desk. How did Abby do that? It was like being spanked with a velvet glove. She shook her head. Abby was the best. Fanta was lucky to be able to learn from her. She would keep everything she said in mind. And, if she played her cards right, maybe she would be able to find out more about Greg than anyone might expect.

* * *

Fanta waited until evening to phone Romy. She sat at her kitchen table and hit the redial button. After a few rings, a sleepy voice came on the line.

"Hullo?"

"Hi there!" Fanta said energetically. She needed Romy's full attention. "It's me, Fanta. Is now a good time to talk? Are you alone?"

"Yes, I'm alone. I was sleeping," Romy grumbled. "We had to do the haying today. I just hate it."

Fanta knew exactly what Romy meant. The stings and itches brought on by haying were legend. "And, uh, Deirdre is not there?"

Romy made a *pffft* sound. "No, Deirdre isn't here. Is she ever? She's probably sucking up to Lana. Or chasing after..." Romy sighed. "Who knows what she gets up to."

Fanta paused, thinking of Romy sharing the motorhome with Deirdre. If it were herself and Deirdre, it would be like a cage match, with only one of them crawling out alive.

"Listen, I was chatting with Dave today. Asking questions. He told me Greg was planning to move out of Two Gates. Maybe take a bunch of clients with him. Is that true?"

"You're asking questions?" Romy perked up. "That's great, Fanta, thanks! I knew you would do it. Sorry, what did you want to know?"

Fanta repeated herself. "This is important, Romy. This is new information that has just come to light."

"What? Everyone knew Greg was planning to go. He was talking to all the clients about it. It wasn't really very nice of him, the way he was handling it," Romy grizzled.

"What about Terry? What did he think of Greg's plans?"

"Oh, please, I'm hardly Terry's BFF."

Fanta scrambled to think of another question. "Was Greg planning on going into business with Lana?"

"Yeah, Lana gave me all the deets and then we had matcha tea and organic crumpets." Romy harrumphed. "I have no idea."

"Okay, well, what was Greg saying to you guys?" Fanta was at her wits' end.

"Are you serious? Greg never talked to me about any of it," Romy snorted. "I would have just been flung in a tack trunk along with the rest of the equipment." She paused. "I thought you'd be better at this stuff, Fanta."

"I have to ask these things, Romy, for clarification purposes." Fanta regrouped; she needed to regain control of the conversation. "So Dave knew all about Greg's plan and...was he angry?"

"Are you kidding? He was freaking out. He was constantly trying to corner Greg so they could talk about it. Even at Greg's hotel room that night, Dave was pounding on his door, yelling for him to open up. It was out of control, it was causing problems for—"

"Wait a minute," Fanta cut in. "Dave was fighting with Greg the night of the murder? He didn't mention that. How do you know?"

"I didn't say they were fighting. I don't know if Dave ever went into Greg's room. I was across the hall. I just heard a lot of noise and looked out. And there was Dave, going ballistic, demanding to speak with Greg. I was sick of the whole thing, so I just closed my door."

"You didn't tell me that before," Fanta said accusingly.

"You told me there was nothing you could do!" Romy cried in exasperation. "Don't go all spymaster on me now."

Fanta tamped down her irritation. "You must have spoken to the police. Did you tell them about Dave? At the door?"

"Of course I've spoken to the police." Romy sounded cagey. "But, you know, Dave's my boss and—wait a minute." There was a pause. Then Romy whispered, "I hear Deirdre's car pulling up. I better go."

The call cut out. Fanta leafed quickly through the notes from her conversation with Dave and hesitated, confused. She had scribbled down a lot of information. But maybe it wasn't the whole story.

Chapter Eleven

"The drug bust has got to be on the front page, guys, how could it not?" Sue was arguing fiercely. "The Toronto reporters are on it and it's been upfront in all those papers, not to mention their online coverage. They're kicking our butts." She took a deep breath. "I've got some fresh local perspective that I think will put us back on top of this thing."

The morning meeting was in full swing. Fanta hovered on the edge of the group. It seemed to her that, even in the few months she had been working at the Newser, the meeting had become even more heated. Of course, media was a competitive business, but now there was so much pressure to feed the online news site and keep fresh content in the printed publications. From what Fanta knew, most newspapers were operating at a loss, with advertisers turning to other channels and circulation revenues dropping. The Newser hadn't laid anyone off, but there was not much hiring going on. That meant the same amount of work, or more, was being done by a smaller group of journalists.

Fanta thought about her stories, which were usually in the back pages or the weekend editions or buried at the bottom of the website. She was never top of the news. Not to mention, she'd just been hired. She might be first up for the chopping block. But surely readers welcomed lighter material and positive stories from their own community. She lifted her chin. She wasn't just some irrelevant expense.

"What about the dead man at the horse show?"

At the sound of Abby's voice, Fanta snapped her attention back to the meeting. Sue was still fielding questions about the police beat.

"It was in our backyard, I think people would want to know more," Abby said. "Could we get some sort of exclusive?"

Sue looked pained. "So, the police have shared some more of the details of the forensics report," she said, notebook in hand, "but really, there's not much new. Like I said, the guy was hit from behind with a blunt object. The forensics seem unclear as to whether he was standing, kneeling, or sitting at the time he was attacked. If he was standing, then it's likely that his attacker was fairly tall. But it's all pretty inconclusive."

Sue looked around the group, a sudden gleam in her eye. "Here's the zinger, though. Apparently, the police interviewed Grenier's parents. They live somewhere in Quebec. Anyway, I guess the mom let drop that Grenier was planning to get married."

Abby pounced, hoop earrings swinging. "That's exactly the sort of thing I'm talking about." She turned to Fanta. "Outside of the hard news, what do we know about him? Could we write a profile of his career, his life? Promising young athlete, life cut short, that sort of thing. I saw a pic of the guy and he's pretty handsome. That helps."

Fanta's thoughts churned. This was new. Greg must have been going to ask Lana to marry him. So things had been getting serious. Leave it to Deirdre to throw herself at a soon-to-be-engaged man. It probably just added to the intrigue and required a whole new level of lingerie. She looked around and realized people were waiting for her to speak.

"Oh! Well, it's definitely a tragedy and a great loss for the horse show world," she stumbled out. Eyes rolled. Douglas looked bemused. She plowed on. "Greg was well-liked and respected by the horse community. I think a profile of him would be a great idea, Abby. I'd be happy to take that on."

"That would be appreciated. There are lots of horse people in our coverage area, and something like this would be up their alley," Abby said briskly. "Let's think about it for the front pages." Fanta glowed with pride. She already had one interview under her belt. "Oh, by the way, Fanta, could you come and see me after the meeting?"

Her stomach dropped. Now what? Had Abby completely lost patience with her? Was she about to lose her job? Would she be able to keep Des? Her mind went into warp speed, conjuring all sorts of worst-case scenarios. She caught a few sympathetic looks from the group. A small smile played on Douglas's lips.

After the meeting broke up, Fanta poked her head in Abby's office. Her heart fluttered in her throat.

"Come in, Fanta, I have something to discuss with you."

Abby stood, motioned Fanta to a chair, and closed the office door. Fanta sat carefully, holding her breath, eyes tracking Abby as she rounded her desk. Her white bubble-sleeve blouse was totally on point.

Returning to her seat, Abby launched in. "Listen, you know we're trying to find new revenue sources and appeal to a wider group of readers and advertisers." Fanta steeled herself. This was surely the end of her career at the Newser. Abby continued, "So what we have in mind is a new magazine, a lifestyle thing with content about home decor, reno ideas, anything along those lines. Glossy, full color, with a great digital presence." Abby waved a flawless hand. "People seem to lap this type of thing up."

Fanta wasn't sure where it was all going. "Um, that sounds nice," she offered.

"I was hoping you could run with it, Fanta. Generate content, mock up a look and feel, work with the graphics and design staff." Abby paused, observing her. "You would need to think about advertorial content or other revenue ideas. Feel free to reach out to the advertising folks; I'm sure they have things in mind. Of course, don't forget the whole online component. Really, it could be your baby." Abby regarded her. "What do you think?"

Fanta was thrilled. Not only was she keeping her job, but the magazine sounded like the sort of project she loved. Style and design! She could already think of several story ideas and the perfect art to go with them.

"Oh, that sounds amazing, Abby, thanks for thinking of me," she replied. "I'm going to talk with people here, like you say, and put together some concepts for you."

"That would be great, thanks," said Abby. "Just keep me in the loop." She offered a discreet wink. Her eye featured just the right amount of mascara, the perfect shadow. "And thanks for your help with that other story. You've got this."

* * *

Fanta's fingers hovered over the keyboard. Given her session at the dance studio with Larry and Babette, she planned to write the feature in a sexy, teasing tone. The perfect lead was just on the edge of her brain. She couldn't quite grasp it. No matter! It would come to her. In the meantime, a nice coffee and a trip to the saddlery store would be just the ticket. She needed some fly spray for Des. She grabbed her purse and walked confidently out of the newsroom. She was an editor now, and everyone else would just have to deal with it.

Stepping through the door at The Mane Connection, she inhaled with pleasure. She loved the musty place, filled with every piece of horse equipment imaginable. Not to mention fun knick-knacks and clothing. The aroma was heavenly—mostly leather, with an undertone of that new clothes smell and a touch of molasses.

Fanta started to browse the racks. Maybe a new pair of riding gloves? How about a nice blanket for Des? She looked at the price tag and drew a sharp breath. The blanket would have to wait. She had new responsibilities at work, but there had been no mention of more money. She shook her head. Idiot. She had been so pleased at Abby's offer that she hadn't thought to ask about pay. Then she smiled. She was in too good a mood to be angry with herself. And she actually liked mac and cheese from a box.

Turning to check out the latest in riding breeches, she spotted Terry Miller in the saddle racks. Fanta observed him. His stylish work clothes were rumpled and baggy. He could probably buy whatever he wanted in the store, ten times over, yet he looked dejected and disinterested. Fanta herself felt confident and effervescent. Maybe she could lift his spirits and, at the same time, find out more about his relationship with Greg.

She pushed through the overstocked store. "Terry, it's good to see you. Looking for some equipment?" she called cheerily.

Terry turned toward her. "Oh, hi, Fanta, yeah, it never ends, right? Always something to spend your money on." His morning shave looked angry and sore.

Fanta winced. "I was going to grab a coffee at that new place next door. Did you want to join me?" she offered.

Terry nodded. "That sounds nice. I can't seem to decide on anything here, anyway." He shrugged as he looked around at the million attractive things he could purchase.

Together, the two of them made their way to Demi Tasse Roastery, which was quickly becoming a neighborhood hot spot. Shouldering through the door, Fanta noted the modern farmhouse style, featuring tables and chairs in golden wood tones. Plants added to the natural vibe and macrame hangings created a boho feel. A large butcher-block counter showcased an array of sweet treats. The smell of freshly brewed coffee was to die for.

She gazed in wonder. She was a lifestyle editor now, and it was her job to take it all in and share it with loyal readers. A total influencer. Amazing! She could already see it: *Hey there, North City style mavens! Be sure to check out the region's newest coffee shop, featuring all your favorite drinks and sweets, and just DRIPPING with urban chic! Take my word for it, you won't be disappointed.*

With a winning smile for the guy at the cash register, she selected a "gutsy cup" that promised to keep her brain cells hopping. There was nothing like a good dark brew. Terry opted for a mocha with a dollop of whipped cream. They found a sturdy wooden table, and Fanta took a first sip of her aromatic coffee. Buoyed by the caffeine rush and everything going on at work, she started telling Terry all about her new role.

"I mean, there's so much happening with kitchen renos. Then there's this whole living outdoors trend," she bubbled, "I think I could do some great coverage of the fab new patio furniture. And who wouldn't want a fire pit or water feature?" The funky café was fueling her creativity, almost like a muse. She turned to Terry, who was staring listlessly at the parking area. His eyes were red and his face was flushed. She needed to tone it down.

"How are you, Terry? It must be so upsetting, Greg's death. I can't even imagine," Fanta tried. As it was, she didn't have the heart to quiz him about the events of that night.

Terry's eyes welled with tears. "If only you knew," he sniffled. "I'm not sure, maybe you guessed, but I always had a thing for Greg. Like, a crush." Terry blinked rapidly and waved his hands in front of his face. "Although of course he wasn't, you know, interested."

"Oh! I'm sorry you went through that." Fanta had never thought of Terry as anything but a talented amateur rider. A bit prickly sometimes. And loaded with money. She'd never considered his romantic inclinations. Suddenly, she felt a surprising sympathy for him. She was intimately familiar with one-sided crushes. "No wonder you were upset with Greg at the show last week. The whole thing must have been…a lot to deal with."

Terry straightened in his chair. "Last week was different. I had accepted that Greg would never feel the same way about me, but I wanted him to take me seriously, to take my riding seriously. Pearl and I have done well together, and I've just bought another horse to start in the jumpers, but Greg didn't have the time of day for me. You know, I paid a lot of money to ride with him. Horses, equipment, boarding, training, vet, farrier—I don't have to tell you how it all adds up."

Fanta was quick to nod. She knew all too well.

Terry rolled on. "I also felt he wasn't being completely above-board with me. That sometimes I was over-paying or that his fees just seemed too rich. I wanted to talk to him about it, but he never even had time for that."

"I'm sure you—" Fanta began.

"But here's the kicker," Terry ran over her. "I found out that Greg was going to hire that blonde newbie, what's her name, Chessy, to come to Two Gates as his assistant. His *protégée,*" Terry spat the word out. Fanta could practically see it lying on the table like a glob of spit.

"Where would that leave me? Taking lessons from *her?*" Terry glared at Fanta. "Just because I don't have blonde hair, long legs, and big—"

Terry stopped abruptly and dropped his eyes. "Sorry, I know that Chessy is from Bay Ridge. I think she's very good, but how much was I supposed to take? Of course, Greg was thinking about leaving Two Gates and starting out on his own. I would have gone with him if he'd asked. Now he's dead, and I have to start again with someone new. I just don't know what to do next."

Terry slumped in his chair. His mocha had gone cold and the whipped cream had congealed. Fanta wasn't sure how to help him.

"You know," she tried with a chuckle, "I always had, like, the biggest crush on Greg." She rolled her eyes exaggeratedly, trying to make light of her words, create a shared experience.

Terry nodded. "I know."

What? Fanta had not been expecting that. Her stomach started to undulate. Did the entire horse world know she'd been aching for Greg?

"Sorry? How did you know that?" She tried to keep the panic from her voice.

"Oh, you know, gossip. The grooms are always going on about something." Terry waved a hand dismissively.

Fanta drew herself up. She didn't even want to contemplate what Terry might have heard from Deirdre. But, she was trying to help him. It wasn't about her right now. "Anyway, I can totally understand that you might have felt overshadowed by Chessy. Or perhaps you even felt that way about Lana."

"Oh, yeah. You would get it, coming from Bay Ridge. I mean, Chessy is the best they have," Terry proclaimed. "But whatever. I'm pretty good, too. And I think I deserved a chance."

Fanta clamped her mouth shut. She was either going to continue to coddle Terry, or give him an almighty kick in the pants. She drew in a deep breath. On the plus side, she had barely asked a single question, and she now had all sorts of fresh dirt from Two Gates. Terry would just have to cope with his own life.

Terry pushed aside his wilted mocha. "This has been great, but I better go now, thanks for listening." He stood, adjusted his wrinkled work shirt and tie, and headed for the door. Fanta watched him climb into his shiny BMW and drive away with a spray of gravel. Terry was possibly an ass, but he didn't seem like any sort of criminal. Still, he had obviously harbored strong feelings where Greg was concerned. He would definitely feature on her list of suspects, along with Dave, Lana, Deirdre, Chessy, and pretty much anyone who had crossed Greg's path.

She got to her feet and gathered her purse. Her brilliant image of Greg was fast dissolving into a pulpy mess. It was depressing. Then she remembered the fly spray. She made her way back to The Mane Connection and stood uncertainly just inside the front door, trying to recall where the spray was located in the store. She peered down the aisle. Oh no. Sally Morelli was approaching. Sally was a big gossip who used her job at the tack store to recirculate all the latest tittle-tattle from the horse world.

"Hey there, Fanta, keeping well?" Sally said, strolling toward her. She had glossy hair, big green eyes, and a smattering of freckles. Over her t-shirt and jeans, she wore a work apron with The Mane Connection logo. Fanta wasn't fooled by her casual manner. Sally was always on the hunt for inside information.

"Can I help you find anything?" Sally drew close and lowered her voice. "Was that Terry Miller I saw you speaking with? He looks like a wreck. What a time it's been. Greg's death is all anyone can talk about!"

"Yes, I guess it's been quite stressful at Two Gates, maybe for a while now," offered Fanta, resisting the pull of the rumor mill.

"That's an understatement," replied Sally with a dramatic eye-roll. "Dave was in here the other day in a panic, trying to figure out how to cut costs on equipment. Greg was really putting him in a tight spot."

Sally peeked over the racks to check if her manager was in sight before moving even closer to Fanta. "So what's up with Terry? I'd heard that he and Greg were at odds. In fact, someone said that Greg felt uncomfortable around Terry. What's with that?" Sally goggled at Fanta. "Terry always strikes me as one of these rich guys who bellyaches about every penny. It would have driven me nuts. Or maybe Greg thought Terry had a crush on him—awkward!" Sally laughed delightedly.

"Right, well, Terry and I were just catching up," replied Fanta. She started to move away. Sally touched her arm and lowered her voice further.

"I sure wouldn't have minded hooking up with Greg," she whispered. "And I was not the only one, I can tell you. You wouldn't believe the stories I've heard. Lana had some competition on her hands, that's for sure. Where there's smoke, there's fire, and Greg was hot, hot, hot!" Sally's round face flushed.

"Well, I should be on my way, if you could just point me to the fly spray?" Had Sally forgotten the guy was dead? Fanta's childhood vision of Greg was already in tatters without Sally piling on.

"Aisle four, Fanta, and don't be a stranger!"

Chapter Twelve

Fanta drove along the country road on her way to Bay Ridge. She had carrots in her purse for Des, and she'd already changed into jeans and a t-shirt. The radio was on and the summer breeze blew through the car, making her feel happy and carefree. All in all, it had been a good day at work. She could barely believe she was going to be the editor of a new lifestyle magazine; it was just too exciting.

As she turned into the familiar drive at Bay Ridge, a great satisfaction swept through her. There was nothing like a summer's evening at the stables: the smell of fresh-mown hay, the late afternoon sunshine, the pure contentment of horses grazing in the pasture, tails swishing. She drew a deep breath and pointed the Honda up the laneway.

Apple trees, which not long ago had been thick with spring blossoms, lined the lane on either side. Spacious paddocks could be glimpsed through their gnarled limbs. The big wooden barn loomed up ahead. Its board-and-batten sides and metal roof were supported by a thick stone foundation. The loft was filled with hay bales and the odd piece of farm equipment. It was an old, traditional barn, and Fanta loved it. So different from the metallic structures at Two Gates.

On her left was the big stone farmhouse where Penny and her husband Hank lived. It had a rambling porch and windows that always shone with a warm glow. Penny often groaned about the endless repairs that were needed, but Fanta knew she wouldn't trade the older house for any McMansion. There was a son, too, who was away at university. Fanta had heard that he had ridden as a child but had become captivated by the world of medicine.

Apparently, he was a natural hand with the horses. Penny probably hoped he would come back home one day.

After a show, the horses usually got a few days off to unwind. It was one of Fanta's favorite times at the stables. She loved to hang out with Des. It was fun to bathe and groom him, or simply walk him around the property on his lead rope. It was a time for both of them to relax. Fanta didn't like to dwell on it, but Des was an older horse, so she liked to take extra care. This evening, she planned to take him for an easy ride on the trails that crisscrossed the wooded ridge behind the barn. It would get her back in the saddle and Des at least starting to think about work. The next show was coming up, and they would begin training again soon.

She parked the Honda in the small lot and strolled toward the stables. Penny buzzed around in the barn, feeding the horses. There were always chores to do, on top of her lesson schedule.

"Hi there, Fanta, how are you on this beautiful evening?" Penny called. "Your boy has been out most of the day and eaten his supper. I'm sure he's keen to see you." She always sounded far less intense at home than at the horse shows.

Dobie trotted out of the barn. The Doberman pinscher had turned up at the farm a few years ago. Thinking she might not be able to keep him, Penny had called him simply Dobie. But no one had claimed the dog, and the name had stuck. Now Dobie was part of the Bay Ridge family. He was a good boy, but maybe not the brightest. He had learned, after a few close calls, to cohabitate with the horses. He did have a certain odor. Fanta tried to give him a wide berth. Dobie pranced around her, tongue lolling and eyes sparkling.

She stepped into the stable, Dobie at her heels. Penny and her husband had done a great job renovating the barn so that it was light and airy, despite the low ceiling. The main aisle was intersected by a smaller one, creating quadrants that contained the horses' stalls, the tack and feed rooms, a wash stall, and an office.

Fanta felt a surge of joy as she spotted Des. He nickered as she approached. Leading him out of his stall, she tied him in the aisle and set to work with her grooming kit. The brushing and combing gave her a chance to look Des over for cuts, scrapes, or bites. Horses might be big and strong, but they were delicate creatures.

Penny stopped to pat Des. "Sorry we didn't have much time together at the show. It's just so crazy busy these days—which is good, don't get me wrong." Penny gave a harried laugh. "I wanted to say how well you did. The first show of the season is never easy, but you two had some great moments and you rode well. Two ribbons! I was really pleased, and I hope you were, too. It always comes back to the same thing: keep him moving forward in that balanced canter. If you have that, the rest should come naturally."

"Thanks, Penny, that means a lot," Fanta replied with a smile. "I know I made some mistakes, but I was happy. I always enjoy riding Des, no matter what."

She put the curry comb in her grooming kit and got out a dandy brush. Maybe Penny would know something about Greg's death. "You must have heard about Greg," she said, running the brush over Des's coat. "What a horrible thing. Have you learned any more about it?"

"Oh, no, nothing at all, I wouldn't know a thing." Penny propped her calloused hands on her hips. A straggly ponytail fell down her back, and her jeans and t-shirt needed to hit the laundry basket. "Of course, I knew that Greg was thinking about moving out of Two Gates. Maybe taking some clients with him. That would not have been good for Dave."

Penny winced. She knew all too well the vagaries of running a horse stable. She swiped a hand across her cheek, leaving a dirty streak. "Greg was a nice rider, but I'm not sure he was always the nicest person."

Fanta was surprised at Penny's frank assessment. "Someone mentioned to me that Greg was going to ask Lana to marry him," she said casually.

"Oh! Well, that's nice. Or I guess it was. Kind of sad now," Penny said, shaking her head.

"I'd heard that Chessy and Greg knew each other. I hadn't realized that." Fanta glanced at Penny before picking up one of Des's hooves to clean it out with a metal pick.

Penny frowned. "You've sure got your ear to the ground." She shrugged.

"I don't think that Chessy knew Greg well. I doubt she was interested in him romantically, if that's what you mean. It's possible that Greg knew about Chessy. She's making a name for herself in the horse show world. She's a real talent. So maybe Greg saw that." Penny stopped to consider. "I hope that Chessy wasn't planning a move to Two Gates. That would have been a real loss for us here."

Fanta felt her usual irritation whenever Chessy's superior riding skills were mentioned. Then she remembered something else. "That reminds me, what happened with Chessy's stirrup that day?"

Penny's brows drew together fiercely. "That was unacceptable. I have no idea how that could have happened. We all check the equipment thoroughly every day. And the strap was quite new. No, it must have been some sort of defect. Rotten stitching or something. I'll be speaking to that saddler, you can count on that."

Penny brushed her palms together briskly. "Anyway, best be getting on. You get that horse out for a good walk. We'll start schooling again on the weekend."

Dobie trotted up beside Penny, lowered his head, and vomited up something that looked like the inside of an apple pie, without the nice aroma.

"Ach, he's been eating the fallen apples again," said Penny, carefully moving her boot away from the steaming mess. "One more thing to clean up."

She disappeared down the aisle in the direction of the broom and wheelbarrow, Dobie following cheerily. Fanta turned her attention back to Des.

"I don't know, Dessie. There are some strange things going on, don't you think?" she murmured, doing up the last buckles on the bridle.

Des twitched his ears and nodded his great head.

She pressed her cheek to his forehead. "Let's go and forget about them for a while." Fanta turned toward the barn door, Des in tow.

* * *

Riding along the forest trail, Fanta could think of no other place she'd rather be. A cool breeze ruffled the tree canopy, birds sang and flitted among the branches, and Des's hooves made a pleasant thumping sound on the dirt path. She let him grab a few leaves to chew as he swung along. Penny would not approve of such poor manners.

As much as she tried to empty her mind, it stayed stubbornly full. What was happening at Two Gates? She attempted to sort through everything she'd learned. Greg was planning to depart Two Gates, leaving Dave in the lurch. Greg was fooling around on Lana, leaving her angry and betrayed. Greg was ignoring Terry, leaving him in a snit. Greg was leading on Deirdre, leaving her…well, who cared. Fanta tried to slot it all together. She puffed out a breath. Who didn't want Greg dead?

There was a great snapping of twigs and rustling of leaves. Des's ears pricked forward and his head rose. Fanta tensed in the saddle. It sounded like a large animal approaching. There were no wolves or bears in the forest. Were there? She squinted through the tree trunks. Des's nostrils flared. A big brown creature was coming through the woods to their right. What should she do? Flee? Freeze? Play dead? No idea. Then she glimpsed a hot pink polo shirt and a horse with a fiery bay coat. It was Chessy riding Kash through the forest.

"Chessy!" Fanta called.

Chessy turned in the saddle as Kash reached the path. "Hey, Fanta, I guess we both had the same idea." Her blonde hair was tucked beneath her helmet and she wore chaps over her jeans, much like Fanta.

"I thought you were a grizzly bear for a moment." Fanta felt like an idiot. Chessy would never be frightened of anything in the forest. She assumed an airy tone, "Isn't it beautiful out here? I just love these trails."

"It sure is, sorry to scare you," Chessy called back over her shoulder as she and Kash led the way down the narrow path. Fanta contemplated Chessy's strong shoulders and supple back. She seemed like a nice person. When the track widened, Fanta rode Des up beside Kash. This was her chance to put things right.

"Listen, I'm sorry if I upset you when I asked about Greg the other day. I didn't mean anything by it."

Chessy glanced at her. "That's okay. Maybe I overreacted." She paused. "But just to set the record straight, I was not involved with Greg, at least not in the way you thought. Actually, he'd asked me to join his team as his assistant coach."

Chessy grew silent. Fanta waited for her to go on.

Chessy shrugged. "Anyway, I guess it doesn't matter now, with his death and everything." She looked steadily down the path. "I wasn't sure it was a good next step for me anyway."

"Oh, why's that?" Fanta was surprised. It sounded like a great opportunity to her.

"Well, I think you know, Greg had a bit of a reputation." Chessy hesitated. "He was with Lana, but I'd heard that he had a few interests, let's say, on the side." Her face hardened. "I didn't want people to think he offered me the job because of my looks. For all I know, maybe he did. I want to be recognized for my riding, not my appearance. I guess it's why your question upset me. It just proved my worries."

"Oh, I am sorry," Fanta responded quickly. "I think you're an awesome rider and Greg's barn would have been lucky to have you." She paused. She did think that. Why did she have to be jealous about it? Maybe it wasn't so easy being Chessy after all.

The horses' hooves moved rhythmically along the earthen path. Fanta felt a sudden urge to confide. "It's just that I've been thinking about Greg's death and trying to make some sense of it. I've been on a bit of a fact-finding mission. It probably won't come to anything."

"Well, be careful," Chessy said. "Greg seemed to stir up a lot of strong feelings wherever he went, and I'm not sure he cared too much about it, one way or another."

Back at the barn, Chessy and Fanta groomed and fussed over their horses. Fanta learned that Chessy shared a room in town with some of her friends at college. Fanta described her work at the Newser and told Chessy about the new magazine. Chessy talked about her vet tech studies and her job search. Together, they tried out some of the dance steps that Fanta had learned, twirling up and down the aisle, arms entwined, laughing.

As she led Des to his stall, Fanta thought how nice it would be to have a new friend. She gave Des his treats and a kiss on the nose. "Don't worry, Dessie, you're still my best friend."

Chapter Thirteen

Fanta settled in her recliner in front of the TV. She had enjoyed a cold mac and cheese salad at home. She still had a smile on her face from her evening at Bay Ridge. When her phone buzzed with an incoming text, she clicked it open. It was from her mother in Florida.

Hi Honey how are you doings? Your dad and I art well. Loving this floridly sunshine

Fanta chuckled. Her mom was a retired schoolteacher. She was a wiz at spelling and grammar, but her attempts to keep up with technology produced mixed results. Fanta tapped on her mom's number. It was tedious and bizarre to text with her. She would just call. She was bursting with news about the home and lifestyle magazine.

"There you are, darlin', I'm so happy to hear from you. How are things?"

Her mom's voice was raspy. A few years before, the doctors had found what turned out to be non-cancerous lesions on her vocal cords. The scare had prompted Fanta's parents to move to Florida to escape the Toronto winters.

"I'm good, mom, and I have some news," she said brightly.

"Oh, what's that, honey?" Her mom sounded wary.

"I've been put in charge of a new magazine at work," Fanta announced. "It's going to be a lot of fun. I already have some great ideas."

"Honey, that's wonderful, good for you."

Her dad's voice came from somewhere in the background. "What's up with Fanta?"

"She's going to be working on a fancy magazine!" her mom shouted into the phone.

There were a few beeps and some rustling sounds. "Sorry, honey, you still there? That was your dad wanting to know how you are. I told him about the magazine."

Fanta opened her mouth to reply. Her dad's voice cut in again. "Is she earning any more money?"

"Now, Frank, that's not really what's important, is it?" her mom called out. "Men, that's all they think about is money," she whispered to Fanta. "How's that horse of yours?"

"He's super, mom. We had a show last week and we did well."

"That's nice, honey. Glad to hear it."

Her mom had never been much into horses, despite the endless hours she'd spent driving Fanta to various stables. She'd always been there, though, even through the worst of the pony club days. Fanta had a weird thought. Her mom was her mom, but she was more than that. Fanta pictured her working as a schoolteacher, helping to support the family, keeping everything going at home.

"Listen, mom, I was hoping you could give me some advice," she ventured.

"That sounds exciting, honey. Do you have a new boyfriend?"

Fanta's brow creased. Why did everyone ask her that? "No, mom, this is about work. You keep telling me I should do more at the Newser, not just features and stuff. So now I'm the editor of this new magazine. How do I get people to take me seriously?"

"That's easy. Just show up on time and work hard. Really, that's all there is to it," her mom said breezily. Then she added hastily, "Oh, and be careful what you wear. I know you younger generation like to express yourselves, but the workplace is not the place for it. These short skirts and high heels. My heavens. And the blouses I see on women these days." Her mom huffed in disbelief. "No, honey, it's best to stick to something plain and simple. Us women, we have to be extra careful about these things."

Fanta thought of Abby and her impeccable clothing. Although her heels were on the high side.

"Okay, but there's got to be more to it than that." Fanta's work wardrobe was pretty boring, and it hadn't done her any favors so far.

"Well, let me see. You know, I've found that it's important to speak your mind. Don't be rude. But there's nothing worse than having an opinion and not expressing it, then finding out you were right all along. There's no going back, honey. It's better to say something and be wrong than to be silent and be right."

Fanta tried to get her head around that as her mother continued.

"Oh, but now you've got me thinking, here's a good one. Always try to see things from the other person's perspective. Goodness knows that's gotten me through forty years of marriage," her mom tittered. "Seriously, though. You mark my words, Fanta honey. If you want to appear mature and professional, that's the way to do it. And when you put your mind to it, you may realize that there's a whole other side to someone that you'd never considered."

There were more bumps and rustling on the line. "Anyway, darlin', I'd better fly! Your dad has steaks on the grill, and you know how that can go. Bye bye, honey, so great to talk to you."

Fanta stared at the phone in her hand. Her mom's advice seemed like something out of a bygone era. But she was right about one thing. Fanta was pretty sure she knew quite a few people with more than one side to them. And they all seemed to have known Greg Grenier.

* * *

"Okay, thanks everyone, let's get to it." Abby dismissed the morning meeting and headed toward her office. Her cotton poplin shirt dress was the ultimate for a summer day at the office.

Fanta abandoned the wobbly chair and plodded back to her workstation. It had been more of the usual. She had hoped the news team might show her more respect as the editor of a new magazine. Plus, she'd taken Abby's advice to heart and tried to make her update to the group succinct and compelling. Yet she had the same sense of simmering embarrassment, frustration, and anxiety that followed every morning meeting. She had worn her nicest knee-length skirt, sensible flats, and a button-up blouse. She had done her best to see things from Douglas's perspective. She still wanted nothing more than to throttle the guy.

"What's with this new magazine I'm hearing about, Abby?" he'd asked in his abrasive voice.

Fanta had listened smugly as Abby outlined the glossy publication and told everyone that Fanta would be the inaugural editor. Douglas had frowned and given his pen a series of rapid-fire clicks with his thumb.

"So it's some sort of promo thing?" Without waiting for an answer, he'd added, "Well, at least we're not wasting editorial resources on it then."

Fanta sat at her desk and fumed. She was as much a part of the editorial team as any of the other reporters and editors. She stared unseeing at her computer screen. The notes that she had typed out yesterday from her ballroom dancing interviews swam before her eyes. She needed to get writing. The draft layout of her birdwatching piece also awaited her attention. And the clock was ticking for her to produce a menu of creative concepts for the new magazine. She had been so excited about it, but now, with Douglas's remarks fresh in her mind, she didn't know how to feel. Still, unless she wanted to get fired, she had to get it in gear. It was all about keeping her focus. That, and trying not to jab Douglas with his own stupid pen.

Her thoughts circled back to Greg's death. The more she learned, the more she wanted to get to the bottom of it. Plus, she had told Abby she would write a profile about Greg. That was no longer just some ruse she'd been using. She clicked out of her interview notes, ignored the birdwatching layout, and pushed creative concepts for the magazine from her mind. The next person to interview seemed obvious. She started to compose an email.

"Dear Ms. Taylor," she typed. *"My name is Fanta Delaney, and I am a writer at the North City Newser. I am also an avid rider and compete at many of the local shows. I have long admired your accomplishments in the show ring."* Fanta did a mini-gag. *"This past week, I was sad to hear of the death of professional rider Greg Grenier. My editor and I have discussed developing a piece on Mr. Grenier that would showcase his riding career and feature interviews with people*

who knew him well. I understand you were close to him, and I was wondering if you would grant me an interview. I can be reached by return email. I look forward to hearing from you, and please accept my condolences on your loss."

It had been easy to find Lana's email address on her website. Fanta re-read her message. A bit fawning, but honey always attracted more flies, as her mother would say. Still, Fanta felt nervous. Lana was a high-profile professional rider, and she obviously had a temper, judging by her outburst with Deirdre. Fanta gave herself a mental shake. She would not be intimidated. Lana was only human, like everyone else.

Her finger hovered over the send key. Could she handle an encounter with Lana? She pressed the button and the message disappeared into the digital netherworld. She would soon find out. Now, she had to get back to business.

She brought the ballroom dancing notes back on the screen. The quotes she had gathered from Larry and the others were fantastic. One had described dancing as the vertical expression of the horizontal desire. Could she print that in the Newser? She had also learned about the different styles of dance. The cha cha had originated in the religious dances of West Africa, while the paso doble was based on the Spanish bullfight. The precursor of the Viennese waltz, the volta, had been banned from the French court in the seventeenth century as immoral. Dancing truly was an expressive art with a fascinating history.

Fanta stared at the blinking cursor. She needed a red-hot lead. It had been on the tip of her tongue just yesterday. She flexed her fingers over the keyboard. *"At first, Roberto was too rough. Then, too gentle. But when he got it just right, Wanda felt wonderful."* Her cheeks flushed. That should hook a reader or two. Was it too much? Well, that's what her sources had told her. She was simply passing on other people's views. That's what reporters did. Her story would capture more attention than anything Douglas or the rest of them had ever written. They could only dream that zoning, taxes, and sewer lines could be so sexy.

Thoughts of passion and romance turned her mind back to Lana. Maybe a quick peek at her email wouldn't hurt. To her surprise, Lana had already replied.

"Hello, Ms. Delaney, thank you for your note and your sympathies. I would be happy to speak with you about Greg, my partner in love and life. Why don't we meet at High T tomorrow at 10am? I hope this works for you. I look forward to meeting you and telling you all about my fabulous Greg. My heart is broken, but I feel he would want me to do this in his memory."

Partner in love and life? My fabulous Greg? Fanta shuddered. This was definitely not the Lana she had heard going off on Deirdre. This sounded like a whole other Lana. It would be interesting to meet her. Replying in the affirmative, Fanta turned her attention back to the world of dance, where it was not always clear who was leading and who was following.

Chapter Fourteen

The lunchroom at the Newser was a far cry from the inspiring style of Demi Tasse Roastery. Fanta gazed around at the linoleum floor and dingy white walls. Limp posters hung from a bulletin board and the plastic window blinds boasted a thick layer of dust.

North City style mavens! You may not be able to afford the latest trends, but a mop, rag, and duster are always your best friends!

Fanta unzipped her lunch bag. She would eat her sandwich quickly and get back to her desk. At least she had the room to herself. Her phone buzzed on the grubby tabletop.

She reached for it, took a moment to put herself in a professional mindset, and answered briskly, "Fanta Delaney here, North City Newser." That was good. A magazine editor needed to be completely on top of things.

"Is that you, Fanta?" It was Romy. "You sound kind of, I don't know, weird or something."

"It's me, Romy." Fanta was irked. "You know, I'm at work right now. Things are busy."

"Got it, sorry. I won't keep you. I thought you might be having lunch. You know, it's noon. I just wanted to see if you'd found out anything." Romy sounded eager.

"Right, well, I have been asking questions and I think I have made some headway," Fanta replied primly.

"Oh, that's great," Romy rushed out. "Like what?"

"Of course, you understand that these are conversations I've had in confidence. I can't just blurt stuff out to anyone."

"Whatever, I'm the one who told you to ask questions. So, what have you found out?"

Fanta pursed her lips. "Well, I did speak with Terry."

There was a pause. "And?" Romy prompted.

"Let's just say he was upset. He felt that he was being overcharged at Two Gates. And he didn't think that he got enough…attention from Greg. I understand there was a possibility of Chessy joining the Two Gates team as Greg's assistant coach. Terry wasn't too thrilled about it."

There was another pause. "That's it?"

Fanta bridled. "That's quite a lot, don't you think?"

"Well, the Chessy bit is new. I didn't know that." Romy seemed to think about it. "That might have been nice. She's a good rider. Assuming that's what Greg saw in her."

Fanta felt a surge of loyalty to Chessy. "I'm sure it was, Romy. Chessy is extremely talented," she said crisply. "But back to Terry. If you ask me, he doesn't have it in him to whack Greg over the head. It's not in his character."

Romy barked a laugh. "You didn't see him leaving the hotel that night. He looked like he could have whacked a few people."

"What? You didn't tell me you'd seen Terry at the hotel." Fanta was irate. Romy was once again withholding important intel.

"Yeah, when I was coming back from the show. I got in late—I don't go to the parties at the bar, Fanta—and Terry went charging by me and out the front door. It was like he was totally losing it. Of course, he didn't see me. He usually doesn't."

Fanta was flustered. "Well, okay, but in any case, Terry must have gotten over it. He told me had every intention of following Greg to his new barn."

Romy chuckled. "The joke was on Terry, then, because I don't think Greg planned to ask him to go."

Fanta wanted to bash her head into the chipped wall of the lunchroom. "Romy! You have to tell me this stuff. How else am I going to figure out what happened?"

"Sorry," Romy said contritely. "What else have you got?"

Fanta glanced around to make sure she was still alone. "Well, we already know that Dave was angry that Greg wanted to leave Two Gates. It sounded like Greg wasn't being very nice about the whole thing."

"Right?" Romy jumped in. "Plus, I told you that Dave was pounding on Greg's door that night. It was a bit over the top, even for Dave." She gasped. "What if I'm working for a stone-cold killer?"

"Oh, Romy. Again, I find it hard to picture Dave killing his friend. It was a business thing, not some broken heart or something."

Romy grumbled softly, "Well, Greg broke everyone's heart."

Fanta had to agree. "But here's something," she said. She was pretty sure what she was going to say next would be news even to Romy. "My sources tell me that Greg was going to ask Lana to marry him," she said triumphantly.

There was a pause. "Huh."

"Huh? This is big news, Romy. Greg was going to commit to Lana. They were in love. They were going to go into business together. He was everything to her."

"Yeah, well—"

Fanta cut in. "Then she finds out he's been less than faithful. She saw him that night at the bar with Chessy. She's heard rumors about him fooling around. She's in a jealous rage. She confronts him in his room—wait, didn't they share a room?" The thought suddenly struck her.

"Oh no, they always had adjoining rooms," Romy said in a matter-of-fact way. "They had different schedules, you know."

"Okay, so…" Fanta struggled to reconstruct the crime in her mind. "She gets into his room, she's angry—she has a temper, in case you hadn't noticed—he's broken her heart and her hopes for starting a brand new business with him are dashed. So she hits him."

"It could work," Romy said skeptically. "You said he was going to marry her?"

"Right." Fanta's own temper was rising.

"So that may have been true. But I don't think he was going to go into business with her. Yeah, no. I'm pretty sure Greg wanted his own business. It was going to be Greg Grenier Inc., not Lana Taylor Stables. Take my word for it."

Fanta struggled to keep her cool.

Romy added cheerily, "Anyway, nice job. I gotta go now. I have to get back to work here. Super busy." The call ended abruptly.

Fanta crumpled her sandwich wrapper and lobbed it at the big plastic garbage bucket, where it bounced off the side and onto the floor. It had been bad enough to be lumped together with Romy in pony club days. Now it was simply excruciating.

* * *

Fanta scrutinized the updated blurb about Greg's death on the Newser's website. The police had released Greg's name publicly, but Sue hadn't added any other details. What about how he'd been killed? Or the fact that he was going to get married? Fanta grumbled. She didn't know much about crime reporting, but it seemed pretty dull sometimes. Then she had a thought. Maybe everyone was waiting for her to write up the nice profile, add some personal detail. That could be it.

She imagined Abby stopping by Sue's desk. *"Sorry to interrupt, Sue, you do a good job and everything, but it's Fanta's piece that people will really want to read. You just stick to the facts. Let Fanta write the interesting stuff. Be sure to share what you have with her. Fanta can take it from there. Have a nice day now."*

Fanta shook her head. Like that was going to happen. It was fun to think about, though. She peered over at Sue sitting at her cubicle. Fanta had thought about strolling over, asking for a quick update on Greg's case. But there had not been an opportunity. Sue had been on the phone pretty much all afternoon, listening intently, talking loudly, gesticulating wildly. Fanta was pretty sure she'd heard a swear word or two. She'd decided to steer clear.

She turned her eyes back to the draft of her ballroom dancing article. Here she was writing about foxtrots and rumbas, while Sue pursued grisly murders and nasty highway accidents. It all seemed grossly unfair.

Her phone lit up on her desk. It was a text from a number she didn't recognize. Probably some hustler asking for her banking information, social insurance number, and the password to her entire life. Fanta threw a skeptical glance at the little message.

What's happening with Greg?

Fanta jumped in her seat, her crusty office chair squealing. Who was it? And why were they asking? She sucked in a breath and looked frantically around the newsroom. Sue's chair was empty and her computer turned off. Fanta's head swiveled. Abby's office was vacant; only a gorgeous Burberry raincoat and matching umbrella were left hanging on a coat rack. Fanta turned around. No! There was no way she would go to Douglas with anything remotely interesting. She shuddered. It looked like he was using the tip of his pen to clear the wax out of his ear as he sat at his desk, staring at his computer.

She looked back down at her phone. Was there any way to trace the number? She had no clue. It would probably take money. Fanta snorted. The Newser could barely afford extra tissue in the bathrooms, let alone sophisticated IT services. It was all up to her.

Who is this? she thumbed out carefully. Now was not the time for a typo. She waited for a response. The little dots pulsed.

Lana is worth a look.

Fanta gaped at the screen. The response was enigmatic. Lana was worth a look because she had killed Greg? Or Lana was worth a look because she was, well, good-looking? Fanta tried to think it through. Who could be texting her? Wait! Who had her number? Well, duh. Anyone who read the Newser, that's who. Dammit. It could be any cranky reader out to rile up the media. They were a dime a dozen.

She looked back at the texts. Maybe she should have asked a better question. She did a quick mental review of any crime drama, thriller, or horror movie she'd ever seen. She had asked what everyone asked: Who is this? It was obvious. She'd try again.

What do you know? she typed laboriously.

Never you mind. The answer came zinging back. **Good luck.**

Fanta tapped out desperately, **Please keep in touch.** She wished she were faster with her thumbs. At least she was being polite. Abby would like that.

Fanta stared at the screen. No response. She was pretty sure that was that.

She stuffed the phone in her pocket. She'd keep the whole episode to herself. Nothing had come of it, after all. Maybe the mystery person would contact her again. She'd handle it better next time. Now, it was time to go see Des.

Chapter Fifteen

It was another gorgeous summer evening at Bay Ridge. Fanta trotted Des around the large oval track behind the barn. He was happy to stretch his legs. The exchange of texts at the office replayed in her mind like a series of flash cards. Should she take any of it seriously? Obviously, a killer wouldn't reach out to chit-chat about the crime, with a reporter no less. It seemed like just one more thing to add to all the stuff happening in her life—the tensions at work, the stress of the horse shows, the financial worries. For some reason, she was also concerned about her parents. She couldn't imagine life without hearing her mom's cheery voice.

Des swung along in the canter, a light sweat coming up on his neck. Fanta concentrated on maintaining a steady pace, just like Penny instructed. Dobie had followed them out to the track and was immersed in his own world, running in and out of the underbrush, chasing errant creatures, and inspecting any fragrant delights that lay in his path. More than once, he stopped to roll, legs thrashing, a look of pure enjoyment on his face. Penny would be thrilled.

Refreshed, Fanta rode back to the barn, where she dismounted and secured her stirrups on the saddle. Dobie disappeared into the stable in search of Penny. Fanta led Des through the open door. Just down the aisle, Jeremy Jepson, the local farrier, had one of Kash's front hooves propped between his knees and was busy rasping and trimming.

Fanta tied Des in the aisle. Penny stood nearby, Dobie panting beside her.

"How have you been doing, Jeremy?" Penny asked, fondling Dobie's ears. "Keeping busy?"

Jeremy dropped Kash's front hoof and straightened his back slowly. He was a muscular man with short salt-and-pepper hair. "Aye, getting on. Lots of work to be done."

He surveyed one of Kash's back hooves before picking it up. "Show season, so everyone wants things done yesterday," he muttered.

"I can imagine," Penny said mildly.

Jeremy started in with the rasp. "It's sure a strange time over at Two Gates."

Fanta's ears perked up. Farriers heard all sorts of stuff on their rounds.

"Hmmm," Penny offered.

"That Greg is all anyone can talk about." Jeremy nipped off some excess hoof, stepped back, and straightened.

"I liked the man; he had a great feel for the horses." Jeremy picked up another hoof. Then suddenly he tittered like a schoolgirl. "Lots of long faces among the ladies. Not a single one who didn't have an eye on him."

Fanta slunk behind Des. The last thing she needed was to be held up as Exhibit A.

Jeremy's muscular arms see-sawed with the rasp. "That Lana is pretty good," he grunted. "Though she has her work cut out for her with those two grooms."

He let Kash's hoof drop to the ground. "They've got a lot of attitude, all three of them. Old Dave, caught in the middle."

Penny's eyebrow rose fractionally.

"Things are looking up, though." Jeremy set to work on the last hoof. "The clients are staying put. Still, Dave seems tense. Something else bothering him, maybe." Jeremy studied the hoof clasped between his knees. "I know that Terry Miller gets on my nerves. Always dickering over my invoices." He hissed out a breath as he straightened. "Guess that's why he's got more money than me."

Jeremy stepped back to admire Kash. "What about this horse here? How are you getting on with him?"

"Well, he's coming along, that's for sure," Penny started.

Fanta listened closely. It was just as she'd thought. There was no money to be made training and selling horses. Penny and Chessy should listen to her for a change.

"And we've already had lots of interest, so we should do well." Penny shrugged. "Still, after all these years, I can't believe how quickly everything adds up."

Jeremy guffawed, resting his hands on the big leather pouch slung low around his hips. "Ain't that the truth." He rolled his thick, sunburned neck. "Speaking of money, that Lana may be having a few problems with the books." His brow furrowed and he threw a glance at Penny. "Sorry, listen to me, runnin' my mouth. Not my business to tell."

Penny nodded. "I'd heard Lana was in some trouble."

"Good thing her parents are around to help." Jeremy gave a short laugh, wiping his hands on the front of his thin black t-shirt. "Just hope they'll pay my bills."

Fanta pulled the comb through Des's mane. This was new. Lana having money problems? She would never have guessed. But if Penny knew, it must be true. Forget the big storybook romance. Maybe Lana had seen Greg as one giant meal ticket, one that was at risk of slipping through her grasp and fluttering away in the breeze.

"What's that noise?" Jeremy demanded.

Dobie was scratching his ear vigorously with a hind paw, emitting a long, low groan, his expression sheer ecstasy. His shiny black coat showed more than a few crusty patches, and a faint odor was detectable, even in the stable aisle.

Jeremy hooted, "Nothing like a good scratch for whatever's itchin' ya."

Penny untied Kash and returned him to his stall. Then she and Jeremy moved down the aisle to look at another horse, their voices fading.

Fanta stroked Des's cheek. "That was interesting, don't you think?" she whispered. Des blinked his big dark eyes. "Even my parents don't pay my bills anymore." She straightened his forelock. "We'll see what Lana has to say tomorrow."

Fanta led Des into his stall and closed the door softly. She wrapped her fingers around the metal bars and gazed in at him as he pulled big mouthfuls from his hay net, chewing happily. "I'll see you soon, Dessie, you be good now."

Chapter Sixteen

Fanta set out for the office the next morning with her favorite travel mug full of hot, strong coffee. She'd had an excellent night's sleep and was filled with renewed energy. The day lay before her, ripe with promise. She would work on her spicy ballroom dancing feature. She would jot down creative and inspiring ideas for the magazine. She would pen a compassionate and nuanced profile on Greg. And she was prepared to ask Lana pointed and informed questions. A failing business. A fickle boyfriend. A rosy future about to go south. Awesome! She wouldn't just take whatever Lana might dish out.

She swung into the parking lot at the Newser. She could see it now. She and Lana, meeting in some frumpy, granny-style tearoom, doilies on the tables, a plump cat sitting in the front window. Over weak tea and soggy sandwiches, she would shred Lana's coy carapace with her razor-sharp questions. Lana would sag in her overstuffed chair. *"You're right, I did it, I killed Greg,"* she would sob. *"He always answered my booty calls, so I just tapped on the door, he opened it, and I let him have it! Whammo!"* Lana would judder with the pain and remorse of it all. *"Oh, Fanta, I've deceived the police, but you saw right through me. What a superb reporter you are!"* Then Fanta and the tearoom ladies would corral Lana, truss her up with some apron strings, and hustle her off to the authorities. Case closed!

Fanta snagged a primo parking spot next to the back entrance to the building, hopped out of her car, skipped up the steps, swung open the heavy door, and bumped directly into Gary Stillwater, one of the top advertising reps in the office. He was possibly one of the most boring people she had ever encountered. His hair oil smelled like overripe fruit, and his face reminded Fanta of the frowning men depicted in ancient Roman busts.

Gary stood unmoving in front of her, the two of them snugged together in the cramped corridor like a hesitant couple. "Fanta, so glad to have caught you. If I could have a moment." Gary's voice was almost as oily as his hair.

"Um, well, hi, Gary. Now's not the best time, really. I have to pop out for a meeting in a few minutes and I have a few things to do first." Fanta tried to squeeze past him, flattening herself against the wall.

"I wanted to talk to you about this new magazine." Gary ushered her, meek as a lamb, to the chair in front of his desk. "What I have in mind is an emphasis on home construction and renovation. That's what sells these days. It would open up a whole new area of advertising for us. You know, lumber, heavy equipment, the latest in hardware—and not the computer kind, ha ha."

Fanta cringed. "That's great, Gary, but I haven't put too much thought into it yet. I was leaning more toward interior design, food and lifestyle, trends in outdoor living, and home-based pastimes." The stunning photography and artfully written pieces passed through her mind's eye.

Gary was undeterred. "Not much in the way of advertising there, Fanta. I think we need to stick to nuts and bolts—ha ha. Practical how-to articles, maybe some columnists from the community who could buy an ad or two." Gary swung his arm in a way that was probably meant to be encouraging and collegial. "What we'd really need from you is solid advertorial content— really pump up our advertisers and let everyone know what great products and services we have here in the region."

Fanta shivered. Her morning high was suddenly as flat as the lukewarm coffee in her travel mug. Her creative control was at risk of slipping away, and the thought of writing ad copy all day made her blood run cold. Her journalism career at the Newser would be doomed.

Gary opened a desk drawer and pulled out a thick publication like Fanta's dad used to get from the local hardware store. "Let me show you what I have in mind. There's all sorts of good promotional material in here." Gary flipped through the flimsy pages filled with cramped text. His fingernails were curiously long and yellowed.

Fanta shot to her feet. "Okay, Gary, you know, I really appreciate your views," she said, backing rapidly away. "I think I'll need to touch base with Abby. Just to get her thoughts, you understand. Then we'll circle back. Great chat, thanks."

Fanta hightailed it to her desk. She threw herself into the grubby chair, which wailed in complaint, and dumped her purse at her feet. Waiting for her computer to power up, she twirled an old pen between her fingers. Now the pressure was really on to get some concepts going for the magazine before it turned into a handyman's catalogue. She pulled up her ballroom dancing story and squirmed as she read it over. She sounded like a romance-starved singleton. Or a horny teenager. Douglas would have a heyday.

She glanced at the time. It would all have to wait. She had to head to her meeting with Lana. She'd wanted to be in a calm and thoughtful frame of mind, but instead she felt harried and insecure. What else was new? She dashed off an email to Abby explaining that she wouldn't be at the morning meeting as she was conducting a key interview for the Greg Grenier piece. Then she reached for her purse and rushed out the door.

High T was on a busy street with plenty of historic charm. Floral baskets swung from Dickensian street lamps and leafy trees threw shade onto cobbled sidewalks. The restored Victorian home featured spindles and corbels and gingerbread trim. It offered indoor dining and a small outdoor area with clusters of white bistro chairs and tables. Fanta scrutinized the building as she hurried across the street. Somehow High T had a modern, zen-like feel, even as it screamed old-world style. She wasn't sure she liked the combo.

North City style mavens! Not sure I'm lovin' whatever's going on at High T. Can you say juxta-posed? LMK what you think!

Fanta wove her way through the crowded outdoor patio and took a seat at a table set tightly against the wall. She glanced around. Only the beautiful people ate at High T. Parking had been a beast. She had shoehorned the Honda into a barely legal spot. She squirmed on the iron chair. It was ridiculously small and hard. She hoped her buttocks didn't hang out on either side.

After several minutes, Lana appeared at the entrance, wearing a breezy summer dress and open sandals, her curly hair pinned artfully on her head. She looked like she'd just stepped from a limo or out of the beauty salon, not searched desperately for parking and come dashing down the cobblestones for fear of being late.

Fanta stood and waved. In her workaday clothes, she was probably invisible among the well-heeled tourists and natty professionals. Lana twiddled her fingers in greeting and swayed through the crowd. Fanta tried to square the fairy princess version of Lana coming toward her with the fierce and foreboding one who thundered around a jumper course at speed on a fiery stallion. In their own ways, the two versions were equally scary.

"Hi, Lana, it's great to meet you. I'm Fanta Delaney. I appreciate your time today." Fanta reached out a hand. Too late, she noticed a big ink stain on her thumb.

"Oh, Fanta, the pleasure is mine." Lana laid her fingers briefly in Fanta's palm. "You mentioned you were writing an article about Greg. You're from the Newser? That's so nice. While it will be difficult, I am so looking forward to sharing my memories with you." Lana perched on the small chair, tanned legs crossed.

They ordered finger sandwiches, petit-fours, and green tea from a waiter with attitude. Fanta reached for the translucent teacup with its scrolled handle. She felt like some giant and peculiar animal out of Alice in Wonderland.

"So, how did you and Greg meet?" she started. "Oh wait, I forgot my recorder." She put her teacup down hastily, pulled the device from her bag, and pressed the little silver button. "I hope you don't mind, it's for my notes."

Lana made a sweeping gesture of consent. "Of course. Well, Greg and I met through riding. We both competed at the highest levels of the sport and, after crossing paths a few times, we were just drawn to each other. What appealed to me was his skill and empathy with the horses." An impish smile curled across her glossy lips. "And, of course, he was oh-so handsome, as

I'm sure you know." She batted lightly mascaraed lashes.

Fanta maintained a neutral expression. She was a member of the media, not a gossipy girl at a sleepover playing kiss-and-tell.

Lana took a sip of tea, savoring the fragrance, balancing the tiny cup on the tips of her fingers. "You know, I'm based in Vermont, so Greg and I didn't start dating seriously right away." She put the cup down with a light clink on the gilt-edged saucer. "Long-distance relationships! I'm sure you know how it is. So difficult for busy professionals. But we kept meeting at the same competitions and realized we were on the same schedule. We just…fell in love." Lana leaned forward dreamily, her chin on her hand.

Fanta sat back. The iron chair was sending pulse waves of pain into her lower back. "I see. And did you have plans for the future?" She grunted as she rearranged herself on the seat.

"Well, between you and me, we were thinking about getting married, going into business together." Lana popped a petit-four in her mouth and chewed delicately. Then she picked up a lacy napkin, dabbed the sides of her mouth, and assumed a saucy tone. "We were going to combine forces, in more ways than one!"

Fanta's stomach heaved. Somehow, picturing Greg in a loving, committed relationship was worse than imagining him chasing women all over the horse world. Fanta braced herself. She needed to poke the bear.

"That sounds wonderful, Lana." She poured them both more tea, her mind leaping ahead. "As I mentioned in my note to you, I also ride horses here in the area. Of course, I'd heard that Greg was planning to leave Two Gates. You're saying he was going to go into business with you? At Lana Taylor Stables?"

Lana waved dismissively. "Of course, what else would he do?"

Fanta drew in a deep breath. "Well, perhaps he wanted to go out on his own?"

Lana's eyes popped over the top of the crustless cucumber sandwich she had just raised to her mouth. "That would never have happened," she said, swallowing forcefully. "Why do you ask that?"

This time, Fanta made the airy hand motion. "Oh, no reason. Just a line of inquiry."

"The answer is no. I have an established business. Greg would have been foolish to start out on his own. I think you can understand that." Lana wiped her hands roughly with the elegant napkin.

"Yes, certainly." Fanta nodded thoughtfully. "Of course, I've seen firsthand that running a stable is hard work. Not only do you have to be a good rider and coach, but you also need a head for business. Greg seemed to have all of those things."

Lana crossed her arms. "As I said, Greg was devoted to me. We were going to get married and start a life with horses together under the Lana Taylor banner." She frowned petulantly. "Please get that correct in your article. I assume I'll see a draft of whatever you write."

"Oh, I'm afraid that's not how it works. The free press, media independence, I'm sure you understand." Fanta smiled ingratiatingly and threw a glance at her recorder to make sure it was ticking along. "But I do want to make sure I've got things straight. Are you saying that you *needed* Greg to go into business with you? Because, as you've mentioned, you have a seemingly successful operation of your own. Lovely horses, family money, established stable. Perhaps there were…problems?"

Lana slapped her sandaled foot on the flagstone. "That's not what I'm saying at all. I'm perfectly capable of running my own business. But Greg and I wanted to be together, in every way!" She leaned over and shouted the last bit into Fanta's recorder where it lay on the table among the dainty tea paraphernalia. A few heads turned. Lana sat back in her chair, flustered. "You media people, you can't get the simplest things right. I have half a mind to call this off."

Fanta held up a placating hand. "I'm sorry, Lana. I promise you I'm just trying to get the facts correct. And, of course, I realize what a tough position you must be in now. You've lost your fiancé and your future business partner." Fanta tut-tutted. "Where do you go from here?"

Lana appeared slightly mollified. "Yes, it's been very difficult." She blinked rapidly and picked up her teacup. "I'm not sure what the future holds, but I plan to keep riding and competing. That's what Greg would have wanted."

Fanta picked up a sugar cube with tiny tongs and plopped it in her tea, swirling it around with a miniature spoon.

"Speaking of Greg's wants," she said, with a slight lift of her eyebrows. "I may have mentioned, I ride at Bay Ridge Farms. Chessy MacKay is a friend of mine. It seems Greg asked her to be his assistant coach. Do you plan to extend the same offer?"

Lana choked on her tea, her face reddening. "Greg was a savvy horseman," she gasped, struggling for words. "He knew…talent when he saw it. Chessy is a strong rider. Greg had…all the best instincts."

"I think you're right." Fanta nodded, allowing Lana to pull herself together before she discharged the next volley. "Then again, Chessy is so gorgeous. Not sure I'd want my boyfriend to be hanging out with her twenty-four seven!" she said with abandon, sending a silent apology to Chessy.

Lana sputtered. "I'm not sure what you're suggesting. I thought this was supposed to be a nice retrospective on Greg. His life, his career. Not his…personal issues." Lana gestured at the recorder. "I think we're done here. You can turn that thing off."

"Absolutely, sorry to overstep." Fanta grabbed the little device. "Just one more thing. I assume you've spoken to the police. They think foul play is involved." Did people say that? The term sounded like something from the nineteenth century. "Is there someone who'd want to harm Greg?"

Lana stood abruptly, the iron chair scraping on the flagstones, her napkin falling from her lap. She looked like a little girl having a meltdown at a friend's birthday party.

"I'm not sure what you've accomplished here," she said with a sob, "but I don't know a single person who'd hurt Greg. He was our…my…darling." She turned to go and then whirled around, her face slick with tears. "How could anyone have done it?"

Lana rushed from the restaurant. Fanta sat back, exhausted, pooching air through her lips. She clicked off her recorder and gathered her things. Before she could lift herself out of the agonizing chair, the waiter laid the bill on the table, as carefully and discreetly as a sacred gift. Fanta flipped open the little folder. Apparently, tea for two was as much as she spent on groceries for a week.

Chapter Seventeen

The late afternoon sun beat down on the parking lot. Fanta trailed out of the back door of the office and toward her car. She'd put in a full afternoon of work at the Newser. Now, she just wanted to hop in her car, dial up the AC, and make straight for What's Your Beef, the local greasy burger joint. She needed something substantial and revivifying after the slim, soul-sucking pickings at High T. Her budget would just have to take the hit, again.

She pulled into traffic, almost cutting off yet another desperate driver. After the run-in with Gary and the encounter with Lana, the afternoon had actually gone well. She had revisited her ballroom dancing feature and decided to stick with the R rating even if it did make her look like a randy schoolgirl. Plus, she'd approved the birdwatching layout and spoken with Abby about the home and lifestyle magazine. Abby had been sympathetic to her concerns about advertising influence.

"I get it, Fanta, I really do, and I appreciate your take on things," she'd said. "But in this instance, I think compromise is the way to go. We need to use this magazine as a money-making venture, but of course it needs solid content to attract readers. If those readers can find some of the items they're reading about at our local businesses, all the better." Abby smoothed her hair behind one ear, revealing a sparkly diamond stud that was the perfect complement to her vintage tie-neck silk blouse. "But let's not be limited by that. We need to strike a balance. Just let me know if you'd like to meet with me and Gary. Then we can put together an approach that works from both perspectives."

Fanta left the Honda in the weedy lot at What's Your Beef, not far from a trio of overflowing dumpsters. Of course, Abby had come up with the best and most common-sense answer. Still. She pushed through the doors of the burger shop. She would just have to succeed, despite Gary.

She planted herself in front of the counter and gazed up at the menu. Now was not the time for watery popsicles or featherweight sandwiches. An attitude adjustment was needed. She ordered a two-patty burger with all the fixings and a heaping serving of French fries from the pimply guy at the cash register.

With her order on a plastic tray, she slid into a quiet booth with a wide, cool bench. She breathed a sigh of relief. Then she picked up the burger and took a whopping bite, letting the grease drip down her chin. A dab of mayo stuck to her nose. The carbs began to work their magic. She felt placid and dull. Was there someone hovering behind her? She would dispatch them with a steely glare. Swiping her face with a napkin, she glanced around.

"Romy?" Fanta almost choked. "Is that you?"

Romy stood awkwardly in the aisle wearing the polyester uniform of What's Your Beef, complete with burgundy visor and apron.

Fanta gestured with her soiled napkin. "What's with the outfit?"

"I work here now, Fanta." Romy slid into the booth opposite her. "With Greg gone, there's just not as much for me to do at Two Gates." She shrugged. "So I got a few hours here."

Fanta readied the burger for another attack. "Well, don't let me get you in trouble. I'm sure you're on the clock." She took a shark-like bite.

"Oh, that's okay, I'm on a break." Romy shrugged a skinny shoulder. "I saw you here and thought I'd say hello." Her face creased. "I don't see too many people I know here. They're not much into burgers or fries." She studied Fanta's meal dispassionately.

Fanta mopped her face with the soiled napkin. She should have grabbed more of the things. And a milkshake might have been nice. She eyeballed Romy. It didn't seem like she was going to budge anytime soon.

"I saw Lana today," Fanta said, chewing.

Romy eye-rolled. "I wish I could see a whole lot less of her. I'm totally sick of being ordered around by the vixen of Vermont. What did she say?"

"The vixen of Vermont? Good one, Romy. Why's she ordering you around? Doesn't Deirdre work for her?" Fanta sprinkled salt on her fries. Deirdre wouldn't be caught dead at What's Your Beef. Possibly one of the place's top selling points.

"Deirdre," Romy sneered. "She's useless. Either she's super nasty or she's just plain lazy. I don't know how she still has a job. At least she's toned it down with the clothing. We were all getting sick of the Victoria's Secret half-time show. Except maybe Greg," she finished in a grumble.

Fanta chewed another mouthful of burger. It was best not to think of Deirdre's underthings while eating. "Maybe Lana and Deirdre will head back to Vermont at the end of the show season." She added a blob of ketchup to the fries.

"Yeah, those two are weird. It's like some kind of hate-hate relationship." Romy glanced up at a big wall clock and then back at Fanta. "Where did you see Lana?"

Fanta swallowed and picked up a few fries. "At this place called High T. I don't recommend it. Very fussy."

Romy snickered. "That's where Lana takes people she's trying to impress." Her brow creased. "Why did she meet you there?"

Fanta bridled. She pointed a French fry at Romy. "I am a public persona, a member of the media. All sorts of people would like to get my attention."

Romy shrugged, eyes flicking to the wall clock again. "So what did Lana say?"

"Oh, just what you might expect." Fanta waved the stained napkin. "She and Greg were in love, they were going to go into business together, she's lost without him. That sort of thing."

She picked up the burger and took another bite. Somehow, it was fast losing its appeal. Her dress pants felt like they were being shrink-wrapped onto her body. She pictured herself sitting in the booth like an overgrown garden slug. Why did everything so good have to turn out so bad?

"Lana was in dreamland," Romy was saying. "I don't think she could see half of what was right in front of her."

Fanta put the burger down and fingered a few of her fries. "Like what?"

"Oh, come on. Everyone knew Greg had a whole bunch of other stuff on the side. Other women. Other…activities. He wasn't very nice that way." Romy seemed at pains to admit it. "I mean, even Deirdre. Who do you think she bought the undies for? It sure wasn't the rest of us. Deirdre was delusional. As if Greg would have hooked up with her."

Fanta surveyed Romy with her formless clothing, the visor askew on her head, her wispy hair escaping the cheap elastic. It was just like in pony club days, when the two of them would huddle together, dissing and dissecting everyone's romantic liaisons. Like they'd had anything on offer.

"Well, we both know Deirdre plays dirty," Fanta commented. "I'm sure she got a thrill out of getting it on with Greg right under Lana's nose." She swirled the fries in the ketchup. She really should have selected a healthy salad.

"Greg would never have *gotten it on* with Deirdre." Romy wrinkled her nose in distaste. "And as for Lana, well, I know she's upset over losing Greg, but she doesn't need to take it out on everyone else. We're all just trying to keep going. Me and Deirdre, we're either being yelled at or ignored completely. Deirdre might deserve it. I don't."

Fanta didn't have any trouble picturing Lana as a lousy boss, even after her showy display of coy civility at High T, a display that had quickly dissolved into a temper tantrum. She looked over just as Romy's lower lip trembled and her chin scrunched.

"I really liked Greg. I know he wasn't always a nice guy, but I was so proud to work for him. He was so great with the horses. And then I found him…I found him that morning…like that. I can never forget it!"

Romy heaved out a sob. Tears slipped down her child-like face. Fanta wiped her hand and laid it over Romy's on the table.

"No one thinks twice about me, the mousy girl," Romy cried, trying to control her voice. "But I have feelings, too. I'm not stupid. I know when things aren't right. I just wish I could do something, that someone would listen to me, that I had a voice. You know what it's like, Fanta." She pulled her hand away and dashed furiously at her eyes. "I gotta go now."

Romy slid out of the booth and headed rapidly toward the kitchen, her crepe-soled work shoes squinching on the linoleum floor.

Fanta bundled up the leftover fries and the last bites of burger in the paper wrapping. Romy was right, she knew exactly what it was like. And now, not only was Greg dead, but plenty of people were suffering. Was she helping, or just making everything worse? She got up, pitched the remains of her meal in the nearest trash bin, and made her way to the parking lot.

* * *

Fanta sat in her bed, propped against the fleece reading pillow her mom had bought her for her birthday. It was plushy and soft, and it always made her feel comfy-cozy. On her phone, she swiped through picture after picture on Greg's social feeds. Greg and Lana, Greg and Dave, Greg and Terry. Everyone looked happy, successful. Big trophies were being hoisted or giant ribbons pinned on horses' bridles. Greg was back-slapping corporate bigwigs or giving Lana's hand a squeeze, treating her to a big, sunny smile. Fanta was gratified to see Deirdre loitering in the background in many of the pics, a bulky backpack or overstuffed grooming bucket making her look sad and put-upon, a step away from the high-octane world of the others.

Fanta laid the phone on the coverlet. What had gone wrong at Two Gates? She thought back to the meeting she'd had with Lana. She'd been pleased with her interviewing skills…for the most part. She'd done her research, been prepared. But it had felt uncomfortable, pressing Lana, getting under her skin, forcing her to flee the restaurant in tears. Was that the type of reporter she wanted to be? She smoothed her hand on the cool cotton sheet. Maybe she didn't have what it took to be a hard-nosed journalist. Maybe she didn't want to.

She turned her head toward the window. The light of the streetlamp glowed through the curtains. She was no expert in reading people, guessing their inner thoughts, but her heart told her that Lana was truly grief-stricken. She might be a good actress, but her distress over Greg seemed real.

Then there was Dave and Terry. Much as she'd told Romy, Fanta couldn't picture either of them smacking Greg with a blunt object over pricey invoices, hurt feelings, or even a business blowout. If Chessy had wanted to join Greg's barn as his assistant, she had every reason to want him alive and well. Even Deirdre, with her sights set on seduction, didn't stand to benefit from Greg being dead.

Fanta put her phone and the reading pillow aside and clicked off her bedside light. The whole thing seemed immense and unknowable. She snuggled under the covers, feeling the long day wash over her. She couldn't help but wonder if there was something—or someone—out there that she hadn't even thought about.

Chapter Eighteen

"*When Wanda first started dancing with Roberto, she felt like she had been whisked off to another planet.*"

Fanta jabbed the delete button. She pounded out another sentence.

"*As soon as Wanda looked into Roberto's eyes, she knew he would be the one to whisk her off her feet.*"

She wanted to crack her head into the computer screen. Maybe Roberto could step on Wanda's toe; at least that would be funny. Better than her pathetic attempts at steamy romance.

It was Friday morning in the newsroom, and Fanta wished she were anywhere else. She'd tossed and turned all night, second-guessing everything she'd done, playing it all out in her mind again and again, this way and that. Now, here she was at her desk, changing her sexy opening sentence into something G-rated. She was totally wimping out.

If she could just make it through the morning meeting. She'd promised Abby she would perform better. She had to really sell herself and her stories, not just duck and weave. Any minute now and—

"Let's go, guys." Abby appeared wearing pleated knee-length shorts and a short-sleeved shirt with a geometric pattern. Somehow, she made the golf attire look like stylish office apparel. Fanta hustled over to join the group and slipped into the wobbly chair.

"I've got a corporate event at Broadhead Links, so we'll make this a short one," Abby launched in. "Nice job on the drug bust, Sue. What else is on the go?"

"Thanks. Yeah, just an update on this Grenier guy. Seems the police are planning to hold a press conference next week. Don't know what that's about. But I do know they've been interviewing a bunch of people," she glanced at her notes, "like the girlfriend, the business partner, some of the clients, I guess? Not sure how this horse business works. Basically, anyone close to the guy."

"Okay, that's interesting. What about that profile, Fanta? Any luck there?"

Fanta was quick off the mark. "Yes, absolutely, Abby. I've also talked to a lot of the people who were close to Greg, including one of his clients—that is, someone who boards their horses at Two Gates and got coaching from Greg." She smiled at Sue. It was nice to actually know something. Sue nodded perfunctorily. "I'd like to gather a bit more info, but I think I can pull together a profile pretty soon."

"Great. And I see the birdwatching piece is teed up for the weekend?"

"Yup, ready to go, and I'm putting the finishing touches on the ballroom dancing feature. I think you'll like it." She would have to sort out the wreckage of her story when she got back to her desk.

"Super, and the magazine?"

Fanta hesitated. What could she say about the magazine? She tried to think what Abby would do. "I'm going to set up a meeting with you and Gary for Monday morning, so we can get on the same page. I have some great ideas after speaking with the design team and I'm sure Gary will have some valuable input, too." Fanta surprised even herself with her smooth response.

"Sounds good," Abby replied. "If you want to get back to work now, Fanta, feel free. It's a gorgeous day, try to get out of here early if you can." Abby looked around the group. "That last bit goes for everyone."

Fanta was about to scurry back to her desk, but hesitated. A serious reporter would want to know what was happening with the other beats. She decided to stay put. Abby gave her a curious look that seemed almost impressed.

The other reporters and editors went through their updates. It was interesting to hear everything that was being covered in municipal politics, the business community, and sports. Abby asked great questions that brought the issues into focus. Douglas was a jerk, but he was on top of his work. He gave a rundown of the analytics that suggested how stories were performing with readers. Fanta made a note to herself to learn more.

Returning to her desk, she knew exactly what she would do. She would stick with her original version of the ballroom dancing story. She was sick of doubting herself. Then she would set up the meeting for Monday morning. She and Abby and Gary would meet and share their views in an amicable and professional manner. Over the weekend, she would work on concepts for the magazine, keeping the advertising perspective in mind. Perhaps she could begin to draft her profile on Greg. It didn't have to be complicated.

All that done, she glanced around the newsroom. It was coming up to noon. Fanta decided she would take Abby at her word and head to Bay Ridge for the afternoon. There couldn't be a better day for it.

* * *

Fanta pulled into the twisty lane at Bay Ridge. Her favorite song was playing on the radio and her hair blew in the breeze from the open window. It had been so nice to leave the office, like being set free. She could hardly wait to see Des. She would ride in the outdoor ring before having a jumping lesson with Penny the next day. She wanted to work on maintaining Des's balance and rhythm. She needed to build her fitness in the saddle. Really, the list of things she had to improve was long.

Lyle and Sara were grooming their horses in the aisle as Fanta stepped into the barn.

"Hey, Fanta, how's it going? Skipping out on work?" Lyle called.

"My boss gave me the afternoon off, actually." Fanta stopped to give Lyle's horse Trifle a scratch on the forehead. Lyle and Trifle had won the championship in their division at the recent show. Lyle had the ability to sit quietly in the saddle and let the horse shine. Fanta knew it wasn't easy.

Lyle pulled a comb through Trifle's mane. "Ready to do it all over again?" He waggled his shaggy eyebrows. "Next show's coming up. You and Des

126

better get out there and kick Terry's butt. We can't have Two Gates beating us all the time."

"As if, Lyle. No one's gonna win over Pearl," Sara's voice droned from farther down the aisle. She stepped out from behind Rose. Her face was scrubbed clean of makeup and her hair was scraped back in a ponytail. "Plus, Two Gates has such a better program than us. More training, more support. I mean, Penny's good but…My parents are seriously considering finding me a spot at Two Gates. Well, they were. With Greg gone, I don't think it's worth it. I might as well just stay here, for now."

"I'm sure Two Gates would be happy to have you, Sara," Fanta said pointedly. "Don't let us stand in your way."

"Yeah, don't let us keep you, Sara!" Lyle crowed.

Fanta ducked into the tack room to get her equipment before going to find Des in his stall. He nickered as she approached. She opened the door and offered him a carrot.

"Are you happy to see me or just the treats, Dessie?" she teased, giving him a kiss on the nose. "It doesn't matter. I love you just the same."

Avoiding Lyle and Sara's bickering, she soon had Des groomed and saddled up. She led him out to the large mounting block at the front of the barn. It was like a mini set of stairs that allowed her to get into the saddle more easily. Once she was settled, she asked Des to start down the sandy path to the large outdoor ring. Penny spotted her and strode over to open the gate.

"Hey there, Fanta, come and join us."

Penny had her eye on Chessy, who was turning Ollie toward two big jumps with one stride in between. Ollie's canter was controlled and powerful. Chessy waited for the perfect takeoff spot. Ollie snapped over the first fence, took one giant stride, and launched over the second obstacle.

"Super, that was just the ticket!" Penny called, her voice booming across the ring. "Keep her light in your hand like that and she'll respect those rails."

Fanta asked Des to start walking around the ring. His head bobbed and his ears twitched as he plodded along, as easygoing as ever. Chessy thundered by on Ollie, the picture of strength and energy, a warrior princess. It was almost impossible not to feel completely overshadowed.

"I'm going to give Des a light ride on the flat today," Fanta said to Penny as she rode past.

"Great, that's exactly what he needs," Penny replied briskly.

Chessy pulled Ollie to a walk and turned to ride alongside Fanta and Des. Ollie's coat was slick with sweat and a light foam was coming up on her neck.

"I meant to say, you and Des did great at the show," Chessy offered.

"Thanks, it was fun," Fanta said modestly, reaching down to pat Des. She glanced over at Chessy, with her pink polo, helmet, breeches, and boots, like something out of the glossy horse magazines. Fanta was suddenly acutely aware of her simple jeans and t-shirt.

Then she did a double-take. Ollie had a bonnet on her head that covered each ear to protect against flies and dirt. That wasn't surprising, but such bonnets were usually black or brown. Ollie's featured the colors of the rainbow.

"Wow, that's quite the headgear," Fanta laughed. She wasn't too surprised. Ollie looked big and intimidating, but she was actually the stable pet and was often outfitted in the latest trendy horse-wear.

"It was either that or a pink one with a unicorn horn in the middle," Penny guffawed. "Nothing but the best for our Ollie! Don't worry, we'll use the plain one for the show ring," she added, more than a hint of mischief in her eye.

Chessy smiled and shook her head as Ollie walked placidly beside Des on a loose rein, poking her big pink tongue out the side of her mouth.

Penny was on her way back to the barn. "I'll let you get on with it, Fanta. Unless there was something you wanted to ask me?"

"No, I'll be fine, thanks."

Chessy waited until Penny was out of earshot. "So, I just wanted to mention, Lana reached out to me."

"Really?" Fanta immediately thought of the rendezvous at High T. Obviously, the bit about Greg wanting to hire Chessy had been a newsflash for Lana. "What did she want?"

"She wanted to inform me that Greg's offer of assistant coach was officially rescinded," Chessy said in a faux-snooty voice. Her lip curled with a hint of amusement.

"*Noooo*," Fanta breathed. Still, it was hardly surprising. Maybe the twenty-four seven dig had hit home. "But that's okay because you weren't going to do it anyway, right?"

"Probably not, so I'm not upset or anything," Chessy said, practical as ever. "Lana did let me know that she'd offered the role to Terry. She said he was thrilled to accept."

"I can imagine," Fanta said, picturing Terry sitting in a funk at Demi Tasse. "So, does that mean Lana is the new pro at Two Gates?"

"No idea." Chessy smoothed Ollie's mane to one side. "It's interesting, though. Greg told me that he didn't want to offer the position to Terry." Chessy shrugged. "Probably not something he should have shared, but whatever."

"Yeah, he had his reasons," Fanta said, pondering this latest news.

Chessy gave her a curious look. "Anyway, I thought you'd like to know. I'll let you and Des get on with things." Chessy turned Ollie away and headed for the gate.

Fanta picked up her reins. "Can't say I'm surprised, Dessie," she whispered. "What about you?"

Des nipped at a big horsefly that had alighted on his shoulder, sending it buzzing away. Fanta asked him to trot forward. Everything drained from her mind as she set to work.

Chapter Nineteen

Fanta led Des into the barn. She had ridden for almost an hour, and they were both sweaty. She tied him in the aisle and started to remove the saddle. She looked over at the empty wash stall. It was the perfect time to hose Des off with warm water, maybe even some sweet-smelling shampoo. He always loved to be fussed over. Her own cooldown would have to wait.

"That horse needs a trim!"

Just as Fanta was backing Des into the wash stall, Marcia Jaczek, the senior groom at Bay Ridge, appeared out of the tack room with the horse clippers. Her white t-shirt showed off her tanned, muscular arms and some colorful tats. Her bottle-blonde hair was scooped up under a baseball cap that threw a shadow over her sharp face.

"I'm gonna give Des a once-over." Marcia elbowed Fanta aside. "These fuzzy ears and old-man whiskers will never do for the show ring."

"Sure thing, thanks, Marcia." Fanta stepped back. Marcia rode roughshod over pretty much everyone at Bay Ridge, but she worked hard to keep the horses looking and feeling their best. Fanta had learned it was best just to keep out of the way.

Marcia turned on the clippers. Des was unperturbed by the light buzzing sound and started to snooze. It was late afternoon, and evening chores would begin soon. Penny came to stand at the wash stall, Dobie at her heels.

Marcia's nose wrinkled. "Good grief, what's that dog got all over him?"

"Oh, you know, whatever stinks, he rolls in it." Penny glanced down. Dobie looked happily back. "There's one more thing to do: put this dog through the wash stall."

"That would be a full-time job," Marcia muttered, running the clippers over Des's muzzle. Then she cleared her throat and spoke up, "That reminds me, Penny, there's a ton of work to do here these days. You know Deirdre, right?" She glanced at Penny. "She was Greg's groom. Before that, she groomed for Lana. Now she's back working with Lana. Sorry, it's a bit confusing." Marcia focused on her trimming. "The thing is, she's looking for a new gig. I guess it's not all roses with Lana. Plus, I don't think Deirdre wants to be based in Vermont."

Marcia stepped back to scrutinize her handiwork. Des snoozed, his lower lip twitching. "Anyway, I told Deirdre I'd put in a word for her here, in case you're interested."

Fanta felt a massive thundercloud roll over the day. She wouldn't be able to cope if Deirdre came to work at Bay Ridge. She felt panicky just thinking about it. Every day would be some fresh misery, just like in pony club times.

"Hi, guys, looks like a party. Can I join?" Bonnie came around the corner with some buckets to rinse out in the wash stall. Her jeans and t-shirt were dirty, but her curly hair shone and there was a slick of gloss on her lips. "Did I hear you mention Deirdre?"

"Marcia says she's looking for work," said Penny. "What do you think?"

Bonnie swirled water in each bucket. "Hmm, well, there's always stuff to do. And we're just starting the show season, so maybe another pair of hands would help." She fiddled with the water taps. "But, to be honest, I'm not sure about Deirdre. I've known her for quite a while, from when she first worked with Lana in Vermont. She was a lot of fun then, but now...I don't know, she's different."

Deirdre? Fun? Those were two words that simply could not exist in the same sentence. Fanta rolled her eyes. Leave it to Bonnie to see the best in everyone.

"Oh, what happened?" Penny asked, just as Marcia drilled out, "Different? How is she different? I haven't seen any difference."

Bonnie had obviously learned a long time ago how to cope with the powder keg that was Marcia. "I'm not sure, but ever since Deirdre came back to work with Greg, she just hasn't seemed like the same person," she replied, carefully cleaning each bucket.

Fanta blinked. Deirdre seemed like exactly the same person to her. Mean, petty, childish. She couldn't even conceive of another Deirdre.

Bonnie continued, "Maybe she was interested in Greg? Hoped to hook up with him? But, you know, he was obviously with Lana."

Bonnie had a long-time boyfriend who would probably soon be her husband. The land of frustrated desires and broken hearts—Fanta's home turf—was likely foreign to her.

Bonnie shrugged, letting water drain from a bucket. "Like I say, she used to be fun, playful. She talked a lot about some guy she was dating. Sounded like they were pretty committed. Now she just seems so…unhappy. And kinda, well, desperate. Throwing herself at whoever. That's why I thought she might have been making a play for Greg."

Marcia opened fire. "Deirdre wouldn't have wasted her time with Greg. The guy was a playboy. His relationship with Lana did nothing to stop him," she argued aggressively. "No, Deirdre was too smart for that. Did you know her mom was a senior IT person, somewhere or other, before she died?" Marcia shook her head crossly. "Here's a thought. Maybe Deirdre just wants to stop grooming and do something else with her life. Maybe that's what's got her preoccupied. Nothing wrong with that."

Bonnie set out the buckets to dry at the entrance to the wash stall. "I'm sure you're right. If it helps, Penny, I'd have no problem with Deirdre coming here."

"Well, it's time for chores; let's talk about it another day." Penny walked down the aisle, Dobie at her heels.

Marcia clicked off the clippers and took them back to the tack room. Fanta moved into the wash stall and let the warm water flow over her fingers and then onto Des's legs.

"What do you think, Dessie? We'd have to make a run for it if Deirdre ever came here. Maybe you could come and stay at my place."

Des swiveled his ears and tossed his great head. Joking aside, Fanta couldn't bear the thought of being hustled out of Bay Ridge and taking Des away from all that was familiar. No. She was the horse owner now, and Deirdre would be the groom. And she would not let Deirdre forget it.

*** *** ***

"In other news, the North City Police will provide an update on the death of well-known local horseman Greg Grenier next week. Grenier died under suspicious circumstances at the Carleton Hotel last week. Police are asking for the public's help and encourage anyone with information to step forward."

Fanta clicked off the radio. Traffic was crazy. Everyone was leaving town for the weekend. She stopped at yet another red light. The news report replayed in her mind. She had information about Greg's death. By her count, there were a few people who had reason to harm him, maybe not with any—what did the police say?—premeditation. Should she step forward?

She pictured herself center-stage at the next morning meeting.

"After extensive interviews and thorough investigation typical of a top-notch journalist and supported by my comprehensive understanding of all things horsey, I was able to pass on significant intel to the police, who were forever grateful for my assistance. Based on my foolproof evidence, they wrapped things up quickly. Mystery solved!"

Or something like that, it needed work. Abby would be impressed, Sue would be awestruck, and Douglas could get bent.

Then she thought of Dave, Terry, Lana, or even Deirdre being hauled off by the police. Something about it didn't feel right. Fanta sighed. The police were speaking to all the same people she was, and then some. Surely they had the same information? She pulled into her building's parking lot. She would wait until after the press conference to see if she had anything new to add.

She cut the engine. She looked forward to a Friday night in her sweats with a glass of wine. Her phone chimed with an incoming text. She pulled it out of her purse.

Hey honeys, bin thinking abut your qvestion. Got some idees. It was her mom.

Hi mom. Like what? She should never have asked her mother for advice.

ok so, heer goes. Never ave a bitch buddy.

Fanta gawked at the message. Her mother's texts were indecipherable. She jabbed the phone icon. Her mom picked up immediately.

"Hi, honey, I thought I might hear from you."

"I got your text, mom. What are you talking about?"

"It's just something I remembered from when I was a working girl. Office life can be tough. I had one boss…well, he was unpleasant, let me tell you. And then this one colleague. She was such a thorn in my side. Anyway, I became friends…well, not really friends…with this other teacher, Doris. All we did was complain about everybody. We'd go for coffee or lunch and bitch, bitch, bitch. It felt good at the time, but I have to tell you, it was so poisonous."

Fanta paused. "So, I shouldn't do that?"

"That's right! Doris was not my friend. We didn't help each other. We were bitch buddies." Her mom's voice held more than a hint of triumph.

"I see." Fanta tried to take it in. Was there anyone like that in her life? She opened the car door. It was stifling sitting inside with the windows up. "Well, thanks for passing that on, I'll definitely keep it in mind." Or not. The glass of wine was calling. Her t-shirt was stuck to her back.

"And never be afraid to say when you've made a mistake, honey. If you're wrong, you're wrong. Better to admit—"

"That's super, mom. Listen, I have to—"

"Here's another one! Always take the high road, Fanta honey. You'll be glad—"

"Mom! I gotta go now. We'll speak soon, don't worry."

Fanta shoved her phone in her back pocket and hustled in the back door of her building. She would always love her mom's cheery voice, but sometimes she just couldn't stand talking to her.

* * *

Fanta sat in her Adirondack chair on the balcony, nursing a glass of cheap wine. There was nothing like a relaxing Friday evening in summer. She leaned forward and peered down at Mrs. Hooper's balcony. She hadn't seen the elderly lady or Lottie for a few days. Fanta liked to keep an eye out. Hopefully, someone would do the same for her one day, when she was old and gray. Fanta couldn't really picture it, but she had a vague idea that it would happen.

She could hear the burble of a TV, possibly coming from Mrs. Hooper's apartment. Fanta cocked an ear. It sounded like the type of game show that Mrs. Hooper liked—lots of dinging and clapping, a cheery host, excited contestants. Suddenly, there was a short, sharp bark.

"Oh, Lottie, dear, that little squirrel is on television, not here in our living room."

Fanta relaxed. That was definitely Mrs. Hooper. A thought struck her. She'd promised to care for Lottie if Mrs. Hooper went away. She hadn't heard any more about it. Maybe she and Lottie should go for a few walks, get better acquainted. She tried to picture herself coaxing Lottie out of the apartment and away from Mrs. Hooper, the little dog growling, maybe even nipping. She didn't know much about walking dogs, but she would put it on her to-do list.

She'd brought her work phone with her out to the deck with the ambitious idea of answering emails, setting up some interviews. One afternoon out of the office and her inbox was a mess. She remembered the mysterious texter. It mightn't hurt to get back in touch. The whole investigation was becoming a jumbly pile of gripes and hearsay, like a tangled ball of yarn found at the bottom of a knitting box. Fanta poked at her phone. She imagined the texter as an ageing armchair detective, probably sitting at home looking for ways to keep busy after finishing the crossword and the Wordle. She started a thread.

Are you there?

An answer shot back quickly. **What do you want?**

That was a bit harsh. Fanta decided to lay it on the line. **Do you know who killed Greg?**

I told you to look at Lana.

The armchair detective obviously took things seriously. Okay. **I did. She's heartbroken.**

Yeah right.

A tad dismissive. Fanta couldn't think where to take it next. How much did the person know about Greg's life? She'd find out. **What about Greg's business partner Dave? There was a disagreement going on there.**

Something to think about.

Very cryptic. It was kinda fun, in an exasperating way. **And Greg's client Terry? He was upset with Greg.**

He never had a chance.

Ouch. Okay, she would go for a real flyer. **Greg had this groom, Deirdre. She was into him. Maybe she felt rejected.**

Hardly! Deirdre is smokin'. Greg knew something good when he saw it.

What? Who was this person? Obviously misguided. But reasonably informed. What would a smart journalist do? Go for the big open-ended question.

I can't think of anyone else. You?

I'm not surprised. Good luck.

Fanta blinked. It was like playing a rigorous tennis or ping pong match and missing the last shot, watching it go sailing by. She looked at her phone, which had gone mysteriously dark, and then at her wine glass, which was empty. Time for a refill. Or maybe a switch to chamomile tea. If she went to bed now, she was pretty sure she wouldn't be able to stop her brain from analysing the whole exchange, along with everything else weird happening in her life.

Chapter Twenty

Fanta stared at the page in her notebook. Why did the ideas that seemed so great in her head look so silly on paper? She sipped her coffee. It was Saturday morning and she was working on concepts for the magazine. She needed to nail it. She snorted. If Gary had his way, the whole thing would be about nails—nuts and bolts, hammers and pliers, and who knew what other brutally boring items.

She wriggled her bare feet in a patch of sunshine. She was sitting on her deck in her Adirondack chair. For the umpteenth time, she looked around in satisfaction. She'd splurged on the whole set-up; the chair, the waterproof cushions, the outdoor rug. What had once been an unappealing cement balcony was now a comfy spot where she enjoyed the rustling of the leaves and the twittering of the birds. A squirrel fixed her with a beady eye and let loose a stream of chatter.

Fanta returned her attention to the page. She started writing. *"What's your neighbor got that you don't? Get in on the region's hottest design trends."* That could be fun. Of course, every issue would have an editor's note where she would have a stylish headshot and an insightful opinion. Fanta kept writing. *"Behind the gates: Local personality so-and-so takes us on an exclusive tour of their fabulous home."* There were more than a few impressive mansions in the area owned by big-name people. Or, even better, *"Divine equine: Equestrian establishments to die for!"* Lots of horse stables were stunning showcases of design and landscaping.

She heard a screen door being pulled back. It sounded like it was stuck on the track. It must be poor Mrs. Hooper. Fanta looked down through the railing. The scraping and struggling continued, and then Fanta saw Lottie trot out. The little dog looked up and growled.

"That you up there, Fanta dear?" Mrs. Hooper came into view. She wore another old-fashioned house dress with an apron overtop. She grasped the balcony railing with one hand and peered upward.

"Hi, Mrs. Hooper. Yes, it's me." Fanta sketched a wave. "How are you today?"

"Not so good, dear," Mrs. Hooper replied shakily. "I've not been doing well." She strained her neck to better see Fanta. "I'm not sure I'll be able to take my trip after all." In the morning sun, Mrs. Hooper's eyes looked weak and watery.

"Oh no, I'm sorry. Your daughter must be so disappointed."

"I'm sure she is. Not half as disappointed as I am, though."

"How can I help?"

"That's so nice of you, Fanta dear. I was hoping you'd ask, actually." Mrs. Hooper blinked up at Fanta. "If you wouldn't mind, dear, Lottie here could use a nice walk every once in a while."

It was like Mrs. Hooper had read her mind. Fanta shifted her gaze to the little dog. They stared at each other.

"I think I could do that, Mrs. Hooper. Maybe this evening? Lottie and I could go for a spin."

"Oh! That's wonderful, Fanta dear. We'll be waiting for you." A dinging noise sounded from inside Mrs. Hooper's apartment. "There's my timer for twelve o'clock. My lunch is ready. See you tonight."

Mrs. Hooper shuffled away, Lottie following. Fanta questioned her own sanity. Then she started. Noon! She had a lesson with Penny in just over an hour. She still had to drive to Bay Ridge and get Des ready. Fanta jumped up, changed into her riding clothes, and dashed out the door, grabbing some carrots on the way.

* * *

"Nice job, Fanta, you rode well. Give Des a good grooming." Penny walked briskly through the barn on her way to the outdoor ring.

"Thanks, Penny, that was fun."

Fanta's jumping lesson had gone perfectly. She and Des had practised keeping a steady pace toward the fences. Penny had set up a course of obstacles with plenty of twists and turns. Fanta and Des had navigated it all smoothly.

"You're gonna kill it at the next show!" Penny called as she disappeared out the barn door.

Fanta smiled. If only. She knelt on the cement floor, slicking oil on Des's hoofs. Then she put the oil away in her grooming kit, gave Des a once-over with the brushes, and went through his long tail with the curry comb. She unclipped the ties and led him into his stall.

"You heard the lady, Des, we did well today." She leaned her forehead against his. "We'll get there, don't you worry."

She offered Des some carrots and turned to look out the barn door at the sunny afternoon. It would be nice to hang around. Maybe she would watch some of the lessons. There was always something to learn, whether in the saddle or the barn. With a last pat for Des, Fanta started toward the gazebo near the outdoor ring. A few people were there already. She recognized Marcia and Bonnie, taking a break from the chores. Someone with long brown hair and a baseball cap was with them. Fanta squinted. Deirdre.

Fanta hesitated. Should she just turn around and go home? No, she would not let Deirdre get the better of her anymore. Besides, if Deirdre planned on working at Bay Ridge, there was no time like the present to lay out the rules of engagement. Was that the same thing as battle lines? Either way. Fanta made her way to the gazebo and pulled up a plastic chair.

"Hi, ladies, enjoying the weather?"

"Hi, Fanta, yes, it's beautiful." Bonnie looked stressed. "Have you met Deirdre?"

Fanta crossed her legs, the picture of calm control. "Oh yes, Deirdre and I go way back."

Deirdre gave Fanta a dark look.

"So Deirdre, how are things with Lana?" Fanta inquired.

"Okay." Deirdre shrugged. Her face was impassive.

"Marcia mentioned you were looking for work here," Fanta said jauntily.

Marcia glared at her. Bonnie looked worried.

"It's good to have options." Deirdre shrugged again. She turned to Fanta. "Sometimes you need to know when to *move on*."

Marcia and Bonnie exchanged a tense look.

In the ring, Lyle was riding Trifle under the hot sun. Penny had him practising without stirrups. It was great for balance, but it was a workout. Lyle looked like he was about to pass out.

"That will put him out of commission for a while," Marcia cackled. Fanta joined in. She would not let Deirdre get under her skin. No, this time the offensive was hers for the taking.

"Don't think I can't hear you!" Penny shouted from the center of the ring.

Fanta turned back to Deirdre and assumed a light, conversational tone. "I understand you wanted to get together with Greg. I didn't know that. You know, hitting on your boss is never a good idea. Besides, you were a little late to the game, don't you think?"

Bonnie gasped.

Deirdre stared like a cobra. Then her blasé manner returned. "Yes, Greg and I had a close relationship. He trusted me. At least I wasn't like you, moping around after a guy you'd never met," she said. "You never stood a chance anyway. Greg wouldn't have given you a second look."

Fanta felt all the old anger and hurt spew up like lava from a volcano. "Well, he sure gave Lana a second look," she said scornfully. "And then he never had eyes for you. Talk about the also-ran. You didn't even get out of the starting gate."

"Whoa! Let's keep it civil, guys," Marcia warned.

Deirdre stood abruptly, the plastic chair scraping over the wooden floor. "I'm outta here."

"I'll go with you." Bonnie hopped up. She looked close to tears.

"That's right, enough chit-chat. We'll walk you to your car, Deirdre." Marcia took control.

Fanta watched the three grooms head toward the parking area. In front of the barn, Dobie sat alert, nose quivering. He had been taught to stay away from the cars. Penny had struggled to train him, since he liked to greet people when they arrived. Fanta could remember plenty of times when Dobie had clambered onto her lap as she tried to get out of her Honda.

She was about to turn back to the ring when Dobie gave one loud bark. Then he launched himself into a full-on run, straight into the parking lot. He pulled to a stop beside Bonnie, who seemed to sway on her feet. Dobie quickly lay down, positioning himself under Bonnie just as she dropped to the ground. Her body shook convulsively. Marcia and Deirdre knelt beside her, obviously unsure what to do.

"We need some help here!" Marcia shouted.

Fanta turned sharply to the ring. Penny was folding her large frame through the wooden rail fence. Fanta jumped to her feet and joined Penny as the two of them sprinted into the parking area. Bonnie's body was beginning to relax, the jerking movements subsiding. Dobie maintained his position, cushioning her from the hard ground. When Bonnie started to regain consciousness, she slipped off Dobie. He lay by her side, alert but calm.

"Bonnie, we're here. Are you okay?" Penny spoke urgently, her hand to Bonnie's cheek. She glanced at the dog. "Oh, Dobie, what a good boy, you were such a good boy." Penny was as emotional as Fanta had ever seen her.

Bonnie tried to sit up. "What happened?"

"You had a seizure, Bonnie. Don't try to get up, just sit for a minute." Penny waited a beat. "Have you had a seizure before?"

"I'm not sure. I think so, maybe." Bonnie was confused. She laid a hand on Dobie's back. "I think he's done this before, helped me like this."

"Yes, I rather think he has," said Penny with a tight smile.

Deirdre and Marcia helped Bonnie to her feet. Fanta stroked Dobie's neck.

"No more work for you today, my dear," Penny said, leading Bonnie toward the farmhouse. "We'll phone the doctor to see what she has to say. Marcia, please take care of the chores. Give my apologies to Lyle. And make sure Dobie is fed and his water dish is full."

"Absolutely, don't even think about it," Marcia replied.

Dobie followed Penny and Bonnie to the house and flopped on the front porch, where he yawned and flapped his ears.

"I'll say goodbye. I've got work to do." Marcia nodded and headed to the barn, where Lyle hovered in the doorway holding Trifle.

Deirdre and Fanta stood together in the parking area. Fanta felt a hot wave of shame wash over her. How petty their arguments were. She turned her head. "I'm sorry for what I—"

Deirdre's hands flew to her face as her body was wracked with a huge sob. Tears streamed down her cheeks and spattered on her t-shirt. Before Fanta could say anything more, Deirdre ran to her car, threw herself into the driver's seat, and took off down the lane, a cloud of dust hanging in her wake.

Chapter Twenty-One

"Oh, mom, it was just awful."

Fanta was walking Lottie around the block. The little dog trotted along, stopping frequently to sniff, bark at squirrels, or visit with any stranger who looked promising. It had only taken a bit of coaxing to get her out of Mrs. Hooper's apartment for some exercise.

Fanta held her phone to her ear with one hand and Lottie's leash in the other. "It all happened so fast," she said. "I felt so bad for Bonnie. Nobody knew what to do. Except Dobie!"

"Oh, honey, I'm sorry to hear it. Will Bonnie be alright? Are you okay? Who's Dobie?"

"Sure, mom, I'm okay. I think Bonnie will be, too. Penny was going to speak with her doctor." Fanta looked both ways before crossing the street with Lottie. "Dobie was the real hero. He's the stable dog. I didn't think he was too bright, but I swear he knew Bonnie was going to have that seizure. He ran over and let her fall right on top of him. It was amazing."

"Oh, I see, that explains it," her mom said. "Yes, those wonderful animals can do so much for us. I don't think we know the half of it."

Fanta remembered that her mom used to volunteer with the local therapy dog association.

"I'm walking a dog right now, mom. It's my neighbor's dog. Her name's Lottie." Fanta felt absurdly proud of herself. Mrs. Hooper had equipped her with poop bags, treats, and some sage advice: "Don't take any guff from our Lottie, Fanta dear."

"Well, you enjoy yourself, honey, and say hello to Lottie for me. Don't forget your rest," her mom admonished. "I better jump off, though. Your dad and I are going to a concert tonight. It's the hottest ticket in town!"

Fanta hesitated. "Listen, mom. About yesterday. I'm sorry if I cut you off."

"Oh, pish, honey, don't worry about it. You take care and let me know how everything is going. Bye bye now."

Fanta tucked her phone in the pocket of her jeans. She and Lottie were already back at the apartment building. Lottie trotted up the cracked cement path and scratched at the front door. Fanta opened it and ran after Lottie as she bounded up the steps. At the door to Mrs. Hooper's apartment, Lottie sat and whined. Fanta knocked softly. Slow steps approached, and the door opened a crack. Lottie pushed her way in, tail wagging.

"You're back!" cried Mrs. Hooper. "Come in, Fanta dear. Unless you've got another appointment?"

Fanta thought of the big basket of smelly laundry and the pile of dirty dishes awaiting her upstairs. "I'd love to come in, Mrs. Hooper. Lottie and I had a great walk." She turned to close the door as Mrs. Hooper shuffled into the kitchen, Lottie dancing at her feet. Fanta loitered in the hall, laying the leash and other equipment on the little table. Mrs. Hooper pulled a box of dog biscuits from the kitchen cupboard and offered one to Lottie, who took it gently from her hand.

Mrs. Hooper came back into the hallway, reaching for the door frame to steady herself. "Come in and sit down, dear. What can I get you?"

"Water would be wonderful, if it's not too much trouble. It's still pretty hot out there."

Mrs. Hooper waved her toward the living room. "Come in, come in. Have a seat."

Fanta perched on a velvet couch with scrolled wooden legs and a large lace doily on the back. After a moment, Mrs. Hooper reappeared from the kitchen with a glass of cold water that she handed carefully to Fanta. She walked a few paces to an old armchair and lowered herself slowly. Lottie bustled into the room, licking crumbs from her whiskers. She threw herself down at Mrs. Hooper's feet and sighed contentedly.

"Got a new fella, Fanta dear?"

"Not yet, Mrs. Hooper." Fanta smiled. She glanced at the faded family photos situated around the room. "I bet your husband was one special guy."

"Oh, he was, he was." Mrs. Hooper's gnarled hand smoothed the wrinkles in her skirt. "He was a policeman, don't you know. So handsome in that uniform of his. I loved hearing about his work. It was better than any mystery book. He couldn't tell me everything, of course, but he liked to get my take on things. I was his secret weapon, that's what he said. I had a real talent for solving crimes."

Mrs. Hooper gave a shaky grin. Lottie snored.

"Really? That's interesting." Fanta cocked her head. "Do you know, I've become involved in a bit of a mystery myself. I've been asking around, gathering information, trying to solve it."

Mrs. Hooper looked worried. "You be careful, Fanta dear. You never know, you might get yourself into trouble. My Pete, he was very cautious. You don't want to get the wrong person upset, that's what he used to say. And you never know how things might turn out. That's been my experience." She glanced down at Lottie, who lay pressed against her foot.

"Yes, I can see it might be dangerous," Fanta replied thoughtfully. Could the person who'd killed Greg have another target in mind? She hadn't even considered it.

"Maybe you need a policeman right about now." Mrs. Hooper said with another grin. "A nice, handsome one."

"I'm sure you're right," Fanta smiled. She finished her water and rose from the couch. Mrs. Hooper looked tired.

"I better be going. But I'd like to come back and walk Lottie again, if that's okay."

Mrs. Hooper nodded. One of Lottie's ears twitched.

"I'll leave my glass in the kitchen and show myself out. Goodnight, Mrs. Hooper."

Fanta placed the glass in the sink. The kitchen, like the rest of the apartment, was tidily kept. A dishcloth hung over the faucet to dry, and a few squibs of old bar soap were wrapped in some plastic netting by the sink. Mrs. Hooper obviously knew how to get value for her money. Fanta hesitated in the hall. She heard the TV flip on and the sounds of a game show. She slipped quietly out the door, ran lightly up the stairs, and entered her own apartment.

* * *

A large pile of clean clothing lay on the bed. Fanta sorted through it, hanging items in the closet or stowing them in the chest of drawers. She was exhausted after traipsing up and down from the basement laundry room to her unit. She put the last of the socks away. She would check her phone one more time and go to bed. She pulled out her device and clicked on the email icon. There was a message from Penny to all of the riders at Bay Ridge.

"Hi gang, Penny here. Some of you know that Bonnie suffered a seizure today. I wanted to tell you that she's doing well. The doctor came and prescribed medication. So thank goodness—and Dobie.

"I also wanted to pass along an invitation from Dave LeDans at Two Gates. He's going to host a pop-up tune-up clinic—his words—this Tuesday and Wednesday. One day will be for the hunters, taught by Terry Miller, and the other for the jumpers, taught by Lana. Dave says there will be guest speakers. He wants to keep the groups small, about four or five riders per day, so he's asked some of the barns in the area to send one rider for each session.

"I know it's awkward timing mid-week, but it might be a good learning opportunity. Think about it, and we can discuss as a group tomorrow, maybe 2pm? Thanks, gang!"

Fanta closed the email. That was good news about Bonnie. It had been horrible watching her fall to the ground, shaking. Had the seizure been brought on because of the dust-up with Deirdre? It all seemed incredibly foolish in hindsight. And selfish, too. Greg was dead, murdered even. It was no time to be dickering over childish slights or failed romances.

She headed to the bathroom, where she brushed her teeth and washed her face. She examined her squashed toothbrush and threadbare washcloth. Even Mrs. Hooper would probably replace them with something newer. Then she fell into bed, nestling into the cool sheets. The clinic at Two Gates sounded interesting. Getting coaching from Terry could be good. Her eyes closed. Of course, it would also be a prime opportunity to observe all of her main suspects at close range. At this point, she couldn't think of what else to do.

Chapter Twenty-Two

"How much longer, Penny?" Fanta hated the whine in her voice. She pulled Des to a halt in the middle of the outdoor ring. She had been trotting around without stirrups for ages, and the burn in her thighs was like fire. Sweat dripped from under her helmet, and her breath wheezed in and out.

"Giving up already?" Penny squinted up at her. "Forget about no-stirrups November. This is just-do-it June!" She guffawed. "A few more laps, posting trot, not sitting. I'll spare you the canter work for another day."

Fanta groaned, picked up her reins, and asked Des to return to his trot.

"That's it. Forward, forward! Des looks like he's out for a ride on the trails," Penny boomed.

If only. Fanta was barely holding it together. She could feel her face turning ten shades of red. Every muscle in her body screamed. She trotted along gamely for several minutes. Chessy was also in the ring, riding Ollie. She threw Fanta a sympathetic look.

Finally, Penny held up a hand. "Okay, I'll take pity on you. You should work without stirrups every day, Fanta. You'll learn to love it."

Fanta was too tired to argue. Penny clapped her hands energetically.

"Alright, ladies, let's get these horses cooled out and put away. We're having our meet-up in forty-five minutes or so."

Fanta sat atop Des in the middle of the ring. She had to get off. Normally, she would swing her right leg over Des's back and hop down without a second thought. After the no-stirrups work, she was pretty sure her legs would give way and she would land on her butt in the sand. She took a deep breath, leaned forward on Des's neck, brought her right leg slowly over his back, and slithered to the ground. If she could just remain upright. Her thighs were like fiery Jell-O.

Chessy rode over on Ollie. "You okay there, Fanta?" she said, hiding a grin.

"I'll be alright," Fanta wheezed. "I'm going to walk Des back to the barn. I'll open the gate."

Fanta lurched across the ring, leading Des. By tomorrow, her muscles would transform from fiery Jell-O into frozen bricks. She could hardly wait. She felt a mild frustration. This had never happened to her as a teenager.

Fortunately, Des had barely broken a sweat. Fanta groomed him and returned him to his stall as quickly as possible, leaving some carrots in his feed bucket and ensuring he had lots of water to drink. She had to sit down, and fast.

She went into Penny's office, threw herself into a chair, and sucked water from her bottle. Coming up for air, she looked around the small room. It contained a hodgepodge of horse equipment, paperwork, dog kibble, and junk food. A compact refrigerator hummed in the corner. A scarred wooden desk was paired with an ancient swivel chair, and a dirty couch was piled with horse blankets. Two rickety wooden chairs rounded out the seating options. Barney the stable cat lay on the back of the sofa, pulling at the tatty material with his claws.

Fanta took another gulp of water. Barney the barn cat and Dobie the Doberman. Penny really needed to get more creative with her animal names.

After a few minutes, Penny came in and sat at her desk. Chessy took the wooden chair across from Fanta. Lyle and Sara perched on the couch. Barney regarded everyone with disdain.

"Okay, gang, let's talk about this pop-up tune-up clinic over at Two Gates," Penny started. She paused thoughtfully. "It's a clever idea, really, I wish I'd thought of it." She launched back in, "Anyway, we can send one hunter rider and one jumper rider. Does anyone not want to go? Let's start there."

Sara performed a dramatic eye-roll. "Sorry, Penny, I've got summer school." She pulled her phone from her back pocket and began tapping at it, as if checking her busy schedule and lineup of important emails. "I'm not sure it's the right fit for me anyway."

Lyle mumbled something. Sara swatted at his head, her fingernails long and pointy. "Like you would know, buddy."

"I wouldn't mind taking Ollie for the jumper day," Chessy offered.

Penny cracked open the battered laptop that lay on the desk. "That sounds good. I think you'd get a lot out of a session with Lana."

Fanta wasn't sure what Lana might get out of a session with Chessy. She had to hand it to Chessy, though. Instead of being miffed about the assistant job at Two Gates being offered to Terry, she was perfectly happy to go and learn from Lana. There was a lesson in there somewhere.

Penny's laptop whirred and the screen jerked to life. Underneath a spattering of who-knew-what on the monitor was a nice screensaver shot of the Bay Ridge barn. A vast number of icons littered the cramped display. Fanta felt stressed just looking at them.

"So it comes down to Fanta or Lyle for the hunter session. What about it, guys?" Penny turned to them expectantly.

"I'd really like to go," Fanta said quickly. "Terry is so good with the hunters. Look how well he does with Pearl. I think he could teach me a lot."

"Lyle?" Penny pressed.

"I'm good with that," Lyle drawled. "I'm pretty much perfect the way I am."

Sara took another swat at his head. "In your dreams, big guy."

Penny frowned as she tried to open her email. The laptop hiccupped, and then a window opened on the screen. Penny tapped something out and pressed the send button. She spun around in her chair. "That settles it then. I can trailer each of you over there for the day," she said brightly. She shot a look at Lyle and Sara. "And don't think you're getting out of work. I'm going to keep you on your toes."

Dobie trotted in and sat beside Penny, pleased to have joined the group. A moment passed. Fanta looked around. Was she the only one sensing an aroma that was building and mushrooming like an atomic cloud?

Lyle gagged, throwing his arm over his face. "Oh man, was that you, Dobie?"

Chessy jumped up and made a hasty exit. Lyle and Sara fell over each other trying to get through the door. Fanta hurried out of the room, eyes tearing. Even Barney leapt from the couch and scuttled away.

Penny strode down the aisle, Dobie trotting proudly at her heels. "Just remember, none of us is perfect. Thanks, everyone!"

* * *

The breeze was heavenly. Fanta stuck her elbow out the open car window and gloried in the summer day. She was excited at the prospect of the riding clinic. It was the perfect last step in her investigative process before she went to the police with what she knew. She realized she hadn't asked Penny about the cost. Again! Why did she always forget the money question? Plus, for maximum benefit, she really needed to be there for both days of the clinic. She racked her brain trying to think of how to make that happen. She would have to ask Abby for time off.

Stopped at a busy intersection, she realized she was near her favorite frozen yogurt place. Dead Smooth was a goth hangout, with black chandeliers dripping from the ceiling and dark wood furniture set atop a checkerboard floor. The inky walls featured line art of grinning skulls and jiving skeletons with dabs of yellow, red, and orange. In addition to a wide range of frozen yogurt flavors, Dead Smooth sold great smoothies and bubble tea.

After a small detour, Fanta parked, rose slowly from the car, and headed in. She ordered her favorite smoothie, the Vegetative State, with spinach, mango, and almonds. She chatted briefly with the server, a red-haired guy with black-rimmed glasses and a gold nose ring.

Turning from the counter, she was surprised to see Dave LeDans sitting at one of the tables, an empty bowl and spoon beside him. Huddled over some paperwork, he looked completely out of place in the hip eatery. She walked over.

"Hi, Dave, I haven't seen you here before. Are you a smoothie guy?"

"Oh, hi, don't tell me…Fanta!" Dave punched a finger in the air. Then he indicated the empty bowl. "I'm actually a frozen yogurt guy. This Blowing

Chunks is amazing. It's got these big bits of brownie and cherries. It's healthier than ice cream, right?" Dave looked hopeful. "Anyway, the vibe in here is just so, I don't know, cool."

Maybe Dave had hidden depths. Fanta indicated the other chair at his table. "Can I join you for a minute?"

Dave waved her to the seat. Fanta sat carefully and placed her smoothie on the table.

"I was just at Bay Ridge and we were talking about your clinic coming up," she said. "I'm going to be riding Des in the hunter portion with Terry. But—I feel silly—I forgot to ask Penny how much it costs." She looked at Dave questioningly.

"It's $250 for the day," Dave replied, organizing some of the papers in front of him. Fanta gulped. Seeing her expression, Dave added, "We thought that was pretty reasonable, given the instruction and the lunch. Did Penny tell you there would be a guest speaker?"

"She did, yes." Fanta hesitated. It might be worth a shot. "Listen, Dave, money's a little tight for me these days. So I was thinking, could I be an assistant on Wednesday? You know, set up fences, get the lunch ready, help the speaker, make sure Lana has everything she needs. That sort of stuff. Maybe it could cover my costs for the clinic?"

Dave reflected. There was a smudge of chocolate yogurt on his chin.

"Actually, that could work," he replied slowly. "Romy will be busy in the barn and Deirdre is, well, not always around these days, so an extra pair of hands might be useful." He regarded Fanta with a smile. "I have to tell you, though, Lana can be demanding. Probably not the easiest person to deal with. Just so you know."

"That's super, thanks." Fanta sipped her smoothie. "I guess Lana is still struggling with Greg's death," she added somberly. "It must be tough. How are you doing?"

"Oh, well, carrying on." Dave raked a hand through his hair. "I've been dealing with the police and helping to arrange the funeral." He examined his dirty fingernails. "There's one thing I never thought I'd say about Greg." He sighed.

"I'm sorry." Fanta placed her drink on the table. She looked at Dave. She could picture him pounding on Greg's hotel room door, storming in, confronting him. But picking up a heavy object and swinging it at his college buddy? It seemed less likely. "I'm still working on my story about Greg," she said. "There are a couple of things I don't understand."

Dave's eyebrows rose in a question mark.

"I'm still trying to figure out whether Greg was going to start his own business, or whether he planned to go into business with Lana." She hesitated. "I'm sorry if this is a sore topic for you."

Dave waved it off. "Don't worry. I'm pretty much over it now. Somehow it doesn't seem so important anymore." He stopped to consider. "You know, most people might have thought that Greg would benefit by joining Lana's barn. But that wasn't the case. I think Lana had more to gain by hooking up with Greg." Dave looked at Fanta to gauge her reaction. "This is not on the record, or whatever you guys say, but Lana's business was in trouble. Her parents were refusing to help her out. Quite frankly, she needed Greg more than he needed her."

Dave grinned. "Greg had a good head for business. He was more than just a pretty face." His smile faded. "Anyway, it won't happen now."

He started to gather his papers, hitting the spoon in the empty bowl with his elbow.

"Just one more thing, something I'm trying to sort out." Fanta picked up her smoothie and twirled the straw. "At the hotel. Who stayed where? I guess Lana had a room adjoining Greg's, or so I heard. What about you? Two Gates is a bit of a drive from the horse show."

"Oh no, I never stay at the Carleton," Dave said, shoving papers into a beat-up briefcase. "Too much to do. I might have gone for a drink sometimes, but I always went home after, even if it was pretty late. The barn work doesn't stop just because there's a horse show on."

"Did you talk to Greg that night before you left the hotel?" Fanta asked, watching Dave carefully.

"I might have had a word. I don't remember clearly," Dave blustered. "Greg could be hard to get hold of." He struggled to cram the papers in the case, their edges bending.

"I see. And what about Terry? He lives in the city. Did he have a room at the Carleton?"

Dave laughed. "Terry? He's too cheap for that. Don't tell him I said so."

Fanta had one more question. "I guess Romy and Deirdre stayed at the Carleton? They had to be at the showgrounds pretty early."

Dave forced the briefcase to close, buckled the straps, and patted his pockets, maybe looking for his keys, which lay splayed on the tabletop. "Yeah, absolutely, the grooms always had a room at the hotel. They work late and start early." Dave paused. "Although, I saw Deirdre's car near the motorhome that night." He shrugged. "Greg must have asked her to pick something up, or she had some chore to do. She must have spent the night at Two Gates. Oof, she would have had to be up plenty early the next day."

Dave gave Fanta a puzzled look. "Is this for your story?"

"I'm just curious as to who might have seen Greg last," Fanta improvised. "You know, who might have had the last conversation with him before he…met his fate. It could be a…poignant touch to the story."

"Okay." Dave seemed unconvinced. He stood, clutching his briefcase. Then he spotted his keys and snapped them up. "I guess that's it then. I'll see you later this week."

"Thanks, Dave. See you soon." Fanta watched him hustle out to his truck.

Obviously, someone had gone into Greg's hotel room late that night, after everyone else had gone home. It could have been Terry or Dave, even though neither of them had been staying at the Carleton. If Deirdre had spent the night in the motorhome at Two Gates, then that let her out. No, from everything she'd learned, Fanta could still picture Lana, her love life and career flaming out in spectacular fashion, slipping in from next door and losing her temper with the man she loved. Wasn't the simplest explanation usually the best? There was a fine line between love and hate, at least that's what everyone said.

Fanta finished her smoothie and rose slowly from the chair. A long, hot shower was in order. Then she would fall into bed and be ready for whatever Monday had to bring.

* * *

Fanta moved as quickly as she could around the apartment. She'd had the long, hot shower, but she'd completely forgotten about all the chores she had to finish up. Falling into bed would have to wait a while. She'd eaten mac and cheese with tuna, cleaned the dishes, and then wrestled her old-fashioned vacuum cleaner out of the little hall closet. The upright machine let out nasty puffs of dirt from the overfilled bag as she jostled it this way and that. Finally, she freed it from a tangle of shoes and boots and was about to flip it on when her work phone lit up with a text. Fanta hustled over. Maybe it was the armchair detective. She looked at the screen. Bingo!

What's up with this press conference tomorrow?

The person didn't waste time with civilities. So neither would she. **No idea.**

Don't you media people know this stuff?

Fanta sighed. **A press conference is to tell the press what's happening. Why do it if they already know?**

She rolled her eyes. Readers were so tiresome. Sue might have some inside dirt, but Fanta doubted even she knew what was going to be announced. She watched the screen. The armchair detective seemed chastened. There were no little pulsing dots. Fanta thought about how the person seemed to know about the dynamics at Two Gates. She typed out, **Are you involved at Two Gates? Do you ride there?**

No.

Fanta considered her next move. **I'm going to spend 2 days there this week.**

Good for you.

For…Fanta bit back a choice expletive. Then she noticed a new message.

Look out for clues.

What do you mean? she tapped out feverishly.

Good luck.

Fanta let the phone drop. The whole thing was like a game of cat and mouse. She'd seen that play out at the stables many times. The cat usually had fun, but things rarely ended well for the mouse. Which was she?

Chapter Twenty-Three

Fanta levered herself out of the Honda, hobbled across the parking lot to the office door, and limped into the newsroom. It was time for her Monday morning meeting with Abby and Gary. She felt crabby and out of sorts. Her muscles were killing her. She shuffled to her desk. Like anyone would understand. All these hockey and baseball fans at the Newser likely thought that the horse did all the work. Fanta threw a searing glance at the sports editor, sitting in his comfy chair, surrounded by big league memorabilia. Then there was Gary, whose athletic pursuits probably revolved around lifting and stacking catalogues.

Moving slowly, she stowed her purse at her desk, gathered her notes, and walked toward Abby's office. Gary was already there. The top of his head shone in the fluorescent lighting.

"Good morning, Fanta, come in." Abby motioned her to a seat. Gary nodded as Fanta closed the door and got settled.

"We appreciate you calling this meeting," Abby said. "Gary and I were just talking about an editorial calendar for the magazine. That way, you can plan content and Gary and his team can approach clients. Any thoughts?"

Fanta was incensed. Gary had no business talking about an editorial calendar before she'd even arrived. She sat up straight in her chair. A zing of pain shot through her from head to toe.

"That's exactly what I've been working on, Abby," Fanta said, resolute. "I've made a list of story ideas and photos to go with them." She flipped through her notes. Her thoughts were scattered. She couldn't bring a specific example to mind. "Of course, I'll need flexibility. There will always be hot new trends in home decor emerging." She plastered a smile on her face.

"I like the idea of the calendar, as we discussed, Abby, but flexibility is a no-go," Gary droned. "These are big advertisers. They require time to plan their spend, so we need to get them locked into a regular timetable. They have to know what they're going to get with each issue."

Fanta pushed to the edge of her seat. Her muscles spasmed. Heat rushed to her cheeks.

"Surely we're not going to make promises to advertisers about the content of our magazine?" She looked at Abby desperately. "That's purely an editorial call. I'm okay with a calendar, but I'll need the freedom to write whatever is most timely and relevant for our readers."

Gary's eyes slid sideways and then back to Abby. "Well, since this is a revenue-generator, the most relevant topics are ones that resonate with our advertisers." He flicked a piece of lint off his trousers. "If we can't build the advertising revenues, then there's no point."

Abby indicated a time-out. "Let's not make a battle royale out of this. We need to meet in the middle. That is, editorial should be free to choose content and interview sources, without advertising pressure." Gary opened his mouth. Abby held up a finger. "At the same time, I'll be looking to you, Fanta, to develop the calendar detailing the themes of each issue. That way, the ad team can plan. Let's make sure we're all happy with the calendar before we proceed. Capisce?"

Gary pursed his thin lips. "When can I expect to see the calendar? The ad team has ideas that I want to make sure are on there." He addressed his question to a stain on the floor.

"It's under development, Gary," Fanta said tightly. "I will share it with Abby for her feedback and then come to you. For example, Abby, I have several ideas that I would like to—"

"The two of you will need to work together," Abby interrupted. "Hammer out something you're both happy with, then come to me. Gary's boss will have to be on board, too." She reached for her tablet and rose from her chair, her linen two-piece outfit flawless. "I need to get to the morning meeting."

Gary stood and left the office, clicking the door shut. Fanta remained in her seat. Her muscles ached, her temper was frayed, and she was about to burst into tears in front of her boss. Abby regarded her calmly.

"Fanta, you know how this game is played," she said, pushing a chunky gold bracelet up her tanned arm. "There will always be this tension between the business side and the editorial side. Ultimately, we all need to be successful to keep this operation afloat. Does that make sense?"

"Yes, it does." Fanta let out a long breath. "It's just…remember when you said this would be my baby? Well, it sounds silly, but that's how it feels to me. I want to own it. I have so many plans, I don't want to be held back," she finished in a rush.

"Don't worry." Abby went to the door, placing her hand on the knob. Her wedge-heeled summer sandals were to die for. "Anything else?"

"Well, I know this is really last-minute, but I was hoping to take Tuesday and Wednesday off. It's a horse-riding thing. I can put in extra hours or come in on the weekend." Fanta looked up at Abby.

"Just have your work in on time and in good shape. I'll need to see that editorial calendar from you and Gary by end of week. Let's get to the meeting." Abby opened the door and headed into the newsroom.

Fanta rose reluctantly and followed Abby. She could hardly wait to tell the news team all about her new working relationship with the ad reps. She took her wobbly seat on the edge of the group, a weakened animal cut off from the herd.

Sue hustled over from her desk. "Listen, guys, I can't stay, but I've got an update." Her carrier bag was slung over her shoulder and she clutched her phone and car keys in one hand.

"I'm headed to the press conference, but I just received the news release from the police. It's this Grenier guy. Some interesting developments." She scrolled through her phone with her thumb, keys looped over her finger. "The police have learned that some items were missing from his hotel room. Namely, his wallet, his watch, and an engagement ring."

Sue pushed the strap of the carrier bag up her shoulder. "Seems his mom knew about the ring. It was a family heirloom. I guess he was going to pop the question that night." Sue shrugged. "Looks like the whole thing was a robbery gone bad." She glanced again at her phone. "I better run. I'll let you know if there's anything more when I get back."

"So much for the soap opera." Douglas crossed his arms over his chest.

"Thanks, Sue. Let's get started, everybody," Abby called.

Fanta sagged in her seat. She couldn't even be bothered with Douglas. She stumbled through her update—birds, dancing, cha cha cha—and managed to gloss over the details of the new magazine. She trailed back to her desk. Douglas was probably right. Her ballroom dancing story was about to make her the butt of a million jokes. She was going to be the editor of a giant advertising flyer. And she hadn't even started the profile of Greg, the victim of a random robbery who would be just another crime statistic.

She poked the power button on her computer. She might as well get to work. At least it paid the bills. And she could sit down while she was doing it.

* * *

"Police suspect robbery in death of man at Carleton Hotel"

Fanta stared at the headline on Sue's online story. Other than what Sue had mentioned to the group that morning, there was no new information. Fanta raised her head from her computer and looked over to where Sue was sitting at her cubicle. For once, Sue seemed quiet and calm, typing away at something. Fanta gazed around. The newsroom was relatively hushed. Maybe this was her chance.

"Sue? Do you have a moment?" Fanta hovered beside Sue's chair, feeling awkward and out of place. She rarely ventured into the heart of the newsroom; her desk was like an outpost on the fringes. She was gratified to see that Sue had a pilled navy blue cardigan slung over the back of her chair and pictures of her kids ranged on her desk. She had to be human.

"Oh, hi, Fanta. Didn't see you standing there." Sue looked around, bleary-eyed, trying to readjust her focus. "What can I do for you?"

"Well, I was just wondering about the press conference this morning," Fanta started. "Did you hear…like, is there anything else new that the police shared? That's maybe not in your story?"

Sue frowned as if she might be about to take offense.

Fanta hurried on, "Not that you would miss anything. But…it all seems so slow. And it feels like there's not much being done."

Sue's expression softened. "Listen, I get it, Fanta, you knew the guy, and you want to know what happened. But the police have procedures that they follow, and not all of them are talked about in the press."

Fanta's hopes lifted. Maybe Sue did know something more.

"That's not to say I have any additional info," Sue added, "because I don't. But it would seem the police don't yet have any evidence tying a specific person to the crime. All they know is these items were missing, so that's the intel that they've shared."

"So, it's a robbery then," Fanta said, subdued.

Sue shrugged. "Maybe, maybe not." Her phone sprang to life on the desk. Fanta recognized the theme music from a popular TV crime drama. Sue's face colored. "I gotta get this, but don't give up, Fanta. The game's not over til it's over." She placed the phone to her ear. "Sue Goodwin."

Fanta wove her way back to her cubicle. Of course, Sue was a reporter; she wasn't going to jump to conclusions. But if the police were calling it a robbery, well…As Fanta approached her desk, she saw the screen on her work phone fade to black. Someone was trying to get in touch. She frowned. She would tell the waspish armchair detective to give it up and check out the sudoku. She sat in her chair, picked up the phone, and poked at it.

What's going to happen next?

The person didn't mince words. Fanta was irritated. **Can you be more specific?**

With the stuff! Greg's stuff! FCOL

Two could play this game. **IDK TBH.** Fanta pursed her lips. **The police will keep investigating.** Before she could peck out "Get a Rubik's cube," another message appeared.

Keep your eyes open.

Just as Fanta was banging out WTV, she saw, **Good luck.**

* * *

Fanta trudged up and down the aisles at the grocery store. Despite her best efforts, she'd barely gotten anything accomplished at the office. She'd seriously considered ditching the riding clinic and concentrating instead on getting her work done before the higher-ups at the Newser sent her packing. But then Penny and Dave would be peeved. Whatever. Why did she have to please everyone?

She was in dire need of comfort food. Her buggy was filled with chips, cupcakes, pop, and a chocolate bar or two. A case of mac and cheese was stowed on the bottom rack. She stopped in front of the freezer and considered what flavor of ice cream to add to the mix. She selected the cookie dough and then swung into the produce section. She picked up two bags of carrots for Des and threw in some ready-made salad for herself. After some debate, she cruised down another aisle and chose a cheap bottle of wine.

"Someone's having a party!" trilled the cashier at the checkout.

Fanta dredged up a smile and tapped her debit card without looking at the amount. Yeah. A pity party. For one.

She stowed the groceries in her car and drove home. She already regretted the money she'd spent on food that would do nothing but pile on the pounds and make her sick to her stomach. Her mother would be appalled. She pulled into her parking spot in the dusty lot and saw Mrs. Hooper holding Lottie on her leash. There was a small pile on the ground. Mrs. Hooper was pulling a poop bag out of her apron pocket.

Fanta cut the engine and got out of her car as quickly as she could. Her sore muscles had yet to relax their grip. "Here, Mrs. Hooper, I can do that."

She took the bag from Mrs. Hooper's shaky hand, scooped up the mess, and deposited it in the nearby dumpster.

"Thank you, Fanta dear, you're always such a help." Mrs. Hooper stood unsteadily at the edge of the lot. Lottie sniffed and scratched in the dirt beside her. "How's that mystery of yours coming along?"

Fanta reached in to get her groceries from the trunk of her car, hoping her hands were reasonably sanitary. "Turns out, my mystery might not be so mysterious after all."

Mrs. Hooper raised thin eyebrows.

Fanta managed to get her purse and the grocery bags in one hand and close the trunk with the other. She started toward Mrs. Hooper. "The police discovered that some items were missing from the crime scene. So they think it's a robbery gone bad."

"Oh, well, it happens. Money is a powerful motivator, that's what my Pete used to say."

Mrs. Hooper turned toward the building's back door. Fanta walked beside her, Lottie following on her leash. They went up the stairs step by step, Mrs. Hooper leaning heavily on the railing. When she reached her apartment, Mrs. Hooper turned to Fanta. Lottie sat at her feet, waiting expectantly.

"Of course, someone might be playing a trick, dear," Mrs. Hooper said, her thin chest rising and falling. "I've seen it a few times."

Fanta shifted her heavy bags. "What do you mean?"

"Maybe they want people to think it's a robbery, so they took a few valuables." Mrs. Hooper rubbed two papery-skinned fingers together and peered at Fanta. "Throws everybody off the scent, don't you think? Quite effective, really."

Mrs. Hooper pointed at the wine bottle poking from one of Fanta's bags. "I can see you have a romantic evening planned. Don't let me keep you. Come, Lottie. Fanta has to get ready for her fella. Have a lovely time, dear."

Fanta struggled up the final flight of stairs. The handles of the grocery bags cut into her palms. Her muscles were staging a mutiny. She stopped outside her unit, dumped the bags on the floor, and waggled her key in the lock. She swung the door open. She had a huge smile on her face. Mrs. Hooper was the best! She'd never believed the whole robbery thing. No, there was a killer out there, and she had a pretty good idea where. Fanta grinned. It was game on at Two Gates.

* * *

Fanta crumpled the empty potato chip bag and picked up her phone from the table beside her recliner. She'd planned to prepare mac and cheese with hot dogs, but had gotten waylaid by the dill pickle chips. The nutritional value of either one was probably zero. She pressed Romy's number with a greasy finger. It rang and rang.

"Come on, come on…" she muttered, licking her thumb.

"Fanta?" The voice was harried. Fanta could hear rustling in the background.

"Romy! I'm glad I caught you."

"You haven't caught me, Fanta, you're simply speaking to me." There was a giant *rrrip* sound.

"Right. Listen, I wanted to tell you, I'm going to be at that clinic over there, at Two Gates."

"I'm well aware of it," Romy replied snippily. Her voice was echoey, like she was leaning over, peering at something. A sticky adhesive noise came over the line.

"Right. Well, when I'm there, I plan to do some investigating. Pick up a few more clues."

Romy grunted. "If you say so. It seems to me you're a bit late. I overheard Dave and Lana talking. The police think it was some kind of robbery. It's all over the news. Don't you listen to the news?"

"Of course I do, I'm a—"

"You can't even imagine the drama going on here," Romy barged on. "Lana heard all about some engagement ring that was stolen, and she's just losing it. She and Deirdre are at each other's throats. I think Lana sent Deirdre to Vermont just to get rid of her. As much use as Deirdre is anyway," Romy grouched. There was a clunk, and water swirled in the background.

"That's just it, I think Lana may have—"

"This clinic is like the last thing we need here," Romy steamed on. "Everyone's in a snit. They're all ordering me around. Do this, do that, it all has to be perfect." Romy's voice rose to a high pitch. "Pull-ease! Like anyone cares whether we have one of these bowl cleaner thingies in the toilet. I can't even fit in my shift over at What's Your Beef." There was a sound like something being tossed in a plastic bag.

"Here's the thing," Fanta cut in forcefully. "I'm going to be riding tomorrow in the clinic, but then I'm going to be helping out the next day. You know, assisting Lana. So I'll be able to see if she's—"

"Oh boy, well good luck with that. It will be a miracle if Lana can keep it together. She'll probably take your head off. I hope you know what you're getting into."

Fanta heard a slamming noise and the sound of Romy walking rapidly.

"That's why I think she's our main—"

"I've gotta go, Fanta. I have a list of stuff to do like you wouldn't believe. Maybe I'll see you tomorrow. If they let me out of the dungeon."

Fanta had a thought. "Romy, have you been texting me?"

"What?" Romy spluttered. "Like I have time for that. Just check out the number, Fanta, it's not hard. Besides," there was the sound of a horse whinnying and something clanging on a metal surface, "you keep phoning all the time. Why would I need to text?"

The line went dead.

Chapter Twenty-Four

The alarm pulled Fanta out of a deep sleep. She peeled her eyes open. It was day one of the clinic. She had that jittery feeling of starting a new job or the first day of school. She crawled out of her warm bed and headed to the kitchen, where she made a cup of strong coffee. After stepping into the shower, she pulled on clean breeches and a yellow polo shirt. Back in the kitchen, she stuffed a chocolate cupcake with sprinkles in her mouth, filled her travel mug, looped her purse over her arm, and headed down to her car.

She drove the familiar route to Bay Ridge, the sun glinting off the highway and into her eyes. She waggled the visor down as far as it would go. It didn't help much. She was relieved to turn up the twisty lane at Bay Ridge. In the parking area, Penny's truck and trailer waited to take Des to the clinic. Morning chores were underway. Fanta parked and unfolded herself from the front seat. Dobie stood at the door to the stable, ready to greet her.

"Hi, Fanta, you must be excited about the clinic," Bonnie called from one of the stalls.

"That horse needs to be prepped for trailering." Marcia marched up the aisle carrying feed buckets.

Penny bustled by. "Top of the morning. I'll be good to go in about thirty minutes."

Fanta scratched Dobie behind the ears before stepping into the barn. "I'll be ready," she said. She led Des out of his stall. After a quick grooming, she wrapped thick bandages around his lower legs to protect them during the trailer ride. She put his halter with the sheepskin pads on his head and secured a light blanket over his back. Finally, she took her saddle and bridle from the tack room and packed up her trunk, ready for the trip to Two Gates.

With a last check that everything was underway at the stables, Penny led Des into the horse trailer. He walked in as calmly as ever.

"We're off, be back in a bit," Penny called with a wave.

"Good luck!" Bonnie offered.

The expression set Fanta's nerves jangling. Who knew what the day might bring? She followed Penny and the trailer slowly down the lane, wondering if the armchair detective had thought of the robbery-as-a-ruse theory. Fanta scoffed. The crotchety person was likely sitting at home in a recliner, slippered feet hoisted up, coffee in hand. Useless. Whereas she was about to walk into the heart of the mystery, like a diver plunging into the depths of the sea.

The highways were busy on a Tuesday morning, but soon the forked laneway at Two Gates appeared on the right. Following Penny up the drive, Fanta could see the parking area was crowded with trucks and trailers. She tucked the Honda in a corner and hurried over to help Penny with Des. Other participants were arriving for the clinic. Sally Morelli's horse Paparazzi was being backed out of a fancy trailer. Sally was carrying a shiny tack trunk across the yard. Fanta made a mental note: anything that happened at the clinic would be all over the local horse community in a nanosecond.

A large, shaggy horse alighted from another trailer, glanced around with his head held high, and emitted an ear-splitting whinny. An older man hung onto the lead rope and looked up at the horse with pride. A dark-haired young man led a lovely chestnut horse into the stable, followed by a mop-headed fellow with a wiry bay horse.

Romy hustled out of the barn with a full wheelbarrow and an agitated look on her face.

Fanta stood at the back of the Bay Ridge trailer. Would anyone drop some sort of clue? Say or do anything incriminating? Fanta pushed her hand through her hair. What, exactly, did she expect?

Terry (stomping around in the outdoor ring): I killed him! I have money, talent, and lots of other stuff. I had to whack him on the head just so he'd notice. The guy had to go!

Dave (slapping his palms on the desk in his office): It was me! Greg may have gotten all the girls, but he wasn't going to take my business. No sirree! Maybe now I'll get lucky.

Lana (storming down the stable aisle): I did it! Chasing women, making a fool of me, refusing to shore up my career and pay my bills. The guy was a beast! He never saw me coming!

Fanta scratched her forehead. Her plan for sleuthing seemed completely irrational. She dropped her hand to her side. At least she could enjoy the day of riding.

Penny backed Des carefully out of the trailer and handed his lead rope to Fanta. Following the others into the stable, she tied Des in the aisle. Then she went back out to the parking lot to check that she had everything from the truck before waving to Penny, who turned down the long lane, empty trailer in tow. Fanta returned to the barn to find Des waiting patiently.

Sally hot-footed it toward her. "Fanta! I had no idea you would be attending." She dropped her voice, "I just love being in the thick of the action, don't you? Talk about ground zero. I can't wait to hear all the latest!" She bounced on the balls of her feet.

Fanta smiled benignly. "Yes, Two Gates is the perfect place to learn about riding. It's such a privilege to have both Terry and Lana here." She would stay above the fray, not trade in gossip and hearsay. Sally gaped.

The older man from the parking lot clumped toward them. "Isn't this wonderful?" he bellowed. "I'm Charles. I'm here with my horse Big John." He pointed at the giant animal. "He's, well, the big one." Charles grinned, displaying stained, horsey-looking teeth. Fanta recognized the sweet smell of pipe smoke.

Sally looked like she'd just been introduced to some sort of fungus.

"We ride with the North City Hunt Club," Charles continued, unfazed, "but I thought we could use a little more finesse. Right, John?" he hollered. The horse stomped a massive hoof.

Fanta smiled politely. "Hi, Charles, it's great to meet you."

"Likewise, ladies." Charles treated them to a wide grin before tromping away. Fanta and Sally watched him go. His breeches bagged in the seat and his wrinkled shirttails hung out over his belt. His boots had been through the wars and he had an old-fashioned velvet hunt cap on his head, secured with an overstretched elastic. It looked like a small flask was tucked in his back pocket.

"*More* finesse, did he say?" Sally sneered. "Did he have any to begin with?"

"Hi there, I just wanted to pop over and introduce myself." The dark-haired young man appeared beside them, hovering like a butterfly. He had fabulous eyelashes and full lips. "I'm Danny. So pleased to be here. That's my mare, Gigi." He pointed a gloved hand at the chestnut horse.

"Nice to meet you." Sally looked like a child with a shiny new toy. She poked Fanta with her elbow.

Fanta jabbed Sally back. "Your horse is a beauty, Danny," she said. "I'm Fanta."

Danny nodded, licked his lips, fidgeted on his feet, and blinked his luscious fringy eyes. "So nice to meet you." He flitted away with a quick wave.

"I would kill for eyelashes like those," Sally hissed. "Let's see what Terry makes of him." She gave an exaggerated wink.

"Koko, stop it!" A whiny voice sounded from the other end of the aisle. The wiry horse tossed its head and ground its teeth as the mop-headed man tightened the girth around its belly.

"That's Derek," said Sally, jerking a thumb. "He's in personal finance. Don't approach him unless you want to talk about budgeting and saving for the future." Sally grimaced. Fanta thought Derek could come in handy.

Terry walked breezily into the barn, dressed in spotless breeches, an open-necked shirt, and tall leather riding boots. His curly hair was pasted off to one side with an extra-strength gel.

"Good morning, everyone!" Terry smiled, bobbed on his feet, and held out his arms like a preacher. "I'm Terry Miller—well, I guess you know that—and I'm so pleased you could join us for our pop-up clinic. We hope it will really give you that extra edge in the show ring." He pumped a fist, baring his teeth and flaring his eyes.

The riders paused in their preparations. Charles sported a goofy grin, Danny peeked through his lashes, and Derek wiped his nose on his sleeve. Fanta patted Des as she waited for Terry to continue. Sally stood with her hands on her hips, Paparazzi beside her, decked out in the latest equipment.

"Since the weather has cooperated with us today on this sunny day," Terry stammered, "we'll head out to the sand ring at the front of the stables. There's a mounting block for those of you who prefer to use it. We'll ride for a couple of hours this morning, take a lunch break with a fabulous guest speaker, and finish up this afternoon with some jumping."

Terry gazed around expectantly.

"Super!" offered Charles.

Terry nodded. "Don't worry, though. We won't tire you or your horses out too much." He made a swooping motion toward the stable door. "As soon as you're ready, let's head out to the ring." He paused. "Oh, any questions?"

Danny put up his hand. "Who will be our guest speaker?"

Terry's eyes widened and his face flushed. "That's a great question. We're incredibly lucky to have Dr. Gerald Long along"—Terry gritted his teeth—"sorry, join us, to talk about sports psychology. Something we'll all find useful, I'm sure."

Derek's nasal voice cut in. "When are we going to do introductions?"

"Excellent suggestion." Terry beamed. "Let's head out to the ring, mount up, and then I'll ask each of you to introduce yourself, your horse, and tell us one thing you'd like to achieve at this clinic. Shall we go?"

The group trooped out to the large sand ring, which was surrounded by pine trees and a thick cedar hedge. Everyone except Charles used the mounting block to step up onto their horses and then started to walk around the edge of the ring. In the center, Charles struggled to get his foot in the stirrup in preparation for hoisting himself onto Big John's back.

"In the hunt field, you don't have the luxury of a mounting block," he grunted, his toe slipping out of the stirrup iron. "Best be self-sufficient."

"Quite right, Charles." Terry watched with a pained expression. "Can I...help you?"

Charles finally got his foot in the stirrup and heaved himself up. The leather strap creaked. Big John braced himself. Landing in the saddle, Charles gave a triumphant whoop. "Fabulous, and we're away!"

The giant horse rambled off, zig-zagging through the middle of the ring.

"Alright, everybody, before we start, I'll have you ride in and we'll do our introductions," Terry called.

Once the group had formed a circle, Terry nodded at Derek.

"Hello, everyone. My name is Derek, and this is Koko. We ride for pleasure, sometimes we go to the smaller shows." Derek's breeches and boots were nice but well-worn. "It's difficult to get Koko to move forward, so that's what I'd like to work on today." Koko chewed the bit with a rhythmic squeaking sound, a sour look to his face.

Sally gave the group a big wave. "Hi, everyone. My name's Sally. You may know me from The Mane Connection. Please visit us in-store or online!" Her azure polo shirt was the latest in equestrian fashion labels. "This is my fabulous Paparazzi. I've been riding with the same coach for many years, and I would like to get some new pointers. You never know, I might learn something." Sally smirked.

"You're so right, Sally," Charles bellowed. Big John fussed and circled. Charles brought him around to face the group. "I'm Charles, and this is Big John. We're not fancy like you folks, so we're here to learn some of the finer points of riding."

Charles's lower legs were thrust forward, his seat well back in the saddle. Big John's thick mane flopped on either side of his neck and his forelock trailed down his face. His muzzle was covered in white whiskers. Fanta imagined the pair did not spend much time in a riding arena. Their comfort zone would be galloping and jumping natural obstacles in wide open country, surrounded by a pack of hounds in full cry.

Danny offered a dazzling smile. "I'm Danny, and this is Gigi. She's quite young, so we're looking for experience." Gigi looked shyly at the other horses with limpid eyes. Danny's white breeches and black polo shirt fit him perfectly.

Terry stared, mesmerized.

Sally giggled.

Fanta jumped in. "Hi, my name is Fanta, and this is Des. I'd like to work on maintaining Des's pace and adjusting his stride." Des stood calmly, swishing his tail against the flies.

Terry nodded firmly. "Great. Let's get to work, everyone. Out on the track, please." He stepped back from the group. "We'll spend some time getting our horses warmed up and listening to us."

Over the next hour, Terry challenged the riders with exercises at the walk, trot, and canter. Big John charged around the ring as Charles struggled to communicate the subtle commands. Derek attempted to get Koko moving faster than a shuffle. Danny looked pleased as Gigi took naturally to the work. Sally wore a bored expression as she circled the ring on Paparazzi.

"Alright, let's try lengthening and shortening stride at the canter," Terry called.

Fanta set to work. With pointers from Terry, Des started to respond to her cues more readily. At the end of the session, she rode into the middle of the ring with the others.

"That was great!" she enthused.

"You did well," Terry said, looking pleased.

Fanta patted Des. Then she remembered her mission. She was here to unmask a killer. She looked at Terry. "Greg was the master of stride control," she commented, as if casually sharing a poignant memory.

"That's so true," Sally breathed.

"Who's this Greg?" Charles looked around the group. His hunt cap sat aslant on his head, the elastic strap lost in the folds of his chin. Big John continued to fuss.

Terry's jaw muscles bunched. "Greg was very good, but others of us do equally well."

"He was just dreamy to watch." Sally sighed. "I could have watched him all day."

"Greg was very nice," Danny added, stroking Gigi's neck.

Terry clenched his fists. "Perhaps you don't know, but—"

"Is this Greg available for some instruction?" Charles circled back around on Big John.

"No, he's dead," Derek chipped in.

Charles looked aghast. "Oh, I had no idea. Sorry, everyone. Tactless of me," he stumbled out.

Sally grinned delightedly.

Fanta watched Terry. The pressure was building. Was this where he would topple to the ground, crying, *"Stop, just stop! It was me! I did it!"*

Terry's face was a mottled purple. "That's it for this morning." He made a herding motion with his arms. "Time to head back to the barn."

In the stable, Fanta busied herself brushing Des. Terry stood nearby at the door to the tack room, surveying the riders. Her strategy was to watch his every move, listen to his every word. It wasn't sophisticated, but it was the best she could think of. She ran the comb through Des's mane. Out of the corner of her eye, she saw Charles approach, looking as contrite as a puppy that had just peed on the carpet.

"Terry, you're running a fine show here," Charles started, "and I wanted to apologize for my comments earlier. Quite unacceptable." He cleared his throat. "Was this Greg involved here at Two Gates?" Perhaps seeing something murderous in Terry's expression, Charles backpedaled. "Sorry, impertinent of me, foolish to ask."

Fanta focused on combing. Des snoozed, eyes half-closed.

"That's fine, Charles," Terry replied in the pompous voice that he likely used with his banking buddies. "Greg was the professional rider here at Two Gates. He was a valued member of the team."

"Ah, all the more difficult then," Charles said. "How distressing."

"Yes, it's been a trying time."

Fanta stepped over to her tack trunk, her back to Terry and Charles. Des stomped a hoof and swished his tail. She strained to listen.

Terry was continuing, "I tried to speak with Greg the night that he died."

Fanta couldn't stop herself from turning around. But Terry didn't notice. He was staring at the ceiling, a faraway look on his face. "There was so much I wanted to discuss with him."

Charles nodded sympathetically.

Fanta heard Romy's voice in her head: *"You didn't see him leaving the hotel that night. He looked like he could have whacked a few people."*

Terry added, "My only regret is that we did not leave things on a more positive note."

Fanta stepped back, bumping into her tack trunk, the lid closing with a bang. Did that mean that—

Terry clapped his hands briskly. "Let's get these horses away. Lunch awaits!"

Chapter Twenty-Five

"I'm starving." Sally adjusted the stylish visor on her head and gazed around the parking lot through blingy sunglasses.

The group trekked across the dusty expanse toward the indoor riding arena. They'd left the horses in their stalls with plenty of hay and water. The lunch and presentation would take place in the arena's viewing lounge.

"This meal better be worth the fee." Derek wiped his sleeve across his brow. "So often it's mushy sandwiches and lukewarm pasta. It's impossible to find a good caterer for a decent price. There's just no value anymore."

Charles scuffed his boots in the dirt. "I hope the bar is open."

Danny jerked his chin. "Who's that?"

A tall, thin man with an owlish face was coming toward them. He wore casual office clothing and looked bemused to find himself walking through a stable yard in the hot summer sun.

"Dr. Long, there you are." Terry hastened forward. "We're so happy you could make it. Welcome to Two Gates." He indicated the riders. "This is our group for the luncheon."

Dr. Long smiled encouragingly. "I hope everyone is in the mindset for success!"

"That would be a nice change," Charles said wistfully.

"Well, that's what I've paid for, haven't I?" groused Derek.

Sally peered over the top of her cat-eye sunglasses like a jaded starlet.

"Hello everybody!" Dave stood at the doorway to the lounge. "Come in. Yes, please help yourselves. Lovely to have you here. Just super."

Fanta stumbled out of the glare of the sun into the cool of the lounge and looked around. It was frighteningly similar to the lunchroom at the Newser. A pair of ageing wing chairs and a lumpy plaid couch were arranged near a large window that overlooked the indoor arena. Several rectangular tables were flanked by the type of stackable plastic chairs usually found on a sunny deck or patio. At the front of the room, a podium probably meant to look Romanesque had been constructed out of something resembling a plinth or maybe an outdoor plant stand.

Fanta recoiled. *North City style mavens!...URGENT...Improvising is great, but sometimes it's just makeshift without the F. And, PS, the outdoors belongs outdoors.*

She ventured farther into the room. A buffet lunch was laid out on a table over to the side. Moving cautiously, Fanta took a paper plate and lined up with the others. She glanced over her shoulder at Terry as he chatted with Dave and Dr. Long. What should she do next? Terry seemed on the brink of the big reveal. He just needed one more little push.

Sally appeared at her side. "That was *sooo* awkward," she whispered gleefully. "Imagine not knowing that Greg was dead! How could anyone be so out of the loop?"

Fanta ladled pasta salad onto her plate. With a flick of the wrist, she could splatter it all over the front of Sally's azure shirt. She placed the serving spoon down carefully and surveyed the sandwich selection. Egg salad was always a questionable choice. She almost dropped her tuna roll as Lana strode into the room wearing breeches and a bright red polo.

"*Ooh*, there's Lana." Sally scrutinized her shamelessly. "She looks like she bombed out at the beauty pageant! I heard about the robbery. An engagement ring! Can you imagine? There was probably more than one lady Greg had in mind for that." Sally shivered.

Fanta placed the tuna roll on her plate. Leave it to Sally to put the tabloid spin on Greg's matrimonial intentions. Seriously, who else would he have wanted to marry? Certainly not Deirdre. Greg would have wanted more from his future wife than a fully stocked lingerie drawer and a narrow bed in a motorhome.

Sally plucked a carrot off the crudité platter. "Dave and Terry look positively happy," she said, chewing like a gerbil. "How could they not—*ooh*, there's that little groom. The one that found him. I bet she knows everything. See you later."

Sally plunked her half-filled plate on the table and made a beeline for Romy. Fanta turned from the buffet and looked out over the room. She needed to stick close to Terry. Things were going better than she'd dared to hope. Spotting his water bottle and a plate of food at one of the place settings, she strolled over and slipped into the adjacent chair. As a bonus, she had a perfect view of Lana, who was perched on a wooden stool near the door.

At the front of the room, Terry was feverishly reviewing cue cards, nodding his head and rolling his eyes upward, obviously trying to memorize key points. His turbo hair gel had dissolved, allowing his unruly curls to flop forward. Finally, he took a deep breath, shoved the cards into his back pocket, stepped up to the podium, and launched into an introduction.

"Greetings, everyone. Today, we're fortunate to be joined by Dr. Gerald Long. I won't bore you with a list of his achievements—well, not that it's boring, Dr. Long, but it is long."

Terry flushed to the roots of his hair, where a sheen of sweat was visible. "Suffice it to say, Dr. Long is eminently qualified to speak to us about sports psychology for equestrians."

Terry steadied himself. "I think, as riders, we need three things." He paused, eyes widening, pupils disappearing into pinpricks. He grasped desperately at his cue cards, but couldn't free them from his back pocket. He gritted his teeth and plowed on. "Three things, that's trained skills, a strong riding companion, and a horse with a healthy mindset."

A few people tittered. Terry looked confused but relieved that he'd trotted out some version of his three points. "So, to keep this short, let's welcome Dr. Long."

Terry scurried from the podium, cue cards spiraling to the floor in his wake.

"Bravo!" Charles hollered over a sprinkling of applause.

Dr. Long stepped to the front of the room. "Hello, everyone, I hope you had a successful morning session." His pleasant voice could easily be heard in the large space. "And thank you for that kind introduction, Terry. While I'm not sure I can speak to the horse's mindset, I'd like to help you with yours."

There were some appreciative chuckles. Terry eased himself into the seat beside Fanta, breathing hard.

Dr. Long continued, "Today I'm going to talk about sports psychology as it relates to competing with horses." He surveyed the audience. "Do any of you suffer from nerves or anxiety when riding?"

A few hands went up. Fanta raised hers timidly.

Dr. Long smiled broadly. "Well, you're not alone." He adjusted the wire-rimmed glasses that were perched on his nose. "You'll be glad to know, I'm going to provide some tips for dealing with your feelings."

Fanta suppressed an eye-roll. Dealing with your feelings? Dr. Long sounded like the sort of snake-oil salesman that she was constantly fending off at the Newser.

"A wee drop works well!" Charles shouted, holding up his flask.

Dr. Long went on, unfazed. "You know, sometimes the anxiety we feel is not related to our horse or our riding." He looked around the room. "Maybe you're having problems in your relationship with your spouse or partner."

Lana glowered, her arms clenched tightly across her body.

"Or perhaps there are financial strains, trouble paying your bills."

Dave shifted in his seat. Derek shook his head in disgust.

Dr. Long's face drooped. "Sometimes there can be friction between you and your coach, which can be very difficult to handle."

Terry thumped his pop can down on the table, face red, eyes staring straight ahead.

As Dr. Long began describing a series of coping techniques, Fanta turned to Terry.

"How are things going? I was worried about you after our talk at the coffee shop," she whispered.

Terry kept his gaze on the front of the room. "Quite well. Dave and I have had some great discussions. He's very transparent." Terry's expression lightened.

"How's Lana?" Fanta asked. "She must be so upset."

Terry shrugged. "Lana supports my riding. In fact, she suggested I coach today's session. There's no question of Chessy joining our team," he added snidely.

Dr. Long opened the floor for a Q&A session.

Fanta added, "It sounds like everything has worked out; you've put Greg's death behind you."

Terry snapped his eyes to her. "Of course not. We're all broken-hearted. But we're trying to move on. Greg would want that."

"At the Carleton, when you spoke with Greg, did you—" Fanta started.

"Terry?" Dave called, craning his neck. "Do you want to thank Dr. Long and set the stage for this afternoon?"

Terry jumped to his feet. His chair flew back, metal legs squawking on the cement floor. The plastic seat scraped against Fanta's finger with a lick of pain as exquisite as a papercut. She tried not to gasp out loud. Blood seeped from her cuticle, threatening to drip on the floor. She rose and tiptoed over to where Dave was sitting.

"Do you have a Band-Aid?" She indicated her finger. "I've cut myself."

"Oh, sure, there's a first aid kit in the barn." Dave kept one eye on the front of the room. "Maybe in the office?" He waved a hand. "Feel free to look around. You'll find something."

Fanta hurried from the lounge. Lana glared at her as she went past. Romy sat glassy-eyed beside a delighted-looking Sally.

At the barn, she hustled down the aisle, holding her finger, blood oozing. She stepped into Dave's office and looked around. On top of the file cabinet? Behind the door? On the desktop? There was no sign of a first aid kit. A thought floated through her head like a streamer: wallet, watch, ring. Her eyes darted around the room. There were a million places where a small item could be hidden. She threw a glance into the stable aisle and scurried around the desk, cradling her finger. The blood was trickling onto the back of her hand, sticky and thick. Her yellow polo shirt was shot.

The desktop was neatly kept. She yanked open one of the bigger drawers and stuck her uninjured hand in. Pens, papers, staplers…the usual stuff. She tried the other drawers. Wait, there was something smooth and squishy. A wallet? Excited, she pulled out an old stress ball. Dammit. Hearing no one approaching, she turned to the file cabinets. They were all locked; none of the drawers would budge. A splat of blood landed on the floor. She was shedding DNA everywhere. They'd be able to track her down in an instant.

Abandoning the office, she scuttled across the aisle to the tack room. Everything was impressively neat. The lockers were all closed, some secured with padlocks. She cocked an ear. Someone would come along soon. Another red splat hit the floor. She might as well draw a map of her trespassing. She pulled open an unlocked door, fumbling with the metal clasp. Dirty brushes, hoof oil, saddle soap…nothing surprising. Ah! She spotted a small tin with a first aid symbol. At least she could bandage her finger. She reached in and pulled out the little container. She struggled to pry off the lid, her blood making the metal slippery. Finally, it popped open. She started in surprise. A shiny gold watch was tucked in the bottom. She lifted it out carefully. There was an inscription: *To my darling Greg, love Lana.*

She looked about desperately. Voices were coming up the aisle. She dropped the watch in the tin, wiped her blood off the metal, shoved the tin in the back of the locker, and swung the wooden door closed. Her eyes landed on a big brass nameplate on the front. In block letters, it said TERRY MILLER.

Chapter Twenty-Six

Fanta could barely focus on the jumping exercise. Her brain was tossing around all the new information like a clothes washer with a wonky load. She tried to think clearly. Terry had demanded to speak with Greg about all his grievances, barged into his hotel room, wigged out, and bashed Greg on the head. Then he'd snatched the valuables and gone steaming out through the lobby for all to see. Terry was right about one thing. That was definitely not a positive note.

She gripped her reins. Terry had set up two jumps on either side of a small circle. The riders had to canter around the circle and jump their horses over the two fences. The difficulty increased as two more obstacles were added. The riders had to constantly look around to the next fence while maintaining a steady pace around the circle.

It was tough going under the hot sun. Big John jumped the obstacles haphazardly. Charles was not a bad rider, but the precision of the exercise was too much for him. Gigi drifted out to the right, missing the jumps altogether. Danny struggled to keep her on track. Koko jumped around in a steady rhythm, completing the exercise easily.

"This is not the way we do things at home," Sally whined as Paparazzi sailed past one of the little fences. "The circle is too small, it needs to be widened to allow the horse to achieve its natural stride."

Des was completing the jumping task admirably. Fanta could barely see straight.

"Use your eyes, your eyes!" Terry called. "You have to look for the next fence while you're jumping that one. Look around the circle, now, now!"

At the end of the session, the riders pulled up in the middle of the ring, red-faced and sweating. Except Derek, who smiled smugly.

"That's it for this afternoon, everyone," Terry announced proudly. "I hope today has been helpful. It has been a pleasure having you here at Two Gates."

Fanta wiped her brow. Terry could be an excellent clinician and coach. Unless he was a murderous thief. It was impossible to look him in the eye.

Back in the barn, she tied Des in the aisle and started grooming. The atmosphere was subdued. Charles took a nip from his flask. Derek brushed Koko, looking pleased with himself. Danny fussed over Gigi like an anxious parent. Sally stalked about, ignoring everyone, placing her top-name equipment in her shiny tack trunk. Terry loitered near the tack room, seeming unsure whether to stay or go.

Fanta's hands shook as she knelt on the floor, carefully wrapping the bandages around Des's legs. She just wanted to head out, the sooner the better.

"Hi there, how did it go?"

Fanta jumped. Penny was coming down the aisle.

"Oh, hi, Penny. I didn't see you come in," she stammered. "It was great, I enjoyed it. Terry had some good suggestions. Des was super."

"Fantastic! It's so valuable to get another person's perspective. You know, a fresh set of eyes. We can build Terry's advice in as we move forward." Penny was pleased.

Dave appeared out of the office and strolled toward them. His baggy jeans and polo shirt were marginally cleaner than usual. "Hi, Penny, great to see you. Come to pick up Fanta?" He smiled at them both. "I don't think we were too hard on her."

Fanta fumbled with the buckles on Des's blanket. The day could not end fast enough.

"Great idea you had for this clinic. I wish I'd thought of it," Penny said.

"Thanks." Dave ran a hand through his thick head of hair and pooched out his lips. "Yup, just trying to reboot the business here. Gotta get Two Gates past our recent tragedy."

Penny smiled sympathetically.

"Oh, did you find that bandage okay, Fanta? For your finger?" Dave asked.

Fanta offered a jittery smile. "It was nothing, really, don't worry about it. Just a small cut." She'd stuck her hand under some cold water before riding in the afternoon session. The bleeding had stopped, but her finger was purple and swollen.

"Now that I think of it, where is that first aid kit?" Dave glanced around the aisle. "Terry!" he called. "Fanta was looking for the first aid kit earlier. Where is the thing?"

Fanta dug in her tack trunk for Des's lead rope. She imagined sinking into the cement floor, clicking her heels three times, or anything that would cause her to vanish.

"Hi, Penny, how are you?" Terry joined them. "The first aid kit is in the tack room, Dave. On the wall, behind the door." He paused, cocking his head. "Funny you mention it. There was something that looked like blood on the clasp on my locker. Was that you, Fanta? You should have just asked for a bandage. We've got plenty."

Fanta's eyes skittered around the stable aisle. She couldn't look at Terry. His guilt shone around him like a beacon. Her mind did a quick exercise in logic. If he'd suspected that someone had been in his locker, someone who was bleeding, who might have seen the little first aid tin…had he guessed that the jig was up? And if he knew the blood was hers…

"Thanks, no worries." She cast a desperate look at Penny. "I guess we better get going, right?" She untied Des, snapped the lead rope to his halter, and started down the aisle.

"Sure," Penny said, puzzled. "Well, I'll see you gentlemen later. Chessy will be here tomorrow for the session with Lana. She's looking forward to it."

"That's great," Dave said. "And, oh, thanks for sending Chessy over yesterday with the payment. Much appreciated." Then he called down the aisle, "We'll see you tomorrow too, Fanta. We'll take all the help we can get." Dave and Terry laughed heartily.

Fanta fled from the barn with Des and high-tailed it toward the Bay Ridge trailer. The ramp was lowered, ready for Des to be loaded. Penny took Des's lead rope and led him on.

"You okay? Did something happen?" Penny asked, reappearing from inside the trailer.

"Absolutely, everything's fine. What could—" Fanta stopped, her mouth hanging open. She'd left her tack trunk and her saddle and bridle in the aisle. She couldn't possibly go back. Not with Greg's murderer hanging about, bold as brass.

"Fanta?"

"I just realized. I forgot my stuff in the barn." She wavered, trying to pluck up her courage.

"Okay. Well, there's something I forgot to ask Dave. I can go back if you like."

"Would you? That would be amazing, thanks." Fanta scrambled to help Penny lift the heavy ramp and secure it with the big metal latches. "I'm just going to give Des some carrots. He was such a good boy today."

Penny headed back to the barn. Fanta hurried to her Honda, grabbed some carrots, and returned to the trailer, where she opened the small door at the front. She looked in to see Des, standing in his narrow stall, chewing on a full hay net. She held up the carrots so he could pull them from her hand with his lips.

"What if Terry is here tomorrow, Dessie?" she whispered. Her finger was red and throbbing. It would be nothing compared to what might happen if Terry took a swing at her with the manure shovel.

Des crunched his carrots. Fanta risked a peek into the parking area. A little Fiat was coming up the lane. A gorgeous young woman hopped out, ran over to Danny, threw herself into his arms, and gave him a big smooch. Charles drove by in a wicked Jaguar SUV pulling a two-horse trailer and headed down the drive, Big John's tail hanging out the back.

"I honestly think they're just doomed here without Greg."

Fanta recognized Sally's sulky voice.

"It was certainly very expensive. I'm not sure it was worth the fee." There was no mistaking Derek's nasal whine.

"Terry thinks he's all that. Who's he kidding? I mean, he may have a bit of money, as if that matters," Sally said scornfully. "And where was Lana? She's the pro. She should have been here today." Sally huffed, indignant. "No, Greg was the glue that held everything together. That's plain to see. Dave should just put the place up for sale and be done with it."

"I doubt I'd come back another time," Derek grizzled.

Sally gave a great sigh. "Anyway, it was nice meeting you, Derek. Be sure to drop in and see me at The Mane Connection. We'll get you fixed up."

"Right, thanks, Sally."

Fanta guessed it would be the last thing on his to-do list.

Footsteps marched off in one direction and shuffled off in the other. She turned back into the trailer to see Des, orange goober on his lips, reaching for his hay net.

"I wouldn't want to be Sally's bitch buddy, Dessie," she whispered.

Des pulled a mouthful of hay from the net, nodded his great head, and kept chewing.

* * *

Hunkered in the darkness of her car, Fanta scrambled to get the wrappings off a veggie burger and onion rings. She had stopped at GLOW, a new eatery in a bland building on the side of the highway. The car window was open, and she could hear the soft buzz of the bright neon lighting that gave the diner its name. People were heading into the restaurant or eating in their cars. She had ordered using GLOW's retro intercom system. A wholesome-looking girl with blonde braids and blue braces on her teeth had come out with the meal.

Fanta crammed the food in her mouth. Terry! She couldn't get him out of her mind. Subterfuge didn't seem to be his thing. The guy wore his heart on his sleeve. Still, she supposed he had to be wily to survive in the corporate jungle. So that's why he'd snagged some valuables from the crime scene. But why keep the watch in the barn, in his own locker?

She pictured Terry in the hotel room with Greg.

"Greg, it's this invoice, it's fifty dollars too much. I've gone over it and over it. I know you think I can't ride, but I can add up a bill. And now there's this

Chessy, working underneath you. I can't take it anymore. I've always loved you, but this has to end!" And then, smack! With what? The picture got fuzzy and then cleared to show Terry, tippy-toeing around the room, giving Greg's crumpled body a wide berth and a pitying look, plucking items from atop the tacky hotel desk or the depths of a suitcase.

Fanta gulped down the last bite. She needed a distraction. Wiping her hands, she pulled out her phone and saw that her mom had called several times. She pressed the dial button.

"Oh, hi, honey, there you are. I knew you would get back to me. Seems like you're busy, busy, busy! Is everything okay?" Her mom was upbeat.

"Hi, mom, yes, I'm fine," said Fanta. She'd ordered a lactose-free strawberry shake. She pulled it from the cupholder, stuck the straw in her mouth, and gave it a slurp. It was yummy and thick. "I rode Des in a clinic today, so I'm beat."

There was a pause. "What, honey? You went to a clinic today? You're not sick, are you? Oh dear, I knew I should check in with you more often." Her mom flew into worry mode.

"No, mom, I rode in a horseback riding clinic." Fanta enunciated. A piece of burger was stuck in her front teeth. She tickled it with her tongue. "It's like taking a lesson, but it goes on all day. Des and I had fun. We had a good instructor and we learned a lot." She couldn't imagine the tangent the conversation would take if she mentioned that the instructor might be a cold-blooded killer.

There was another pause. "What's that? But weren't you supposed to be at work today, honey?" her mom asked. "Don't tell me they let you go. And what about Penny? Isn't she your coach? You're not leaving Bay Ridge, are you? Such a lovely spot, what a pity."

Fanta wrapped her lips around the milkshake straw and sucked in a huge draft. An ice floe surged up her nose, into her sinuses, and spread throughout her brain. She gasped, "Listen, mom, I better go. Someone's just brought my meal. Everything's great, don't worry. Talk soon!"

"Oh, honey, that's amazing, are you on a date with a—"

Fanta jabbed the red button. She let her arm flop to her side and leaned back in the driver's seat. She was in over her head in so many aspects of her life. She returned the milkshake to the cupholder. She would go home, take a hot shower, prepare a suit of armor for the next day, and go to bed. She turned the key in the ignition. Wait. She'd missed a whole day at the Newser. She should check her email. She rummaged in her purse and pulled her work phone out. In the pink-purple glow of the restaurant's neon lighting, she saw a new text.

What's happening?

Fanta growled. She was getting sick of the armchair detective. What did the person want? They'd be better off pestering Sue. **What do you mean?** she hammered out.

What have you found?

Fanta's heart plummeted into her stomach, where the shake, burger, and rings were jiggling around on some sort of pulse setting. What had she found? No one knew she'd found anything. Except maybe…Terry?

A new message popped up on the screen…**found out?**

Fanta sighed with relief. She did that all the time, pressed buttons too fast, sent texts full of gobbledy-gook. She felt suddenly magnanimous. The texter just wanted to know, to see justice done for poor Greg. Still, she wouldn't share anything until she knew more. It would be irresponsible. **Nothing conclusive.**

The response was immediate. **Forget it. Good luck.**

Fanta smarted. She tossed the phone on top of her purse and cranked the engine. She wouldn't bother with the armchair detective again; any queries would go unanswered. She started out of the lot. As she slowed for a gaggle of carefree kids and their distracted parents, it occurred to her that, in fact, she was being irresponsible. She'd found Greg's watch, taken from his room on the night of his death. She should be speeding to the police station at that very minute. What was she thinking? But no, that would be reckless. She would stay quiet, spend one more day at Two Gates, and then go to the police with everything she'd learned. No sense doing it in dribs and drabs.

She entered smoothly into the flow of traffic, chuckling as she recalled texts mangled by typos or auto-correct. Her mother's messages were rife with such things.

What have you found?…It swirled in her brain. Her fingers tightened on the steering wheel. What if the armchair detective had not made an error? What if the armchair detective knew all about the three items, hidden away at Two Gates? Fanta drove steadily down the wide road, streetlights flashing by overhead. Her tired brain struggled to take the next step. Wouldn't that make the armchair detective…the killer?

Chapter Twenty-Seven

Fanta squinted in the early morning sun as she drove up the long lane at Two Gates. It was amazing she'd arrived in one piece. Her sleep had been colored by dreams of Terry, dressed like the little man in the Monopoly game. He'd strutted around with his top hat and cane, pulling items from the pockets of his trousers like a magician. First, Greg's gold watch. Then, the missing wallet. Finally, a gigantic diamond ring that twinkled in the light. Monopoly Terry had giggled in delight and swung his arms as if holding a giant baseball bat.

Fanta had vague memories of Lana, dressed like a sparkly mermaid, and Dave, being sick in a corner of the room. A sly cat with long eyelashes and a baseball cap had played with a mouse wearing a polyester apron, while Fanta's mother had called from the top of a tower like Rapunzel. The whole production had been punctuated by a big, angry text reading **I AM THE KILTER!**

She parked in the lot at Two Gates and rubbed her eyes. She'd stopped at Demi Tasse for a gutsy cup and was functioning at a basic level. She stared through the bug-speckled windshield, trying to imagine what the day might hold. Was she in over her head? She'd been trailing down the stairs at her building that morning on her way to the parking lot when she'd been waylaid by Mrs. Hooper.

"There you are, Fanta dear." Mrs. Hooper had been peeping anxiously out from behind her apartment door, Lottie hovering at her ankles. "I was hoping it was you coming down the stairs. I've been thinking about you."

"Oh, why's that?" Fanta had asked groggily, the watch, the texts, and the whole mess tumbling hotly around in her brain like clothes in the dryer.

"Well, I've been thinking about what you told me, and, I have to say, you really should get to the police station. I know that's what my Pete would advise." Mrs. Hooper had spoken quietly, her eyes shifting warily, obviously not wanting to annoy her neighbors with any early morning noise. Her old-fashioned dressing gown had been zipped up to the neck, her wispy grey hair held in place with a few bobby pins, well-worn pink slippers on her feet. "I wouldn't want you to be in any danger, dear."

Fanta had hesitated. Was she in danger? She was only going to spend the day at Two Gates. Hopefully, Terry would not be there. But which Lana might turn up? The cloying version from the interview at High T, or the snitty one from the dress-down with Deirdre at the horse show? In any case, there would be lots of people around. She wasn't going crawling alone through some dark alley.

Mrs. Hooper had leaned out farther, Lottie's head popping around her leg, eyes bright and curious. "In my experience, if someone has gone to the trouble of taking valuables from the crime scene, it could be a very crafty killer, a calculating person, cold-blooded even. Not someone you want to be dealing with, dear."

Lottie had wriggled past Mrs. Hooper's legs and out into the hallway, sniffing the floor and gazing hopefully down the stairs.

Mrs. Hooper had shuffled back a few steps. "You do what you think is best, dear, but be careful, and don't be afraid to ask for help," she'd said, retreating into her apartment. "Come, Lottie, you let Fanta get on with her day. It's time for our breakfast."

Lottie had hurried into the apartment and the door had pushed shut, leaving Fanta to stare at the cheap wood with the tiny peephole in the middle.

She heaved herself out of the Honda. Mrs. Hooper was probably right. Fanta locked the car. Just one more day, and she would follow her advice. She walked slowly across the parking area. The clinic participants were arriving, horses and people milling about. Chessy and Ollie were already in the barn, preparing for the day. Fanta propped her sunglasses on top of her head, hoping she didn't look like a hot mess.

"Hey there, Fanta," Chessy called. Then she did a double-take. "You look worn out. Should I be worried? I hope Lana doesn't work us too hard." Chessy laughed easily, running a brush over Ollie's gleaming chestnut coat. "Did it go well yesterday?"

"Yeah, it did, actually." Fanta felt even more wiped standing next to Chessy, who looked fantastic in gray breeches and a fresh pink polo shirt. Fanta looked down at her baggy jeans and dark blue polo. They were dowdy and formless.

"Doing any more fact-finding?" Chessy asked mildly, with the lift of an eyebrow.

"Oh, yeah, a little." Fanta was surprised Chessy had remembered that tidbit. "I better leave it to the police," she added, with a modest laugh and a pinch of guilt. "Anyway, I should go find Dave or Lana." She sketched a wave and continued down the aisle.

"Good luck," Chessy called.

Fanta cringed. Why did people keep saying that? She paused at the door to Dave's office. Lana sat at the desk, pecking at the computer keyboard with varnished fingernails. She wore an emerald-green polo shirt with tan breeches. Fanta felt a jolt from her subconscious. But no time for that now. She poked her head in the door and smiled enthusiastically. "Good morning, Lana, I'm your hired help for the day."

"Good. Just in time, too." Lana looked up and then back at the screen. She finished something, powered down the computer with a tap, and turned her attention to Fanta. "We've met before, right? You're that writer from the newspaper. The one who was asking me about Greg."

"That's right, yes." Fanta braced herself for whatever might come next.

"What's the paper again? The Newser?" Lana made a dismissive gesture. "I haven't seen anything nice about Greg in there."

"That's right, the Newser. The article is coming along well. Should run any day now." Fanta nailed the smile to her face. The jolt hit her again, kicking loose a bit of memory. "What a lovely shirt. The green really suits you."

Fanta's brain whirred like a sluggish internet connection. "I think I saw you in something of the same color. When was that?" She tapped her bandaged finger on her chin. "Oh! At the bar that night, the night that Greg…that night."

Lana's face fell. Fanta's cheeks burned.

"I'm so sorry, Lana, that was thoughtless of me."

Lana stared dully at the blank computer screen.

"Do you know, I happened to see Greg that night. It was great to meet him." Fanta had the sense of being in a deep pit with a shovel. "He was looking for you, actually. I hope he found you okay." Could it get any worse?

"No, I did not see him that night, as it turned out," Lana said brusquely. She rose abruptly, rounded the desk, and arrived at the door, where she pushed by Fanta and out into the aisle. She surveyed the participants as they readied their horses.

"We've had a cancellation, everybody," she called. "Terry Miller was supposed to join us, but he's had a work emergency. So it will just be four in the group today."

She turned a withering gaze on Fanta. "Since you're here, I want you to set up some exercises in the front ring. Get a dozen or so poles from the shed. I'll be there shortly to tell you how to set them out. Thanks."

Lana turned away and began mingling with the riders.

Fanta made her way to the ring and stepped into the shed. Terry had cancelled. Was he cracking under the pressure of his guilt? Proceeding blithely with his life? Pitching the watch, wallet, and ring in the nearest dumpster and planning a move to a foreign country? Fanta puffed out a breath. At least she wouldn't have to cope with him. On the downside, snitty Lana was out in full force.

She surveyed the jumble of jump materials. Wooden gates and walls, plastic flowers and shrubbery, metal pins and pole cups. The complicated, dirty mess seemed like the perfect analogy for her own life. She stooped to pull a few long wooden poles from a large pile and started carrying them into the ring. They were heavy and awkward and coated in grit. She struggled through the deep sand of the ring with one pole under each arm. Within minutes, her polo and jeans were filthy. She wiped her hands on her thighs and trudged back to the shed. By the time the riders entered the ring, she had amassed a small collection of poles. She stopped to catch her breath, swiping her face with a dirty palm. Her sunglasses slipped down her nose.

Lana strode into the ring alongside the riders. She wore a trendsetting sun hat with a wide cloth band that matched her green polo shirt. She indicated Fanta without actually looking at her.

"Everyone, this is Fanta. She's helping me for the day. If you need anything, don't hesitate to ask her."

Fanta waved limply at the group. Was she everyone's gofer? Chessy tried not to grin.

"Alright, before we start our exercises over poles, let's do a round of introductions," Lana said briskly. She was obviously more comfortable teaching than Terry. "Maybe we could start with you, Chessy." Lana spat the name out like a bite of rotten fruit.

"Sure, thanks, Lana. I'm Chessy, and this is Ollie." Chessy smiled at the group. "We're from Bay Ridge. I ride in the junior jumpers, but I would like to move up, if I can."

"I'm sure you would, thank you," Lana cut in. "Next?"

"Hello all, I'm Keshia, and this is Ranger," said a tall, skinny woman with knobby knees and elbows. Her long-backed bay horse wore a hackamore, or bitless bridle. "Ranger and I have been together a long time, but we're always looking to up our game."

Lana nodded and turned her eyes to the next rider.

"Greetings, the name's Neela. This is Speedball." Neela was a compact young woman with short legs. Her horse wore a complex arrangement of straps, ropes, and other equipment on his head. He was already sweating and champing the bit. Neela sat on him easily. "We've got the speed, I just need to contain this guy a bit better."

Lana turned to the last rider, a tall, friendly-looking man astride a plain bay horse with a super-cute face.

"Hi, everyone, I'm Nick, and this is Blue Streak. I've got the opposite problem from Neela," he said, smiling. "We need to build our speed for those jump-offs."

"Great, everyone, thanks for being here." Lana headed toward the poles heaped in the middle of the ring. "Let's start warming up our horses with some transitions, walk-trot, walk-canter, canter-halt, you get it. I'll let you do your thing and tell you what I see."

She pointed at the poles. "Fanta, I need four of those poles in a fan shape and the rest in an S configuration." She walked briskly away to watch the riders circling the ring.

Fanta looked down at the pile. She knew about a fan shape since she had done the exercise at home with Des and Penny, but she had never set it up before. The idea was for the horse to canter over the four poles, remaining in the center of each one and following the curve of the fan. If the horse was too far to the outside of the fan, the striding became very long. Too far inside, and the striding was too short.

Fanta started fumbling with the poles, making an educated guess at the spacing. Then she turned her attention to the S configuration. How did that work? Did the poles go end-to-end? She had no idea what to do. The sun beat down on her dark blue shirt and sweat flowed freely into the waistband of her dumpy jeans.

Lana bore down on her. "What's taking so long?" she hissed, looking at Fanta's handiwork. "The striding is all wrong here." Lana rearranged the fan-shaped poles. "Where's the S?" Lana shook her head in disgust. "Honestly, even Deirdre would have been better than you. At least she knows what she's doing." She stared at Fanta. "What do they teach you at Bay Ridge? Not much, apparently."

With a dramatic eye-roll, Lana created an S with five parallel poles. The horse would need to canter over them in a snakelike way. Fanta shrugged. It seemed obvious now.

Lana glared at her. "Maybe you could go to Dave's office and get my sunglasses and sunscreen? Is that too much to ask?"

Fanta hurried out of the ring. It was just like at the Newser, where she constantly felt underqualified for the simplest tasks. Maybe cloying Lana would have been better. At least she could have been ridiculed in a genteel fashion. *"Oh, Fanta, thanks so much for that, but of course it's completely wrong and only an idiot would have done it that way. But good for you. So happy that maybe you'll learn something today."*

She walked briskly down the stable aisle, pulling off her sunglasses and rubbing her sweaty nose. Ow! Her eye burned as sunscreen leaked into it. Fanta blinked. Fortunately, there was no one in sight; the barn was cool and deserted. She would find Lana's things and go back to the ring, pronto.

She stopped in the doorway to Dave's office. Should she try another search of the drawers? She was pretty sure she didn't even want to find something else. She placed her sunglasses on top of a filing cabinet and surveyed the room. The desktop was bare. They kept things neat and tidy at Two Gates. She walked around the desk to where Lana had been sitting in the office chair. Tucked beside the computer monitor were a pair of sunglasses with tortoiseshell rims and a tube of expensive sunscreen. She looked again at the drawers. It was tempting, but Lana would lose it if she took too long. Fanta took the glasses and sunscreen off the desk and went back out into the aisle.

She looked both ways. There was still no one around. If the plan was to go to the police, perhaps even that evening, it would be smart to confirm that the watch was still in its hidey-hole. Otherwise, she'd look—once again—like a complete fool.

She hastened to the tack room and stepped in carefully. All was quiet. She took four large strides over to Terry's locker. The metal clasp that she'd grabbed with her bloody hand had been wiped clean. She opened the door and looked in. Terry had done some tidying. She scanned the well-organized items. Her eyes landed on the small metal tin. With trembling fingers, she reached in and pulled it out. The metal shone clean and bright. Had she imagined the whole thing? Or had someone—likely Terry—been quick to realize exactly what had happened? What did that mean for her? Her brain couldn't take it any further. She pushed at the edge of the lid and it popped open with a squeak. The tin was empty.

Chapter Twenty-Eight

Fanta hurried back to the outdoor ring, being careful not to spook the horses. The riders were navigating the pole exercises with varying degrees of success. Speedball barreled through, oblivious to the poles. Ollie clumped along, not showing much interest. Ranger shifted his body this way and that, sometimes tripping on the poles. Blue Streak hopped through, ears pricked and big, dark eyes shining.

Fanta hustled over to where Lana stood in the middle of the ring.

"I'm burned to a crisp out here," Lana said peevishly, snatching the sunglasses and tube of cream. She put the glasses on in one smooth motion, squeezed a dollop of sunscreen on her hand, and began rubbing it on her forearms.

"I just saw a car come up the lane, Fanta. I presume it's our guest speaker." Lana spoke as if addressing a particularly slow student. "Why don't you go and greet her? Show her into the viewing lounge? Help get the lunch set up?" She pinned Fanta with a look from behind her tinted lenses. "Let's make this a success, shall we?"

"Of course, happy to do it," Fanta stammered. She jogged toward the parking lot. If it meant getting out of Lana's orbit, she would welcome Attila the Hun with a smile on her face and a spring in her step.

She arrived in the dusty lot just as a sleek Mercedes sedan pulled to a stop. The driver's door opened. The scent of buttery leather and brand-new car blossomed in the air. A red-soled stiletto poked out. A long leg emerged, clad in spotless white jeans. Then, a perfectly groomed brunette unfolded from the vehicle. The hip-hugging white jeans were paired with a red sleeveless top and chunky accessories. The woman oozed charisma and confidence. She was anointed with some stupidly expensive perfume.

Fanta straightened her filthy polo and tugged at her jeans.

"*Ooh la la*! They have sent someone to greet me, how *charmant*." The woman cooed, plucking a designer handbag worth Fanta's annual salary from the car. A scarf that Fanta longed to touch and hold was tied loosely to the purse strap. "I am delighted to meet you. I am Chantale Lamoureux." She reached out a hand with a red-hot manicure.

Fanta hesitated. It seemed wrong to soil the exotic creature. But what choice did she have? She seized the woman's hand in a firm, assured grasp. "I'm Fanta Delaney, Ms. Lamoureux. How great to meet you. I'm helping with the clinic today. Can I get you anything? Would you like to see some of the morning session?"

"*Mais non, cherie*. I have come to see my old friend Da-veed. Where is he, that wonderful man?" Chantale's gaze swept the parking area as if sprites might come twinkling out of the tractor shed.

Da-veed? Fanta thought furiously. "Oh, Dave, you mean?" She looked desperately from the barn to the arena and back again. "I'm not sure, I—"

"Chantale! How great to see you." Dave appeared from the darkness of the stable aisle and hurried over. "How long has it been? Too long, my lovely." He pulled Chantale into an embrace, his sweaty t-shirt pressed against the woman's silk top.

"Dav-eed, how wonderful that you have invited me here, to this beautiful Two Gates." Chantale's expression went from delight to despair. "But what is this I hear about my darling Greg? I am devastated. It cannot be true, can it?" Chantale's hand fluttered to her throat and she fingered a gold cable necklace. Fanta guessed it was not from the jewelry store in the mall, the one with the fake pearls, plastic baubles, and gaudy beads. The place seemed spoiled for her now.

Dave nodded somberly. "We'll talk about it later, my friend." He glanced at Fanta. "Have you ladies met?"

"*Mais oui!* Fanta has been so helpful." Chantale gave a brilliant smile.

"Chantale and I are old friends from college." Dave grinned. "She and

Greg were a bit of an item, back in the day, isn't that right, Chantale?" He winked. "Now she's a renowned speaker in the horse world."

"What is this, *old* friends? You have not changed a bit, my Dav-eed," Chantale tittered.

"We're going to my office, Fanta," Dave said, looping Chantale's arm through his. "Could I ask you to help the caterer? It will be pretty much the same set-up as yesterday."

Dave and Chantale set off toward the barn, arm-in-arm, reminiscing about halcyon days. Fanta thought the whole dynamic was weird. Hadn't Dave ever wanted to score with Chantale? The two seemed cozy enough. Yet Dave seemed okay with the fact that his pal Greg had zipped by for the touchdown, once again.

Fanta stood in the lot beside the Mercedes, which gleamed in the sun like a spaceship. She'd never heard of a Chantale Lamoureux. What was she going to speak about? High-end fashion? Uber-expensive cars? She didn't seem like the horsey type. The white jeans at a stable were a dead giveaway. She imagined younger versions of Chantale and Greg clinched together in some sort of French maneuver. What exactly had Greg learned at college?

She headed to the viewing lounge, scuffing her toes in the gravel. She would turn her mind to laying out cutlery and napkins, making sure tables and chairs were set up, and organizing the buffet food. If there were a way to screw it up, she would find it. She stepped through the door and saw the caterer had been and gone. There was little to be done except peel plastic wrapping from the serving plates. She looked out the window and saw Chantale approaching alone, walking carefully in her designer heels.

"Ah, yes, but this is lovely." Chantale stepped into the drab lounge as if entering the palace at Versailles. "And there you are, Fanta. Such a fabulous name. So full of life and hope."

Fanta smiled. It seemed impossible to dislike Chantale, despite her beauty, the money that dripped off her, and the fact that she'd bagged Greg when others could only dream.

"Thank you, Chantale. I...I was wondering if I could ask you a question. I'm curious about something."

Chantale stared, enraptured. "But of course!"

"What was it like, in college? With Greg and Dave. They seem a bit like, well, an odd couple. I wouldn't have seen them as friends," Fanta rushed to add.

Chantale threw her head back in a full-throated laugh. "Ah, those were the days! Greg was so handsome, so dashing. Dav-eed was so serious, so studious. You are right! They do not seem well-suited. But indeed, they were the best of friends. It was heart-warming to see them together. Like cheese and wine, caramel and *chocolat*. Everything that is good in life."

Fanta frowned, perplexed. "And…Dave was never jealous? Of Greg and his…achievements?"

Chantale looked enchanted by the question. "Ah, you English. Always so prim, so proper. I will not embarrass you with details. I will play your game. So let me just say that I do not think Dav-eed shared all of Greg's interests. He had a few, one might say, of his own."

Fanta's mouth fell open. Was Chantale saying that Dave was—

"Ah, I see I have shocked you! I am sorry. But do not worry, *mademoiselle*. Where there is love, there is light."

Fanta was stupefied. Her thoughts leaped to Lana, stomping around in the stable aisle, looking for her useless helper.

"Okay, thanks, Chantale. I guess I better pop over to the stables, see if I can assist there." Fanta indicated the dingy room. "Do you need anything for your presentation?"

"*Mais non*, everything is *superbe*." Chantale placed her fingers on her lips and pulled them away in the dramatic gesture of a Michelin-starred chef. "I need only a few moments to prepare myself."

Fanta couldn't resist. "What will you be talking about?"

Chantale lowered her voice to a dramatic whisper. "My specialty, equine psychology. How we communicate with these fabulous animals."

"Oh, awesome." Fanta pointed toward the door. "I'll be back in a second. I'm sure everyone's excited to hear from you."

In the barn, the riders were getting their horses ready for the lunch break. Lana circulated among them, even appearing to engage in a civil conversation with Chessy. Unsure what to do, Fanta headed toward Dave's office. He sat at his desk, looking dispirited.

"Hi, Dave, sorry to interrupt." She popped her head around the door jamb. "The lunch is ready to go. Chantale is in the lounge preparing for her presentation. Can I do anything else? Is everything okay?"

Dave sighed. "Don't mind me." He rubbed his face with both hands. "It's great to see Chantale, but she has reminded me of times past. Things were very different then." He shook his head. "Funny how when you're young you can't wait to grow up, and when you're older you wish you could return to your youth." Dave chuckled. "Well, to parts of it, maybe."

Fanta's heart went out to him. "I just wanted to say how much I am enjoying the clinic, Dave. Terry did a great job yesterday, and Lana is so knowledgeable. It was such a fantastic idea of yours." She hesitated. "Maybe my opinion isn't worth much, but I think you and Two Gates are going to be just fine. Greg was wonderful, but you have what it takes, too. I'm sure you'll get things figured out here in no time."

Dave's face wobbled. He looked down at his work-worn hands. Then he levered himself up from the chair with a grunt.

"Yes, well, Greg may have beat me out in the past, but not this time," he said crossly. He glanced at Fanta. "Let's get this group over to the lounge. I appreciate your views, but there's no point dwelling on ancient history."

Fanta stood, uncertain. Maybe somewhere under Dave's tattered teddy bear demeanor, there was a glowing ember of resentment toward his buddy Greg. And maybe that ember had sprung to life and consumed Dave as he barged into Greg's room that night, ready to have it out.

Dave pushed by Fanta and steamed down the aisle toward the stable door. "Let's go, everybody!" he called over his shoulder.

Fanta hurried after him and over to the lounge. Dave made a beeline for Chantale and started chatting. Fanta loitered near the buffet. Keshia and Neela came in, talking animatedly. Nick sauntered through the door, gazing around appreciatively. Chessy hurried in, probably thinking she was late.

"Ah, but you must be Lana." Chantale flowed toward Chessy, hand outstretched. "I could tell right away. Such a beauty. Truly statuesque, *mais oui*. And so wonderful with the horses. I am so pleased to meet you."

Chessy gaped at Chantale. "Actually, I'm not, I—"

Lana barged through the door and brushed roughly by Chessy.

"Ms. Lamoureux? I'm Lana. It's nice to meet you," she said, scowling.

"Ah, so sorry, so sorry. But you are perfect. So, so...*mignon! Bien sur!*" Chantale quickly regained her composure. "The perfect choice for our marvelous Greg."

Looking at the expression on Lana's face, Fanta wondered if the lights would start to flicker with the approach of the devil himself. She wandered over to join Chessy at the buffet.

"What was that about?" Chessy whispered, placing salad on her plate with plastic tongs.

Fanta shook her head. "It's a long story."

They found seats together at one of the tables. Romy scurried in and perched on a chair near the door, throwing a death stare their way. Fanta made a "what?" gesture in return.

"Hello everyone, and thank you for attending the Two Gates pop-up tune-up clinic," Dave announced from the front of the room. "It's my good fortune to introduce a true friend of mine, Miss Chantale Lamoureux." Dave indicated Chantale, preening before him.

Dave assumed a teasing tone. "Some of you may know that Lamoureux means, in English, the loving one." He waggled his eyebrows suggestively. "Well, let me tell you, it is a fine name for my friend. The tales I could tell. Isn't that right, Chantale?"

Even Chantale looked a bit embarrassed. "Oh, Dav-eed, you must stop!" she giggled.

"Of course, Greg would have known exactly what I'm talking about. Lamoureux! He and Chantale needed no translation."

Dave laughed heartily. Keshia and Neela squirmed in their seats. Nick cleared his throat politely. Romy dropped her head in her hands. Lana looked as if she were about to spit nails.

"Without further ado, I give you, Chantale," Dave concluded, bowing like a circus master.

"I'd run the other way if I were this woman," Chessy commented to Fanta. They watched Chantale sashay to the front of the room as if on the catwalk.

"*Bonjour, le monde!* And *merci* Dav-eed. I am Chantale Lamoureux. So happy to be here." She beamed at everyone, presiding over the room easily. "Today, I will speak with you about the psychology of the horse. So fascinating. But first, I'm sure most of you knew our wonderful Greg Grenier. I wanted to say I share in your sadness at his sudden death. So young. So wonderful with the horses. And so handsome. What woman did not fall at his feet?"

Chantale grinned like a sorority girl. Dave nodded encouragingly. Lana looked as if she were about to initiate a full-on frontal attack.

To most everyone's relief, Chantale launched into a detailed presentation about herd dynamics, equine body language, and how horses perceived and reacted to humans. Fanta listened attentively. How did Des perceive her? As a trusted guide or a bumbling fool? Maybe it was best not to delve into it too far.

"Equine psychology must be a lucrative business for Chantale," she whispered to Chessy. "Did you see the car and the—" she indicated Chantale's clothing "—get-up?"

"Oh, I think it's just a sideline, like a hobby," Chessy said, nibbling salad. "I hear she's a corporate lawyer in New York."

Fanta snorted. It was one more thing to toss onto the pile of life's inequities. As Chantale neared the end of her presentation, Fanta bade farewell to Chessy, grabbed a Nanaimo bar off the buffet, and started toward Lana, dread in her heart. With the jumping exercises planned for the afternoon, she could only guess what might be in store.

Lana was like a wasp's nest poked by a badger. "There you are. Aren't you supposed to be working here today? Typically, that doesn't mean sitting around with the paying guests." Lana threw a crumpled napkin on top of her half-eaten meal. "Really, it would have been preferable if you'd been doing set-up while we were at lunch. Now we'll waste time building fences when we should be jumping."

"For sure, so sorry, Lana," Fanta mumbled through a mouthful of graham cracker, custard icing, and gooey chocolate. Whoever had invented the Nanaimo bar should be knighted. Fanta zoned out, chewing contentedly, letting Lana vent a bit longer.

"And so that's what I'll expect to see when we get out to the ring," Lana concluded.

Fanta realized she'd just missed a complicated explanation of the jumps that would need to be constructed. Ah, well. How hard could it be? They weren't laboring on the frontier of advanced technology. Licking her lips, she headed toward the door, pretending not to notice Romy's knowing look, and trudged toward the ring, where she pushed and pulled heavy poles and jump standards through the thick sand. Her jeans and polo were at some level of filthy she had never experienced. Sweat poured into her eyes, stinging and smarting. She fantasized about ripping the clothing from her body, running down a long dock, and cannonballing into cool, dark water. Finally, she stepped back to view the five lopsided jumps she had placed in a straggly line.

"Honestly." Lana walked into the ring, swept by her, and started making indents in the sand with her heel. "Put the fences here, for goodness' sake. I've marked them for you."

Fanta made the adjustments, grunting and sweating. Then she stood by uselessly as the clinic progressed through the afternoon. Chessy had to work to fit Ollie's big stride into the short distances between the jumps. Speedball flew through as Neela struggled to slow his pace. Ranger jumped in an unorthodox way, his front legs dangling below the knee. Blue Streak and Nick made quick work of the tricky exercises. Blue Streak was much like Des: easy and willing but talented, too. Fanta liked him a lot.

Without any further call for assistance, Lana proceeded to adjust and set out the fences herself. Fanta felt more humiliated than if she'd been shouted at for an hour or more. At least it was fun to watch the horses. And, she had to admit, Lana was a compelling instructor.

"Great job, everybody!" Lana called. "Let's cool out these horses. I'm here if you have any questions." She turned to Fanta. "I think Deirdre is back. If you see her, please send her my way."

"Sure thing," Fanta said, defeated. Lana was treating her as thoughtlessly as she would a bellhop at a posh hotel. And now she had to go in search of Deirdre. Of all the people she did not want to find. Could she just slip into her car and disappear down the drive? Would anyone be the wiser? She squinted in the late afternoon sun. She realized she'd left her sunglasses in Dave's office. Sighing, she retraced her steps once more to the stable.

She stepped into the aisle. It was quiet and empty. Romy was busy sweeping at the far end. Soon, the clinic participants would return, and the barn would be filled with chatter and activity. Lana would be with them, smooth and poised as a flight attendant. Fanta wanted to hightail it out, go home, and salvage what was left of her ego. She approached Dave's office. The door was ajar. Maybe Dave was up to his ears in accruals. She knocked softly and pushed in.

"Dave? Sorry to interrupt, I—"

Deirdre's rounded rump protruded from underneath the desk. Her head came up sharply. She had a broom in one hand and a dustpan in the other. She looked at Fanta as if a skunk had lumbered into the office.

"You have no business here."

Fanta tried to hang on, but the slide into her teenage self was inevitable. "Hi, Dee-Dee, it's always *so* nice to see you. Lana was wondering where you'd got off to."

"What do you want?" Deirdre reached out with her toe to ensure the bottom desk drawer was closed before using her hand to brush wood shavings and horse hairs from the desk's plastic blotter onto the floor, where she rounded them up with the broom into a little pile.

"I'm just here to get something, you can calm down." Fanta plucked her sunglasses off the top of the filing cabinet. If she were smart, she would leave without another word. She continued, "I won't keep you. You must have lots of chores to do. It's been very busy here at Two Gates while you've been away."

"I've been in Vermont, if you must know," Deirdre sneered, depositing the contents of the dustpan into a garbage pail. She stood unmoving behind the desk. "I think you're the one who'd better get going. Now that the clinic is over, it's time for all the wannabes to head home."

Fanta drew herself up. She couldn't think of a single snappy retort. She propped her sunglasses on her head and straightened her polo shirt, which was stiff with dirt and sweat. "I think I will be going. Busy day in the office tomorrow. I'll leave you to do some work. For once." That was the best she had.

Fanta turned on her heel and walked primly down the aisle. If she never came back to Two Gates, it would be too soon.

Chapter Twenty-Nine

Fanta sat at her kitchen table, chin propped on her hand. She'd had mac and cheese with bacon bits, salad from a bag, and three peanut butter cookies. She felt sick. The clinic was supposed to have clarified everything, shone a huge spotlight with a flashing arrow on the perpetrator. If anything, she felt more confused and discouraged than ever.

She should phone the police. How would that go? *"Yes, police? I'm from the equestrian world—yes, that's right, I ride horses—and I know a ton of people who would have wanted to hurt Greg Grenier. Like who? Well, really anyone who ever knew him. Why? Because he was fickle, unfeeling, and kinda mean, although gorgeous to look at and super with the horses and other things. And, oh, I found the watch. Yes, that one. Where is it? Well, that's a good question."*

She spun her work phone around on the varnished wooden tabletop. She'd checked her email. There were some whiny messages from Gary Stillwater about the magazine (addressed to Abby, with Fanta in cc), an off-color comment from a reader on the birdwatching story, and a question from a dance studio about when the piece would run. Fanta sighed. She would never succeed at the Newser. The years stretched before her. At what point would she have to make coffee and refill the water cooler just to keep her job?

"Where there is love, there is light." Chantale had seemed like a wise if giddy woman. What had she been talking about? Fanta picked up the phone and tapped a number.

Romy opened with a yawn. "Yes, Fanta?"

"Oh, hi, Romy. I couldn't think of anyone else to call." Fanta tried to marshal her thoughts.

"Well, how nice that I popped into your mind," Romy responded smoothly. "Although, I did notice that you had little time for me at the clinic these past two days. Too good to speak with the hired help, are we?"

"Hardly," Fanta spluttered, "I was the hired help, in case you missed that."

"Right, and how did that go? I had the impression Lana was thrilled with your support." Romy's voice hardened. "You wouldn't last a week here at Two Gates. And forget about What's Your Beef. You better stick with the reporter gig. Maybe you'll begin to pick that up soon."

Fanta was exasperated. "Okay, enough, Romy. I'm sorry I didn't stop to chat. I'm busy trying to figure out this Greg thing. Asking questions, like you wanted. Quit giving me a hard time." Fanta put her hand to her forehead. Ow! She'd scrubbed so hard in the shower the skin was red and irritated.

Romy sighed. "Alright, I'm sorry. I know you've been trying. I'm just sick of being overlooked. And no one knows anything about Greg's death! Are we all just supposed to forget it ever happened?" she ended on a pleading note.

"No, no, that's why I'm phoning. I've been thinking about Dave." Fanta took a paper napkin from the pile on the table and started to fold it absently.

"Dave? What's he done?"

Fanta hesitated. For all her bluster, Romy seemed naive. Would she understand what she wanted to ask about Dave? "Nothing, I don't think. But don't you find it weird that Dave was never jealous of Greg and all his girlfriends?" She let the question hang in the air.

"*All his girlfriends*? I think that's a bit much. Greg was popular, but no more so than any other handsome guy," Romy said staunchly.

Fanta pressed down on a napkin crease. It was going to be tough sledding. She might as well come out with it. "Right, but what I'm wondering is if maybe Dave is gay. So he wouldn't care about Greg's love life." A thought flew at her from far left field. "I mean, maybe even Dave and Terry were, you know, like, together."

"What?" Romy sounded repelled. "This is my boss we're talking about. I don't stop to consider his…preferences. Oh, gross. Now that's in my head."

"Would there be anything wrong with that?" Fanta asked pointedly. Maybe Romy was not only naive, but also provincial in her thinking.

"Of course there's not anything wrong with it, Fanta," Romy said forcefully. "If you must know, I rather prefer women. Except for Greg, but that was different. He had such…wide appeal."

Fanta's mind boggled. Now who was the provincial one?

"Why are you asking? What in the world does this have to do with Greg's murder?" Romy rattled out the questions.

Fanta slumped. "Honestly, I don't really know. I thought if Dave were jealous of Greg, that would give him a motive. You know, above and beyond the whole stealing clients part. I still think it was Lana. But it could also be Terry. Maybe Dave and Terry acted together, you know, to rid themselves of Greg?"

"Stop, just stop, Fanta," Romy huffed. "I can see how this whole thing has gotten away from you. I'm going to go back to reading my book now, in peace and quiet."

"Deirdre's not there?"

Romy let out a gusty sigh. "No, she's back from Vermont, but she's up to her usual hijinks somewhere. Good luck to her. Now, if you'd let me get back to my book?"

"I should question her." Fanta was startled by the idea. Why hadn't she thought of it before?

"You do that and let me know how it goes. On second thought, don't. I'm pretty sure I've seen the Deirdre-Fanta movie before. It never ends well." There was a pause and some rustling. "I think something is happening over at the stables. I better go. Goodnight."

Fanta laid her phone down. The paper napkin looked like origami gone horribly wrong. She rose slowly from the table. She needed to sleep, reboot her brain. With any luck, things would be clearer in the morning.

Chapter Thirty

"I've got an update on the Grenier case." Sue started the morning meeting with a bang.

Fanta struggled to tune in. She had slept heavily. She felt groggy and tired, like she was underwater, her senses muffled.

"Let's hear it," Abby said.

Sue flipped to a page in her notebook. "The police have made an arrest. The guy's name is—" she glanced down "—David LeDrew?" Her brow furrowed. "Drew LeDans?" She flipped through a few more pages. "No, sorry, here it is. David LeDans. That's the name."

Fanta gasped as if breaking the surface of a deep lake.

"You know this man, Fanta?" Abby's head swiveled her way.

"A little. I just never thought...I mean, I never suspected..."

"Continue, Sue," Douglas interjected, making a rolling motion with his hand.

"What I'm hearing is that the police got a tip. They searched LeDans's office last evening. From what I've been told, they found the vic's watch and wallet. In the desk drawer, apparently."

Sue paused, checking her notes. "I heard, too, that someone saw LeDans banging on Grenier's door the night of the murder." Sue shrugged. "So it looks pretty bad for this guy. The cops haven't given a motive. But it seems obvious that LeDans and Grenier knew each other."

"What can you tell us, Fanta?" Abby asked.

Douglas groaned.

Fanta tried to put her thoughts in order. "Well, Dave was Greg's business partner. Greg had been planning to leave the business and go out on his own. So Dave was pretty angry about that." She shook her head in disbelief. "But that wasn't enough for him to kill Greg. It was just a—"

"Leave it to the police, Fanta," Douglas cut in. "They know what they're doing. They work with facts, not gossip and melodrama. Let's keep the broken-hearted club out of this."

Fanta's face flamed. Abby took over.

"We better get going on our profile of Grenier. The window is closing for us to get something out there." Abby turned to Fanta. "Why don't you finish that up? Come see me if anything."

Fanta hurried back to her cubicle. Douglas! The guy would never disappoint. Dave! She'd been right to wonder about him. But...she still couldn't picture it. Did most killers stash the evidence of their crime in their own desk drawer? There had to be something else at play.

She jabbed the space bar, willing her ancient computer to come to life. She was dying to phone Romy, who was likely in a panic. But Abby was expecting the profile on Greg. She hadn't even started it, she'd been so taken up with everything else.

The screen glowed, ready to go. She took a moment to control her heartbeat. In through the nose, out through the mouth. The mystery of Greg's murder was like a giant hodgepodge in her brain. But she couldn't deal with it now, she needed to focus on other things. Getting the editorial calendar for the magazine underway would be a good first step. All her themes were jotted down, it would be easy to format them. Then she would wrangle with Gary.

She spent the next hour fiddling with calendar formatting. Writing was so much easier. She scanned the newsroom. Gary was at his desk, probably memorizing a catalogue.

"Hi, Gary, could I speak with you?" Fanta indicated the empty chair. Gary nodded.

"So I've developed a draft calendar for the magazine." Fanta placed her document in front of Gary. "I've included a main theme and secondary themes for each issue. And I've left this column," she pointed at it, "for you and your team to complete." She sat back. "Once you and your boss are happy, we can share it with Abby. What do you think?"

Gary looked grudgingly impressed. "It's a good start. Let us see what we can do. If you could share a digital format with me? I'll get back to you as soon as I can."

Fanta stood. "Absolutely. I'll need something back by noon tomorrow. Thanks."

Fanta turned toward her desk. Editorial calendar, check. Collaborative approach, double check. She sat in her stained office chair, spun to face the computer, and opened a new document. The cursor blinked stupidly at her. The piece about Greg would be more difficult. It seemed inappropriate to detail his shortcomings, but neither did she want all the usual quotes about people who died unexpectedly: *"Oh, he was really nice"*, *"She always had a smile"*, *"He was a great neighbor".* She had more interesting comments than that. In fact, a piece about Greg could be quite intriguing, if she could only figure out how to start. She drummed her fingers on the keyboard. Nothing.

She glanced up at the newsroom clock. Maybe she should take a break for lunch, get her thoughts straight. She put her computer into sleep mode and opened the drawer where she kept her purse. She'd tucked a sandwich and some carrot sticks into it. Her bank account was sending clear signals that she was eating out way too much. The High T expense in particular had landed like a stick of dynamite.

Fanta filled her water bottle at the cooler in the lunchroom and chose a seat near the window. Her soggy tuna sandwich was about as inspiring as her surroundings. She squinted at the bulletin board. There was actually a poster for a garage sale that had happened two years ago. She pulled a few carrot sticks from her lunch bag. She resented them deeply. But think of the money she could save. It was nice to live a simpler life. A bit of budgeting never hurt anyone. She crunched vigorously. If carrots were good enough for Des, they were good enough for her.

At least she wasn't Dave, tousled and confused, sitting in one of those interview rooms at the police station just like on TV. Was he spilling his guts? Or sitting there completely baffled? She thought again of calling Romy, asking what was going on, but Romy was probably busy freaking out.

Sue sauntered in, headed for the coffee machine. "I can hear you chewing from out in the newsroom."

Fanta swept carrot off her front teeth with her tongue. "That was an interesting development in the Grenier case today," she commented, an orange blob winging onto the sticky tabletop in front of her.

"Yuh." Sue poked buttons, and dark, hot liquid spewed into her mug.

"I'm struggling with this profile," Fanta continued. "You know, should it be just nice things? Or should I share some of the…less savory aspects of Greg's personality?"

Sue leaned on the counter, sipping her coffee. "Just tell it like it is, Fanta. No one is black or white." She winced as the liquid burned her tongue. "If you want me to read your piece over, I'm happy to do that. It is an active police investigation, after all. We need to be careful."

"Oh, that would be great. I'll take you up on that." Fanta paused. She regarded Sue, with her rough-cut hair and baggy eyes. "What if, hypothetically speaking, someone thought they might know something about the case? I mean, probably nothing the police don't know already, nothing really important." Fanta made an airy motion with her hand, carrot stick between her fingers.

"Hypothetically speaking?" Sue's eyebrows went up. "They should get over to the police station. A crime has been committed. It's no time for fooling around." She shook her head. "Too many amateur detectives these days." Sue's sharp gaze pinned Fanta to her seat. "Hypothetically speaking, would this someone be you?"

Fanta blustered, "Oh, no. I was just, you know, role-playing. Thinking out loud." Another orange bit went flying out of her mouth and to the floor.

Sue let her stare linger. "My advice would be, if this person wants justice for the victim, best not wait around. A lot of things may hang in the balance. This LeDans, he needs all the help he can get."

Sue headed toward the door. "Gotta go." She disappeared into the newsroom.

Fanta forced herself to finish the sandwich and carrots. Poor Dave, caught red-handed. She chewed thoughtfully. Of course, Dave wasn't the only one with access to the desk drawers in his office, either to get stuff out or put stuff in. She knew that well enough. Mrs. Hooper's words floated through her head. A crafty killer, calculating, cold-blooded. Maybe someone else was outsmarting them all. The only question was, who?

* * *

Fanta watched from her desk as Newser employees wended their way out of the building. It was late afternoon. The sun slanted through the dusty window blinds and threw long shafts of light on the floor. The newsroom was quickly becoming quiet and eerie, with only the hum of the AC and the tired computer equipment. Fanta had wrestled for hours with her profile on Greg. It just wasn't working out the way she'd hoped. She'd written about a million leads and discarded every one of them.

"When Greg Grenier met Lana Taylor, he knew she would never be enough for him."

No.

"Greg Grenier and David LeDans were best friends in college. Now, one of them may have murdered the other."

Delete.

"Together, Greg Grenier and his star pupil Terry Miller made a great team, or so Miller thought."

Delete, delete.

Fanta dropped her head in her hands. Her stomach grumbled. The tuna sandwich seemed a long time ago. Plus, it was getting spooky, alone at the office. Who knew what ghosts of journalists past might spring up out of the soiled and flattened carpet tiles, summoned by her rank desperation. She slapped her palm on her forehead. How to write this stupid thing?

Then, inspiration. Of all things, she flashed on the horrific collage that Deirdre had constructed in pony club days. The pictures of Greg, from various points in his career. That was it! She would go back in time, trace Greg's early days as a rider, his first taste of success, his journey through the

213

horse world that ultimately led him to Two Gates, and his sad fate. That seemed safer than a sensational and legally dicey description of current events.

She quickly clicked into all of Greg's social media accounts that she'd followed so religiously. She scrolled and scrolled, searched and searched. She remembered many of the photos she discovered. It was like going back to her own past, as if she needed any reminder. The office grew darker, exit signs glowed in the hallways. Fanta looked up. Were there not any cleaning staff? She rolled her eyes. This was the Newser.

Her eyes began to ache in the blue glare of the screen. A small faded photo glided by and disappeared. What was that? She pressed on her mouse, scrolling this way and that. She hadn't recognized the photo. She had to find it. Her pulse raced. It seemed critically important. Where did it go? Click, click, click—there!

The screen stopped. Fanta froze. There were three figures in the picture. On one side of the photo was a teenage Greg, a bit skinnier, movie-star handsome, smiling proudly. In the middle of the photo was a dark horse with a white blaze down its face, ears pricked, a bridle on its head. On the other side of the photo was a pretty brunette, laughing and happy, holding the horse's reins in her right hand while displaying her left hand to the camera. On her ring finger, a thin gold band with a tiny diamond. Fanta would have recognized her anywhere. Deirdre.

She powered off the computer, grabbed her purse, and ran for the parking lot.

Chapter Thirty-One

The kettle whistled on the stove. Fanta hurried into her kitchen. She was making a cup of tea. She'd already changed the bedsheets, scrubbed the bathroom, and polished any surface she could reach. She'd been trying and trying to call Romy, but she wasn't picking up. Fanta could feel her anxiety rising like a thermometer in July.

She poured hot water over a fresh tea bag, hands shaking. The TV droned in the background. The newscaster had mentioned Dave, hauled in for questioning. Fanta went to sit in her recliner with her mug, jumping at every little noise. Finally, her phone sprang to life. Her heart leaped into her mouth. It was Romy. She grabbed at the device.

"Romy! I need to verify something with you."

"I don't have time now, Fanta, but you kept calling and calling." Romy sounded near tears. "Don't you know what's happened? They've arrested Dave! He's my boss. I wish someone would tell me what's going on."

"But that's just it, Romy. I do know what's going on. And I don't like it."

"What? What are you talking about? How could you possibly know what's going on?" Romy's voice was plaintive.

"I have to ask you something. It's about Deirdre," Fanta started.

Romy cut in. "Oh, please, you've got to get over all that silly childhood stuff! Who cares about Deirdre? It's Dave we have to worry about."

Suddenly, Fanta had a thought. "Where are you?"

Romy groaned. "Here we go again. I'm in the motorhome, Fanta. And before you ask, Deirdre is not here."

"Okay, that's good," Fanta tried to breathe. She had to get her thoughts straight. What was the next question? "At the hotel that night, the night Greg was…killed, did Deirdre stay the night in your room? You two bunked together, right?"

"That's right. And no, Deirdre was not in the room. Of course, that wasn't anything new," Romy's tone got gripey, "I don't think Dave knew half the antics she got up to. I've never known someone so—"

"Okay," Fanta jumped in, "and did you tell Deirdre about seeing Dave outside Greg's hotel room? You know, you said he was pounding on the door."

"I may have mentioned it to her," Romy said, her voice turning cautious. "Do you think she said something to the police?"

Fanta ignored the question. "Okay, and then, you said that you…found Greg the next day. How did you get into his room?"

"Well, I had his room key. The key card thing." Romy drew a steadying breath. "Greg was a sound sleeper. He often asked one of the grooms to wake him if he had to be up early. So Deirdre and I kept the key card in a special spot on the dresser in our room. So we could always find it."

Romy paused. "I just thought of something. That morning, the key card wasn't in its spot. I almost didn't see it. It was actually on the floor. It was as if…someone had thrown it onto the dresser and missed."

"Had that ever happened before?" Fanta's breath was coming fast. It was like being on a runaway train, heading for a hairpin turn.

"Um, *nooo*." Romy's voice rose to a wail. "Oh no! You're thinking it's Deirdre, aren't you? And I'm here in this trailer like a sitting duck, waiting for her to come back."

Fanta heard rapid, muffled steps and then a great banging. Romy screamed with the fear and frustration of a trapped animal.

"I'm locked in. The door is jammed. I can't get out!"

There was a fierce sound of a handle being wrenched up and down.

Fanta felt her own panic bubbling. "Romy, try to keep calm. I know this must be upsetting, but think. Can you get through a window?"

There was a noise like a drawer being yanked open and items spilling everywhere. "Oh, Fanta," Romy sobbed, "the windows have screens on them.

And we don't have anything but plastic cutlery in here. Everything's so cheap." There was a sharp snap. "Plus, the windows are old and don't slide easily. I've tried. It's so hot in here in the summer. This place is a piece of crap." Something got a swift kick. "Ow!" Romy's keening ratcheted up.

"Call the police, Romy. I'm on my way." Fanta sprinted around her apartment gathering her purse and keys.

"The police? What am I going to say to them? I'm locked in a motorhome, please help? They won't even write it down, make a report, whatever." Romy was losing it completely. "Just get here as fast as you can. Before Deirdre shows up to finish me off!"

"Okay. You're not in a burning building, Romy. Just sit tight and have a cup of tea."

As she galloped down the stairs on her way to the car, Fanta realized she was talking to a dial tone.

* * *

Fanta strained to see the road in the half-light of the evening. Shadows were deepening at the sides of the highway and clouds were rolling in, making the darkness come faster. She flipped on the headlights and focused on driving quickly but carefully. Thankfully, she knew the route well. Romy was in no imminent danger. She hoped.

She turned into Two Gates and headed up the long laneway. The barn and outbuildings looked quiet. A tall lamppost spread a weak glow in the parking area. Otherwise, Two Gates was quickly disappearing into the growing dusk. She pulled up as close as possible to the motorhome. Pinpricks of light shone from the windows.

She hopped out of her Honda and trotted over. "Romy, it's me," she called softly.

"Fanta? Get me out of here!" Romy's voice was muffled. She banged at the door.

Fanta squinted in the dim light. "Okay, I can see that someone has rigged the handle so it can't be opened from inside." She peered at the lock mechanism. "Where is the key?"

"Under the flowerpot."

Fanta moved aside a withered geranium. A small key shone up at her. She grabbed it and started to jimmy it around in the lock.

"Hurry up! I'm dying in here," Romy called, her voice straining.

The little key winked and shone as Fanta twisted and turned it. Just as she felt a click, the key fell from her fingers and disappeared into the shadows under the trailer. She dropped to her knees and began pawing around in the dirt and debris. It was a good thing she couldn't see what she was touching.

"Fanta! What are you doing?" Romy cried.

Abandoning the key, Fanta grasped the door handle and pulled with all her might. With a screech and a pop, the lock sprang free, the door shimmied open, and Romy stumbled out, almost falling to the ground.

"Oh, thank goodness, you have no idea. I was just freaking out," Romy gasped. Her wispy hair was plastered to her head. She wore jeans and a pajama top with a rainbow pattern.

"You okay?" Fanta whispered.

Romy glanced around nervously. "I don't know. Where's Deirdre?" she asked, gawking at the shadows. "I don't see her car."

Fanta was about to answer when a gust of wind set the treetops tossing. Romy shivered and shoved her hands in the pockets of her jeans. Then she drew in a sharp breath.

"Oh! I almost forgot. When I was tearing apart the trailer, trying to get out, I found this." She pulled a small velvet box from her pocket and held it toward Fanta. "I was just about to open it when you came."

Romy grasped the little lid and peeled it back with a squeak. Fanta sucked in a breath. A stunning diamond ring sat nestled against a satin interior. The lights from the motorhome set the facets sparkling like tiny fireworks.

"Wow, that must be—"

A shriek pierced the velvet softness of the night like a spear. Fanta and Romy exchanged a look of panic. Animal or human? The flesh prickled on Fanta's arms. Whatever it was, it sounded like it was in trouble.

Romy shoved the little box in her pocket. "That could be one of the horses.

CHAPTER THIRTY-ONE

We have to go!"

They ran to the stable. Romy pulled on the heavy door, and it swung outward with a groan of hinges. They paused on the threshold. Horses rustled and snorted in their stalls, sensing danger.

"Why are the lights off?" Romy fumbled for the switch in the darkness. A shrill whinny rang out as the overhead fluorescents flickered on. The long aisle was empty, the doors to the office and the tack room closed.

Then Fanta heard it. A whimper. Where was it coming from? She motioned for Romy to follow her down the aisle. They glanced in every box stall, looking for something amiss. Nervous horses paced in circles, tossing their heads. Hooves thumped on wooden walls.

"Oh no!" Romy stopped in front of Palmetto's stall, her mouth open in astonishment. "What do we do? Fanta, get over here."

Fanta walked as quickly as she dared toward the stallion's stall, not wanting to spook him by moving too fast. But Palmetto was focused on something against the back wall. Fanta peered in. She could barely believe it.

Palmetto's ears were flat against his head, his yellow teeth bared. He stood four-square, one front hoof pawing the ground. Fanta watched in dread as he lowered his great head and made a snaking motion with his thick, powerful neck. His focus didn't waver from Lana, the intruder in his stall, huddled on the ground before him.

Fanta's thoughts went in a zillion directions at once. She mustered the calmest voice she could manage. "Lana, it's Fanta and Romy, we're here to help."

Lana's eyes moved. Her face was soaked in tears, her blonde hair flecked with straw and dirt. Her legs were curled underneath her and her arms were pressed to her sides. Fanta guessed she was in shock.

"Romy, get Palmetto's halter and a lead rope. Grab some oats in a scoop. Stay as calm as you can. No sudden movements or loud noises." Fanta noticed the bolt on the stall door was firmly latched. What had happened? Why was Lana trapped in the stall with Palmetto?

Romy scuttled off just as Palmetto threw his head in the air and squealed. Lana cowered, gasping and sobbing. Fanta could only watch and pray.

"Here, take these." Romy pushed a halter and lead rope and some sweet-smelling oats at Fanta.

Fanta took a deep breath. "Okay, Lana, I have oats for Palmetto. I have his halter and a lead rope. I'm going to open the door. When he looks at me, I need you to start moving slowly this way. Keep low to the ground, make yourself as small as possible. Do you hear me? I'm going to open the door now, just enough so you can get out."

The bolt clanked. Palmetto's ears flickered. Fanta pushed the door aside, just a bit. She shook the oats. Palmetto turned his head toward her. His nostrils flared crimson as he took in the scent of the feed. Ever so slowly, Lana began to uncurl. Fanta shook the oats again. The stallion eyed the scoop in her hand.

"Hey there, fella. I know we've upset you. But you're okay, you'll be okay," Fanta crooned.

Lana crawled toward the open door. Fanta shook the oats, mumbling soothing words. Just a few more inches, Lana was almost there. Then, as quick as a flash, Palmetto whirled toward the front of the stall and reared up on his hind legs. Lana reached desperately for the door. Fanta dropped the oats and the halter and bent down to grab her. Catching Lana by the wrist, she pulled her roughly into the aisle. Overwhelmed by a wave of relief, Fanta leaned her forehead against the cool metal of the door and sucked in a lungful of air.

Then, a pair of strong hands pressed into her back and she fell, landing flat on her face in the straw. She gasped for air and twisted onto her back. Palmetto was right above her, standing on his hindquarters. His pie-shaped hooves with their sharp metal horseshoes dangled over her head. She had to move! Her brain flooded with panic. Her hands slipped and slid in the straw.

Just as Palmetto came plunging down, fingers encircled Fanta's ankles, and she was yanked out of the stall onto the pavement. The stall door closed with a bang. Palmetto snorted in rage and drove a back hoof deep into the wooden wall.

Chapter Thirty-Two

"We have to get out of here!" Romy shrieked.

Fanta rose to her feet shakily. "What happened?" She dashed tears from her eyes.

"It was Deirdre!" Romy cried. "She came up behind us, just as we got Lana out of the stall. We didn't even hear her. She must have been hiding in the office. She pushed you in, Fanta, and then she"— Romy gestured down the aisle—"ran out the door."

Fanta looked from Romy to Lana. "So, where is she now?" She put a hand to her cheek. Her fingers came away sticky with blood.

Lana's clothing was stained, her hair disheveled, and she had a nasty scrape on her arm. "We don't know. She ran off, like Romy said, but we had to pull you out of the stall, so we let her go." She shook her head. "I can't believe it, but Deirdre pushed me in there and bolted the door. She pretty much left me there to die."

Romy's breathing was ragged. "I think she must have locked me in the trailer so I couldn't help you. We have to get out of here, guys. Who knows what she might do now."

Lana looked in at Palmetto, who was nosing around his stall, looking for stray oats.

"I'll give him some extra time and attention tomorrow," she muttered. "He was just being a horse, and he's a good one at that."

"That's all well and nice," Romy spluttered, "but in case you haven't noticed, we have a killer on the loose. What should we do?"

Lana shrugged. "I just don't get it. Deirdre and I argued, but this is way over the top. We don't fool around with safety when it comes to the horses. She knew what Palmetto was like."

"Forget about that, we have to—" Romy started.

"I think there's more going on here," Fanta interjected. "I think it's quite likely that Deirdre is the one who killed Greg."

There was a beat of silence.

"What?" Lana's face twisted in disbelief.

"Yeah. I found out that Deirdre and Greg were involved back when they were teenagers. I think it was serious. Then he must have started his riding career, and I guess he met you, Lana. So that was the end of his relationship with Deirdre. I'm not sure she ever got over it."

Romy bounced on the balls of her feet. "Okay, so this is great, but like I'm saying, we need to—"

"Really?" Lana was surprised. Then she reconsidered. "That would explain things," she said. "I thought Deirdre was just fooling around, trying to hook up with Greg because…I don't know, she wanted to? I never took it very seriously. I didn't think he'd give her a second look. I mean, she's a groom." Her eyes slipped over to Romy. "Sorry."

"I don't care too much about anyone's love life right now," Romy was wild-eyed. "Deirdre's running around out there somewhere. We're still in danger!"

Fanta nodded at Romy. "Okay, well, I don't believe Deirdre would ever harm the horses. You know, burn the barn down or something."

"Oh no!" Romy wailed.

"No, she wouldn't do that," Lana said firmly. "She always loved the horses."

Fanta nodded again. "Okay, and do we know if she has access to a gun or anything?" The whole conversation was surreal.

"Oh no!" Romy cried.

"I don't think so?" Lana said. "Of course, it looks like I didn't know her very well at all. Or my own boyfriend, for that matter."

"That's *sooo* not helpful, Lana," Romy whined. "I say we hide in the office, barricade ourselves in, and wait for the police to come."

"One of us has to call the police," Fanta said hastily. "Did you want to do that, Lana? I'm going to step out into the parking area and have a look around."

Romy opened her mouth to object, eyes rolling.

"I'm sure Deirdre is long gone by now, Romy. Why would she stick around here?" Fanta added.

"Besides, it's three against one," Lana said. She jerked her thumb toward the office. "My phone's just there, let me grab it." She walked off briskly, returning a few seconds later. "Yes, that's right, Two Gates Stables. As soon as you can. Thank you."

She ended the call. "I'm going with you, Fanta. I can't sit here and do nothing. I want to make sure everything is okay outside."

Lana and Fanta started toward the stable door. Romy hung back, uncertain. Then she hurried after them. "I'm coming with you!"

"Deirdre and Greg, huh?" Lana muttered as they reached the door. "Wow, how could I miss that?" Her lips twisted. "Then again, I'm pretty sure there was a lot I missed where Greg was concerned. It was hard to keep track. What woman didn't have him on speed dial?"

Fanta glanced at her. "He wanted to marry you, Lana."

Lana nodded. Her eyes held a sheen of tears.

The three of them peeped out the door. The parking area was quiet. A halo of light surrounded the tall lamppost. A misty rain fell, creating a sheen on the graveled lot. Crickets chirped in the darkness.

"I feel silly." Lana pushed out and took several steps away from the barn. She turned back to Fanta and Romy, who hovered in the doorway. "I'm going to head over to Dave's house. I think he's out on bail. He needs to know about everything."

Lana started walking across the parking area.

Romy whimpered, her eyes flicking back and forth, searching the gloom.

Fanta stepped out of the barn door and into the lot. "It's okay, there's nothing out here."

Romy scampered after her. Lana waited for them to catch up.

Fanta held out her arms to embrace the night. "Everything's just—"

The desolate parking lot transformed into a brightly lit stage. A powerful diesel engine roared to life in the shadows. Large tires bit into the dirt, sending gravel pinging off a metal outbuilding. With incredible speed, a vehicle hurtled toward them, pinning them in the glare of dazzling headlights. Fanta could only stare blindly.

Romy was the first to move. She pushed Fanta to one side and tackled Lana so the two of them went rolling away, somersaulting over the gravel. Fanta landed heavily on her hands and knees, stones jabbing into her skin. A rush of air touched her cheek and ruffled her hair as a big truck passed within inches. A shriek of pain came from somewhere in the darkness.

Fanta scrambled to her feet, breathing hard. The truck was heading away from her, out of control. It glanced off a corner of the hay shed, its headlights bouncing crazily, sparks flying into the night. Then it lurched drunkenly to one side before careening off in the direction of a big garage, picking up speed. It cannoned through the darkness and, with a horrific bang, crashed into the back of a massive farm tractor.

The quiet of the night flooded back. A hiss came from the crumpled hood of the truck. A light rain pattered down.

Fanta ran blindly through the lot. She found Lana, curled on the ground, holding her ankle.

"Are you okay?"

"Yup, I'm okay," Lana managed. "My ankle, it's twisted or something. Where's Romy?"

Fanta looked around frantically. Romy was walking slowly toward the truck.

"It's Dave's truck." Romy approached the driver's door, which was buckled open.

"Be careful," Fanta called.

"Go, Fanta, go see who it is," Lana urged. "Help them."

Fanta ran to join Romy. The truck was in bad shape. The engine steamed softly, and a gentle dinging came from inside the cab. They peered in the driver's side, just as the headlights flickered and died. Still, it was easy to make out Deirdre's face, lying cushioned on the airbag, her long brown hair falling gently on her cheek.

Romy's hands flew to her face. "Oh!"

"My truck!" Dave ran toward them from the far end of the parking lot.

A whirl of sirens could be heard in the distance, coming closer.

Dave stumbled to a stop. "What happened?" He looked at Fanta and Romy. "What's going on here?" He glanced inside the truck. "Oh no! Deirdre, can you hear me?"

A cry of pain came from behind them. Dave spun around.

"Lana! What in the world? What is happening here?"

Lana lowered herself back onto the ground. "I'm okay, Dave," she puffed. "Stay with Deirdre. She needs your help now."

Deirdre was unconscious but seemed to be breathing steadily. Fanta left Romy and Dave hovering outside the truck and walked over to where Lana sat in the dirt.

"I'm sorry," said Lana quietly.

"For what?"

"For this, for all of it." Lana's breath caught on a sob. "I've been…so selfish. So foolish. I just wanted everything to…no, I just wanted everything. Now it's such a mess. My business is in shambles. And I've lost Greg." Her shoulders shook. "I miss him so much."

Tears streamed down Lana's face. Fanta knelt beside her as a whirlwind of lights and sirens surged up the long lane toward the stable.

Chapter Thirty-Three

Dobie hopped into the back of Fanta's car and flopped happily on the seat.

"That dog is going with you?" Marcia looked at Fanta as if she were nuts.

"Yeah, Penny said he likes going for car rides." Fanta closed the car door. All four windows were cracked to let in the fresh air. She'd learned about Dobie and enclosed spaces.

"Just bring him back in one piece," Penny called from the barn door at Bay Ridge. Bonnie stood beside her, grinning. Marcia shrugged.

"And give Lana our best." Penny waved as Fanta backed her car out of the lot and started down the twisty drive.

She turned onto the country road. A couple of days had passed since the frightening events at Two Gates. Fanta had spent the time resting. She'd been more affected by everything than she'd realized. So she'd sat on her deck in her Algonquin chair, walked Lottie, and chatted with Mrs. Hooper. She'd gone to see a movie with Chessy and her roommates. And she'd checked in with her mom, who fortunately had run out of career advice. She'd spared her mother the details about her night at Two Gates. She would only worry.

But mostly, she'd spent a lot of time with Des. He was the best comfort she knew.

She cranked up the radio and sang along as the summer road unfolded. Wildflowers were thick in the ditches, and the breeze carried the scent of sun-warmed fields. Dobie poked his long snout through the partially open window. He wore a new leather collar with a shiny nameplate. Dog hair swirled inside the car and stuck onto the cloth seats, the dashboard, pretty much everywhere. Goober trails and nose smudges covered the windowpane.

Fanta smiled. Tomorrow she would go back to work. Back to the morning meetings, the feature writing, and the magazine. Back to grappling with her colleagues. She was determined to give it her best. She enjoyed feature writing. She wouldn't let anyone, including her mom, make her feel it was not worthwhile. She even had a few ideas for upcoming articles. Maybe something on body image or bullying. Or profiles of seniors in the community. Feature writers had important stories to tell, too.

"Here we are, Dobie. Let's pay a visit." Fanta turned into the long laneway at Two Gates that was so familiar to her now. The parking area was quiet. Horses grazed in the nearby paddocks. Lana sat in the sun on the wooden bench outside the stable door, leaning against the metal wall, her bandaged ankle propped on a bucket. Romy was visiting her parents in the Maritimes. Fanta hoped she was being spoiled rotten.

She opened the back door and let Dobie hop out of the car. He was excited by the new sights and smells, but stuck close to her side. They approached the stable.

"Hi there, Lana. We wanted to see how you were doing." Fanta pointed to the dog. "This is Dobie. He's Penny's dog."

Lana shaded her eyes against the sun.

"Hi, Fanta. Thanks for thinking of me." She shifted her weight and indicated the seat beside her on the bench. "Did you want to sit?"

"Sure." Fanta made herself comfortable next to Lana. They were both wearing jean cutoffs and summer tops. Lana's was a bit frilly. Fanta stretched her legs out in front of her. Her skin was a fearful white, but so what? The wall at her back was warm from the sun, a fresh breeze fanned her face, and she'd applied SPF one million.

She gestured at Lana's ankle. "Looks like the recovery is going okay."

"Yup, if all goes well, I should be up and about in the next few weeks." Lana watched Dobie sniffing around near the stable door. "I'll miss a few shows, but maybe it's for the best. The horses and I could use the break."

She shifted her gaze to where Palmetto grazed in the paddock. His tail swished against the flies as he tore at the grass with his teeth. "Terry's agreed to ride for me, so I have some time to think about things. You know, really think things through."

"I think that's a smart move," Fanta offered.

Lana perked up. "Dave and I have even talked about my coming to ride here, as the pro."

The ginger barn cat took up position in the stable door, like a bouncer at a nightclub. Dobie stared, awestruck, a kid about to get carded. Lana pointed. "Is your dog going to be alright?"

"Oh, I think so." Fanta had no idea. From what she knew about Dobie and Barney at Bay Ridge, the cat would probably get the best of things.

"How's Deirdre? Has she been able to see anyone?" Fanta asked gently.

An ambulance had taken Deirdre to the hospital that night. She was badly injured but expected to recover. The police were set to lay a whole series of charges against her. Her life as she knew it was over.

"Yes, I visited her in the hospital." Lana hesitated. "I wanted to take her some clothes and things. Her parents are both gone now. I hoped she wouldn't be upset to see me, but I think she was glad to have a visitor." Lana examined her chipped manicure. Dobie abandoned the cat and came to sit near her.

"Deirdre told me what happened," Lana continued. "You were right, she and Greg were involved before he met me. They grew up in the same small town in Quebec. They'd talked about building a life together, even got engaged. They were really young." Lana sighed. "Then I guess Greg went off to college and started to get a bit…distracted. And soon after, he was offered a position with a big horse stable in the States. So that's when Deirdre applied for the job with me. She said she was trying to follow Greg, as best as she could. She knew he was slipping away from her."

Lana paused, fiddling with the ragged edges of her cutoff shorts. "So then Greg's riding career started to take off, he met me and…well, you know the rest. I had no idea about Deirdre when I met Greg." Lana shook her head. "So typical of me. It was probably obvious to everyone else, but I was just so wrapped up in my own little world."

Dobie leaned against Lana's leg. "When Greg came back here to Two Gates to partner with Dave, Deirdre convinced him to take her on as a groom. Probably not one of his best moves," Lana added wryly. "Anyway, Deirdre said she wanted to be near him, even if it wasn't the same. She still hoped she could win him back. But it must have been really hard, seeing him with me and hearing about our plans for the future." Lana's voice trailed off.

Fanta remembered Greg hugging Deirdre after his ride on Dash. She could easily see how Deirdre might have held out hope. "What happened on the night Greg died? Did she tell you?"

"Yes." Lana paused. Dobie pressed himself against her leg. Lana reached out to scratch his head. She drew a deep breath. "She went to his room late that night to talk to him one more time. She got in using the extra key. She pleaded with him to come back to her. Greg told her to leave, that he was with me now. He turned his back on her. She said she felt so…dismissed. After everything they'd been through together."

Lana's voice became strangled. She stroked Dobie's head.

"She was so angry and hurt, she picked up the bedside lamp and hit him. She didn't want to kill him, she barely knew what she was doing. But then… he was gone. She went out of her mind, she said. She saw the engagement ring on the dresser. She couldn't stand leaving it there. She said Greg had planned to marry her. So she took it."

A tear slipped off Lana's nose and onto her blouse. She cleared her throat.

"I guess that's when Deirdre realized she'd committed a crime, that she'd killed someone. She said she panicked. She took the wallet and the watch, which were with the ring on the dresser. She thought maybe it would look like a robbery. Then she slipped across to the room she shared with Romy and left the extra room key. And then she drove back here to Two Gates."

Lana wiped at her tears with one hand. "She said it was impossible for her to sleep across the hall from him, knowing he was…he was…"

Lana tried and failed to contain a sob, possibly thinking of herself, sleeping soundly in the adjoining room. Dobie held steady against her leg.

"I'm sorry," Fanta said, pausing as Lana plucked a tissue from her pocket and wiped her eyes. "So, I guess it was Deirdre who planted the stuff at Two Gates. Did she explain that?"

Lana snorted. "I guess she was thinking a bit more practically by then," she said. "Obviously, she knew we were all under suspicion. And she didn't want to be found with the evidence. So she went into survival mode, I suppose. She tried leaving the things in various spots around the barn, but she needed someone to discover them. Then she heard about Dave being outside Greg's room that night, and she got an idea. She phoned in an anonymous tip, enough to prompt the police to search Dave's office. And she dropped the wallet and the watch in his desk drawer." Lana shrugged. "Voila."

What did you find? Fanta drew in a sudden breath. "I bet Deirdre was my armchair detective."

Lana looked at her, puzzled. "What?"

"Sorry, never mind." Fanta tried to pick up the trail of the story. "What about the ring?"

Lana blinked. "Deirdre said it should have been hers in the first place. She couldn't bear to part with it. So she hid it in the trailer."

Fanta thought for a moment. Deirdre had been crafty and calculating. But cold-blooded? Maybe not. "Deirdre must have been jealous of Chessy, too. I think she ripped the stitching on her stirrup strap that day at the show."

Lana's face fell. "That was me."

Fanta turned to her in astonishment.

"I thought Chessy was making a play for Greg," Lana hastened to explain. "With his death, I wasn't myself. Everything was spiraling out of control— my plans with Greg, my business in Vermont. I just wanted to lash out at someone and Chessy was it. It was the stupidest thing ever. Chessy could have been seriously hurt. I will never forgive myself." Lana pressed her lips together and blinked hard.

Fanta didn't know how to feel. Chessy was her friend. She decided to return to the situation with Deirdre.

"Here's what I don't understand. With Dave arrested, Deirdre might have been in the clear. So why go after you?"

"I asked Deirdre the same thing." Lana winced as she moved her foot on the bucket. "She said that, even though Dave had been arrested, she didn't feel any better. In fact, she felt worse. Not only had she killed Greg, which was the last thing she'd wanted to do, but she'd set up his friend for murder. She said it was all my fault. I took Greg from her, which set the whole chain of events in motion. So she locked Romy in the trailer to keep her away from the barn and pushed me in the stall and left me there." Lana turned to Fanta and added with a humorless laugh, "I guess she hadn't counted on you showing up."

Lana returned her gaze to the paddocks. "I know it sounds crazy," she continued, "but I've had a taste of what grief can do to you, and it sure doesn't make you act rationally." Her eyes dropped to the dusty ground.

Fanta sighed. "Well, I guess we all need to figure out how to move on from here." It would be a long road. She got to her feet. "I should get going, I can see you're tired. I better get Dobie back to Bay Ridge before Penny starts worrying. She sends her best, by the way. They all do." Fanta smiled tentatively at Lana. Friend or foe? She wasn't sure. "Take care," she offered, "I'll see you at the horse shows."

Lana shaded her eyes with her hand and looked up at Fanta. "I'm sorry for how I treated you. You didn't deserve it. And thank you for getting me out of that stall. You were amazing."

Fanta nodded. "Come on, Dobie, let's go home."

Chapter Thirty-Four

"So that's how I figured out that it was Deirdre who killed Greg. She never got over her broken heart."

Fanta had everybody's full attention at Monday's morning meeting. She sat up straight in the sturdy wooden chair someone had offered her. Her mom had sent her some money as an early birthday present, and she'd spent time at the mall buying nice work clothes. She felt polished and professional. Her new black midi skirt was like something out of Abby's wardrobe. She'd even tried a free makeover at the drugstore. The startling geisha girl look, complete with white face powder and dark lipstick, had required an emergency dash into the public washroom.

"It's quite the story," Abby responded. "Let's get some of that color in our coverage. Sue, make sure you get the details from Fanta."

"You got it." Sue gave a thumbs-up. "I've also got a shooting last night in the east end, a robbery at the Quikbits convenience on Main Street, and a nasty accident over on Highway 5. We've already got something up on the site, but I'll get the rest done for posting by noon."

Abby nodded. "Great, thanks. By the way, I liked your dancing story, Fanta. Nice lead."

A blush crept over Fanta's cheeks. "Oh, thanks. I hoped it wasn't, you know, too spicy." She hurried on, "My next feature is going to explore the trend toward body positivity, how people are learning to love their bodies, even if they're not perfect." She wiggled her fingers in air quotes on the last word.

"That sounds like another good one. There was something else…" Abby put a hand to her temple, trying to draw something from her memory. Her burnt-sand blouse with a flowing foulard was a masterpiece, not to mention her classic leather slingbacks in tangerine. "Oh, I know what it was. I got some positive feedback from Gary's boss on the editorial calendar for the magazine. So we should be good to go there. If you and Gary could wrap it up, let's start the first issue." She looked squarely at Fanta. "You're hitting it out of the park these days. Well done."

Fanta beamed. "Thanks, Abby." She'd thought a lot about the new magazine over the past few days. She'd decided it wasn't just going to be about the latest in trendy decor. Instead, her goal would be to inspire readers to find and express their own style and personality. She could hardly wait to get going on the first issue, which would be all about big, bold design choices.

"I agree. Nice job, Fanta," a quiet voice said.

Fanta glanced over in surprise. "Thanks, Douglas."

"But let's not forget that Grenier piece." Abby jumped back in. "I still want to do a profile to complement Sue's news story."

"On it. I'm going to write that up this morning." Fanta felt energetic and engaged, sitting in the center of the group.

"Great, let's go, everybody." Abby dismissed the meeting and headed toward her office.

Fanta went back to her desk. There was a text waiting on her phone.

You take it easily honey. give that dog doobie a pat. And that supee horse

Fanta chuckled. **Thanks mom, for everything.**

A text zinged back. **Luv you. And that dansing story! Your dads and I are talking lessons. Goin to skip the lite fandangos.**

Fanta smiled and tucked the phone in her purse. She pictured her mom and dad twirling around on a dance floor, laughing and chatting, probably stepping on each other's toes. She thought about her own single life. Maybe her mom and Mrs. Hooper were right about finding someone special. It was time to leave silly childhood crushes behind and look for a real person to share her life with. Someone smart, warm, and funny. Someone who loved horses, of course.

Her eyes landed on the calendar pinned to her wall. July. A beautiful bay stallion stood regally in a grassy field, head held high and proud. Fanta thought of everything Des had taught her, not only horsemanship skills, but also confidence and trust. When she went to Bay Ridge that afternoon, she would talk to Penny and get her advice on where to go next with her riding.

But first, it was time to get busy with her career. Whatever else happened, she wanted to be a successful, independent woman. She powered up her computer and settled herself in her pristine new office chair. What could she say about Greg Grenier? It was impossible to believe he was gone. The hard truth of it was really sinking in. She had admired him for so long and assumed so many things about him. She had never stopped to think that he was human, with faults and foibles, weaknesses and worries. Just like herself.

Fanta flexed her fingers over the keyboard. She would portray Greg as someone to be admired, but also as someone who needed a little understanding and maybe more than a little forgiveness. Perhaps readers would relate. She started to write.

Acknowledgments

Writing is a solitary pastime, but sometimes you have to throw your hand out into the universe and see if anyone will grab it. A few people grabbed mine. Cindy Bullard's feedback offered a ray of hope in the dark days of querying. Toronto editor Jess Shulman ever so deftly, ever so subtly, and ever so politely showed me how to stop writing like a journalist. Of course, many thanks to my publisher Level Best Books for taking a chance on the horses. On the personal side, eternal gratitude to all the four-legged friends in my life, past and present, who have given me gifts beyond measure. And thanks to you, Mom and Dad. I wish I could put this book into your hands, but I hope you're up there somewhere having a good chuckle. Finally, a shout-out to everyone who has cheered me on from the sidelines. Here we go!

About the Author

A.V. Howland is an award-winning feature writer and newspaper editor who continues to work in daily journalism, now with a hint of mystery and mayhem on the side. She grew up riding horses and now lives in Ottawa, Canada with two rescue dogs. Of course, she's always looking for ways to get back in the saddle.

AUTHOR WEBSITE:
  Website: avhowland.com

SOCIAL MEDIA HANDLES:
  Facebook: A. V. Howland
  https://www.facebook.com/profile.php?id=61567499282655
  X: HowlandAv https://x.com/HowlandAv
  Instagram: @avhowland
  https://www.instagram.com/avhowland/